Nicholas St Aubyn is the direct descendant of the Bassets, Godolphins and Seyntaubins who feature in this story.

Born in 1955, he won a scholarship to Oxford. A versatile career led him from downtown Soweto to uptown Manhattan, and from a trading floor in the City to a trading estate in Redruth.

During ten years in Cornwall, he stood for Parliament three times, including in the County's only by-election in a lifetime. He was later MP for Guildford.

Custom of the County is Nicholas' first novel and he is now working on the sequel.

The cover reproduces a drawing by William Daniel
of Mullion Cove, The Lizard, Cornwall

CUSTOM OF THE COUNTY

Nicholas St Aubyn

First Edition

Red&BlackPress

redandblackpress.com

Published by Red&BlackPress,
St Day, Cornwall TR16 5HY
Printed and bound in Great Britain by
MPG Books, Bodmin. Cornwall PL31 1EB

A CIP record for this book
is available from the British Library

ISBN 978-0-9564852-1-2 (Hardback)
ISBN 978-0-9564852-0-5 (Softback)

Red&BlackPress supports the Forest Stewardship Council (FSC), the leading international forest certification organisation. This title is printed on FSC certified paper.

Mixed Sources
Product group from well-managed
forests and other controlled sources
www.fsc.org Cert no. SA-COC-1565
© 1996 Forest Stewardship Council
FSC

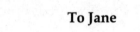

To Jane

Contents

Illustrations

Historical Note

On 9th September 2006, the following press release was issued by the British Department for Culture, Media and Sport:

Culture Minister David Lammy has today announced the re-designation of the wreck site of the St Anthony, located off Gunwalloe Fishing Cove, Cornwall. This will ensure that the whole of the St Anthony wreck site will now be protected under the Protection of Wrecks Act 1973.

The St Anthony was a Portuguese merchant vessel and sailed as the flagship of a fleet bound from Flanders. She sank in 1527 in a storm described, in contemporary evidence, as a great and urgent tempest of winds and weather.

She went down with a mixed cargo including copper and silver ingots and, it is believed, the dowry of Princess Catherine, bride of King John of Portugal and sister of Charles V, the Holy Roman Emperor. The cargo manifest still survives.

Violent disagreements between survivors and local people over salvage from the wreck are extremely well documented, which adds to the historical context of the site. The St Anthony wreck site was discovered in 1981.

Yet, apart from the odd artefact, the fate of the vast treasure carried on the *Santo Antonio* has remained a source of mystery for five hundred years...

This dramatised account is based on real persons, true events and authentic sources.

LIST OF PRINCIPAL CHARACTERS
(the lives of all of whom are recorded)

ON BOARD THE *SANTO ANTONIO*

Antonio Paciecho	Admiral of the Portuguese Fleet
Jeremy de Corfe	Gentleman of the King's Chamber
Diogo Vaz	Ship's Master
Diogo Alvares	Ship's Factor

MARAZION

John Millaton	Captain of St Michael's Mount and JP
James Chynoweth	Officer of Wreck to Sir John Arundell
John Arscott	Archpriest on St Michael's Mount

CLOWANCE

Thomas Seyntaubin	Village Squire and JP
Mary Seyntaubin	His wife
John Moyle	Yeoman Farmer at Clowance

GODOLPHIN

William Godolphin	Local Squire and JP

TEHIDY

Sir John Basset	Landowner and Courtier
Lady Basset (Honor)	His wife (sister to Mary Seyntaubin)

HAMPTON COURT

Thomas Wolsey	Cardinal and Lord Chancellor to Henry VIII
Thomas Cromwell	His Secretary
Arthur Plantagenet	Lord Lisle and Vice Admiral of the Fleet (natural uncle of Henry VIII)

ANTWERP

Roderick Fernandes	Consul to King John III and Queen Catherine of Portugal
Francisco Pessoa	Servant of the King's Chamber (and former Consul)

LONDON LAW COURTS

Anthony Waite	Inner Temple lawyer (cousin to Lisle)
John Densell	Lincoln's Inn lawyer (friend of Lisle)

OTHERS

Sir John Arundell	Landowner and Lord of the Manor
Master Pengelley	Helston shipping clerk
Father Trelobys	Cornish priest
John Keene	London goldsmith
Mistress Holland	Queen of the Southwark bawds
Sir Richard Grenville	Nephew to Mary Seyntaubin and Honor Basset
Mercurino Gattinara	Grand Chancellor to Charles V of Spain

Mount's Bay

Mount's Bay

If a ship or other vessel happens to be lost by striking on some shore, and the mariners thinking to save their lives, reach the shore, in hope of help... instead thereof it happens,... that in many places they meet with people more barbarous, cruel, and inhuman than mad dogs.

Article XXXI, The Rules of Oleron

1

Chapter I

...divers of the mariners and other persons then being within the same ship were there also then piteously perished and drowned

Seyntaubin's Answer to Star Chamber

The three hundred ton Portuguese carrack smashed through the waves. She heaved clear of the last jagged outcrop of life-threatening granite. The *Santo Antonio*, armed flagship of the Admiral of the Fleet, carried priceless royal treasure. Her safe delivery from Antwerp to Lisbon was a vital matter of state. But the lashing of the Atlantic storm had forced her back into the bay. Diego Alvares shouted for the chart.

How like the Cornish, Alvares thought, to call this point Land's End. Ten years in the service of King João the Third, fetching cargo from the farthest reaches of his empire, had taught the ship's Factor more than he cared to know about the real ends of the earth. Yet the heavy seas, as the waves kept breaking onto the reef, had never been more menacing. Alvares thought of his devoted Marina and their four children, no doubt counting towards his return to Lisbon in a few days' time. Rain-soaked under a star-ravenous sky, he sought to fix the ship's position, as fear crossed his mind that day might never come.

In the distance, Alvares could just make out a lamp burning. The chart told him this must be the ancient Benedictine monastery, standing atop St Michael's Mount. Giving a silent prayer of thanks to the patron saint of sailors, he set the course and handed clear instructions to the bosun, who had taken the ship's helm. The arc of the bay was providing the *Santo Antonio* with some shelter from the worst of the Atlantic storm and even the diligent Alvares needed his rest. He went below.

It was no longer monks providing a guiding light to ships passing St Michael's Mount. The island's order had been disgraced. A fortified garrison in the service of King Henry the Eighth now controlled the island landmark. Captain Millaton, a newcomer with no ties to the rebellious Cornish, had recently gained the command, with just a few monks on hand to satisfy the passing pilgrims.

That night, with a high and raging tide to insulate the island from danger, Millaton and his men were lured by the temptations found in any port. As the *Santo Antonio* turned into Mount's Bay, the captain turned towards the beautiful Irish girl undressing herself in his bedroom. Neither he nor his drunken garrison cared to notice that the island's beacon light had been extinguished by the strength of the storm.

James Chynoweth knew soon enough. A Marazion man to the bone, he would never forgive Millaton for securing the one job in the world which he secretly coveted himself. But nothing could prevent him from viewing the Mount, like so many who lived in the houses on the mainland, with a sense of ownership. Little escaped their notice and sharing the news provided keen amusement.

The door to Chynoweth's house burst open. He looked up to find a couple of his henchmen on the threshold standing between him and the gale outside.

"Have you look'd to see, Mr James, that the Mount 'tis now as dark as the devil! Methinks that Captain Millaton is paying more attention to his dick than to his duty tonight..."

"And who's surprised at that? The young Irish wench 'e fetched from Penzance today had many heads turning."

"Well, 'e obviously cares a great deal more for foreign girls than 'e does for foreign galleons," declared Chynoweth. "So where's we to?"

"Bearing a light towards St Hillary, I suppose. There's nought else for it," one of them responded resignedly. "No

Cornishman would be at sea on a night like this, but 'tis right we should be doing something for those caught in the storm."

"Aye and even more so for their cargo, should it choose to come ashore."

The church spire at St Hillary stood less than a mile from the coast. A ship coming into the bay, taking its signal for that on the Mount, would at least be guided away from the most dangerous stretch of shoreline by its lantern light. That, at least, was how the Cornish saw it.

The truth was that wrecks along this coast were commonplace, bringing a toll of death. The Cornish would never lead ships to their destruction, but few in these parts cared for the lives to be saved as much as they cared for "God's grace" – the name they gave the load to be rescued from the wreckage. It was the business of James Chynoweth, as an Officer of Wreck in the pay of Sir John Arundell, the head of Cornwall's leading family, to ensure that such loads were dealt with in the proper way.

As the lantern-lighters made their way to St Hilary, the sleeting rain began its next offensive. This weather had lasted three months now, an unrelenting desecration of crops and cattle throughout the land. At sea, this heavy rain was more treacherous than fog.

The bosun of the *Santo Antonio* was a level-headed mariner. He had every faith in the judgement of Diego Alvares and he was not panicked after the distant light by which they had been charting their path suddenly disappeared, as the rainclouds drew another curtain across the shoreline. God had spared them when they had sailed into the eye of the storm. The sea here in the bay seemed calmer. Even the darkness of a new moon could do nothing to dampen his confidence. When the bitter January cold tore through his clothing, numbing his senses, he turned his thoughts to the girl he was due to meet again in Lisbon.

The light at last reappeared, just as the sea renewed its anger. Gusts of wind had found a new direction into the bay and rearing seahorses tossed the carrack in their wake. He fought to clear his mind of confusion. According to the ship's speed and the light from the shore, they had made too little headway. The *Santo Antonio* must be further out to sea than Alvares had reckoned. The bosun ordered a tightening of the mainsail and the crew, half dead with exhaustion, limply complied. Steering the carrack to port, he sought shelter closer to the mainland, keen for relief from the tempest.

But the *Santo Antonio* was now in great danger. Along this shoreline, reefers stretched beneath the waves far into the bay. As the spring tide beat its rapid retreat, their ragged teeth came closer to the water's surface. The *Santo Antonio* was heavily laden, with a cargo of copper and silver caskets, gold jewels and cloth, along with a full ship's crew of eighty-six men, several passengers and the Commander of the Portuguese fleet. But far from her true course, there was no one to pilot the vessel past this treacherous coast to safety.

Belatedly, the bosun realised that his manoeuvre had rendered the *Santo Antonio* helpless in the force of the leeward gale now raging. Whichever way he swung the wheel, demon-like she headed closer to the cliffs looming through the darkness. At last she seemed to turn, but it was too late. The hull struck the rocks with a mortal blow, the stern lanterns snuffed out and the surging water thundered through the cabins.

The searing crack of timber jolted Alvares out of his slumber. He guessed instantly that the ship's cause was lost. He just had time to snatch her manifest and dash out of his cabin before one of the three masts crashed down and snapped in two. The belly of the carrack began to see-saw on the rocks, as members of the crew lurched from side to side, loose chests and guns on deck cannoning into victims in

6

tempo with the merciless rhythm of the storm.

The shattering of their sanctuary – the naked panic of those who believed they had already survived the worst, to find that the sea can always find further cruel tricks to play – made some men foolish. They went below to retrieve some treasure only to become trapped and drowned. Hurled into the eddy, others grasped some piece of flotsam which the receding tide pulled far out to sea.

Alvares clung to his objective. Wrapping the manifest in an oil cloth, he used a length of stray rigging from the broken mast and carefully lowered his body into the freezing water. Then, steadying himself in the swirl, he pulled along until he could gain a footing on the soft, life-assuring shingle. He had brought the manifest ashore. He would use it to parley with the locals, while he sought help from the Portuguese ships resting in the river Fal, barely ten miles away.

Disaster had struck off Gunwalloe, a long stretch of cove just below the Lizard Point. Nearly half the crew were dead. None of the survivors, least of all Alvares, could imagine the dangers that dry land held in store.

Chapter Two

The Portuguese that came alive to land with the help of goodmen of the county saved the Saturday at afternoon as much goods as did amount to a thousand ducats and above

Pessoa's Petition to Star Chamber

Five miles inland from the Mount's Bay coast that evening, Thomas Seyntaubin was seated in the Great Hall at Clowance. As the logs blazed in the vast open hearth and waged battle with the bitter winter cold, wind swept through the cracks in the panelling which covered the stark granite walls. A couple of spaniels scrapped over a bone, tossed from a sister's plate by a mischievous son, while a stray pigeon swooped between the timber beams above.

To his village, the Squire was a lucky man. Spawned in the bosom of a secure Cornish family, fortune had promoted him to master of his childhood home. Yet, this evening, the laughter of his wife Mary and their young children gnawed at Thomas. A third son, whose future had lain at the Inns of Court in London, he had never expected to inherit the family seat, set in its grounds beside the lake, let alone the farms with their income of forty pounds a year.

Marriage to Mary, a daughter of Sir Thomas Grenville, had brought another six pounds a year, her generous annuity as Devonshire widow. The fact that he was Mary's second husband had never troubled Thomas, while the prompt arrival of their sons and daughters brought much shared joy.

But when Peter, the second of his elder brothers, died from a sudden outbreak of plague, the burden of Thomas' inheritance weighed heavily. The old King had fined Peter severely, for his support of the Cornish rebellions, while the new King's taxes wrought further damage. Treasured family heirlooms had

8

vanished from the vault and heavy mortgage dues had left the farms short-changed. Thomas' plan – another loan to add to his stock and increase his yield – now threatened to destroy him. This rain was merciless.

"A letter arrived today."

Thomas smiled at his wife, in the hope that his abstract musings had gone unnoticed, which of course they never did.

"My sister Honor is paying us a visit," Mary continued. "Now that Sir John is ill, she spends so little time in this part of the county."

"My Lady Basset is always welcome," Thomas replied with a smile. "You know how much I admire your sister, Mary. In truth, I wonder if Sir John realises how blessed he is to have such a gifted wife."

"Sir John has always taken pride in Honor," Mary replied, "even if old age has made him slow to appreciate her as a lady, rather than the sprightly young girl he married ten years ago."

"It's true he's proved a constant friend to all of us. Yet what will happen if this latest illness takes Sir John with it? Honor could be left facing a bleak future as a Cornish widow."

"Thomas, never forget that we have the Bassets to thank for bringing us together in the first place. I rather think Honor's hoping we will do the same for her one day."

The Basset estates far exceeded the Seyntaubins' modest holdings. One neighboured Clowance, while their family seat was in Devon. Thomas struggled to see how he and Mary, living in West Cornwall, could possibly find a worthy match for a beautiful widow blessed with such advantages.

"We could introduce her to my old friend Danvers, I suppose."

"And go to live in Norfolk? Then I would never see my sister and in any case, she'd freeze from the cold. For sure, Thomas, that would be an even crueller fate."

"Then there's Gloucestershire. I heard from John Wye only the other day. He tells me this rain is everywhere, by the way."

"I've heard it too," Mary replied. "Soon the poor will have to sell their brass and bedding, if they are not to die from starving. What we can do for the Clowance men, I daren't even think, my love."

Mary looked tenderly at Thomas through the candlelight. He was beginning to rue the sacrifice of his legal career at the Inner Temple in London to take charge of these farms in Cornwall. His recent appointment as a Justice of the Peace, which had made Mary so proud, simply entrenched his predicament. It was all very well for their nephew Sir Richard Grenville, with his income of a hundred and thirty pounds a year, to be planning beyond the law, to a seat in parliament or a position under the Crown. But Thomas knew that even if Clowance survived this latest catastrophe, he lacked the means to provide for his children's future, let alone to realise such ambitions.

Looking on their happy faces around the table, it would be churlish to reveal his anxieties. Above all, this was not the time to confide in Mary the latest demands for repaying their debt to the Arundell estate.

****

The winter storm, as so often along the Cornish peninsula, was the prelude to a perfect dawn. With the sun clearing above the remaining whispers of grey cloud, only a few hours after the dramatic events of the night, shades of light played on the still surface of the sea. Not daring to hope that the winter weather had finally turned, that morning Thomas Seyntaubin seized this welcome break in the clouds to enjoy one of the rides along the coast.

His tall, lean frame strode out of the front entrance of Clowance, his father's thickset gown worn loosely over his belted tunic. A felt hat fastened his hood, brightened by a single pheasant plume. Smiling as a pair of ducks rose from the lake before him, Thomas turned sharply left towards the stables. Here he found his favourite chestnut mare and spoke to her as she was being saddled. They could attain the shore well before the sea reached high tide at eight, he reasoned, and enjoy a canter along the sands near Gunwalloe. After that, he would ride her inland, before lunch with his friend and cousin, William Godolphin. He earned a snort of approval.

As they trotted towards Gunwalloe, his leather uppers gently squeezing her sides, seagulls soared overhead, crying thanks to the fresh breeze expelling the damp from their feathers. But twenty minutes into the ride, the horse suddenly pricked her ears forward. The squawking seagulls had been overtaken by a rising cacophony of voices. Alerted to danger ahead, as he approached the headland Thomas surmised there must be a riot in progress. He had witnessed the scene of many wrecks in his time and taken advantage of a few. As he wearily leaned over the cliff edge to look down, his mare started to stamp the ground with her front hoof and shy nervously backwards.

Most wrecks measured in hundreds of pounds. But brass and iron guns, silver ornaments and copper blocks, Flemish tapestries and Antwerp jewels – the lavish hoard now floating in from the Cornish sea was a once-in-a-lifetime opportunity for the desperate wreckers he witnessed salvaging in the cove. Word had quickly spread throughout Penryn and Kerrier of the extraordinary providence of God's grace, ensuring no shortage of helpers to rescue the Portuguese spoils.

James Chynoweth, as the Officer of Wreck, would soon hear word. But as Seyntaubin knew, he always bided his time. To Chynoweth, the wise course was to let the excitement abate, before asserting the Right of Wreck which belonged to his master, Sir John Arundell. Survivors from a wreck often paid with their lives in defending their cargo, in the brutal scramble with the wreckers which followed. That was when Chynoweth preferred to take charge.

"Mr Thomas!"

Seyntaubin turned in his saddle and was surprised to find John Moyle, one of the yeomen who worked his farms, staring up at him.

"What in the name of God brings you to this devil's cauldron?" asked Thomas, dismounting to greet Moyle with a firm shake of the hand.

"I was about to ask you the same question, Squire," beamed Moyle. "I didn't know you had acquired the duties of Chynoweth and his men."

"So you mean to tell me that Chynoweth is not taking charge of this rabble?" Thomas scowled. "Look at them, risking their lives to recover the booty and haul it up the beach."

"We know he never does, not if he can leave it until the excitement has died, as y' might say." Horrified by the murder of ships' officers, the Crown had granted the salvage from a wreck to any survivor from a ship. So now not just the officers, but every member of the crew had reason to fear for his life.

"You're right, of course," Thomas agreed in disgust. "The wreckers know they're outside the law and have no means to convert their hoards into ready cash. So in return for a modest outlay, Chynoweth and his fellow Officers of Wreck recover the loot from the wreckers and turn a handsome profit…"

"…all the while citing their master Sir John's legal rights to defend their dealin'. It's a cynical ploy," Moyle rejoined, knowing full well that the far-reaching power of the Arundell estate was even more irksome to Thomas than to himself.

"Problem is, there's an absolute fortune out there and none of the men has ever known anyt' like it," Moyle continued. "What with this talk of famine an' all, they seem t' think 'tis God's way of saving them from starvin' this summer. So there be rogues turnin' mazed right now, at the stuff they've been 'n' told us is bein' held back by them foreigners. They fear the tide will sweep these dazzling riches out to sea."

Thomas looked out at the wreck, embedded between the rocks despite the swell of the tide. He gauged the size of the vessel, while he hazarded a guess at the load it must have carried. When a child, he had often spent a summer's afternoon watching the ships coming into Mount's Bay. He would listen to the seafarers in the Mount harbour to learn more of their ways. There were the Irish fishing boats, the Spanish galleons and the Flemish traders. Then there were the Newfoundland netters, who travelled the Atlantic Ocean to bring back the strangest fish. But even though it was a wreck, he could tell that this was a rarer vessel still.

"Who are they, John?" he asked.

"One of 'em – looked half dead, he did – said some'at abou' King John. Damned if I know…that bastard's been gone long enough, surely?"

Thomas smiled. There were still some uses for his legal training after all. You could not attend the Inns of Court without gleaning knowledge of the courts of Europe, not to mention some interest in the alliances of the world's greatest empire.

"Have you heard of King Charles of Spain, the Holy Roman Emperor?" Moyle nodded. "Well now, he's recently married his sister to the King of Portugal. The dowry is said to be more than a hundred thousand pounds."

"That's a staggering sum, Mr Thomas, why – I can't believe the English Crown can receive that much in a year!"

"You would be near as right, Master Moyle. But for the Emperor, it's just one more loan from the lenders in Antwerp."

A single mast remained standing on the wreck and as Thomas peered, he could detect the colours of the Portuguese flag flapping above those of Flanders. Thomas rubbed the mare's nose. A wild idea had entered his mind.

****

Diego Alvares was beginning to believe that he was already dead. At least, this was as close to torment as he ever wished to come.

13

As the tide receded, the forty-five survivors of the *Santo Antonio* kept being pushed back onto the wet shingle by the rising number of Cornish natives running riot in the cove. The Portuguese dragged the remnants of their cargo with them, but Alvares knew the tide would rise again soon and this mob would be happy to see them drowned in order to get their hands on it. He was starting to have visions of Marina, smiling and waiving in front of him. He bit his lip until the pain seared through the cold. He must remain conscious.

The bosun, who spoke a smattering of English, had been dispatched by Alvares with some silver coins and was last seen making his escape up the path leading towards the Fal River, only twelve miles by land. At least three merchant ships pledged in the service of João the Third were resting there, more than enough crew to strong arm their rescue and recover their royal cargo.

As local scavengers gleefully paraded the assortment of silks and tapestries, court dresses and painted dishes, which the force of the storm had scattered along the cove, Alvares kept glancing between them and the wreck. Its lowest deck was still intact. So far, none of these cunning swine had discovered the true value of the chests still held in there.

Just then the noise subsided and Alvares looked up. A beautiful Welsh mare, at least sixteen hands, was advancing slowly down the beach, cowering at the crowd as she made her way. Her mount was evidently a man of some importance, as Alvares saw the natives begin to murmur words of respect and try to hide their illicit booty as he passed them. A wave of relief swept over the Portuguese. A sense of order was about to interrupt their ordeal.

As he rode through the crowd, Thomas grew in confidence. Moyle had been right.

"Do nothing to stop 'em, 'n' they'll not have the time to be stopping thee either."

Thomas hadn't bargained for the show of deference to his office, but it came as no surprise.

14

"There are vagabonds here, John," he shouted, "whose regular appearance before the Penwith Justices keeps us in office!"

Moyle grinned his acknowledgement. Justice was always harsh, but at least as magistrates Mr Seyntaubin and Mr Godolphin had the wit to show occasional mercy to the local villains, unlike that Captain Millaton. But then perhaps that was because in John's opinion, Captain Jack was a villain himself.

Thomas had grasped the predicament of the Portuguese as soon as he made his way into the cove. A spring tide goes out the furthest – and comes in the fastest. Many times he had chuckled to see pilgrims returning from St Michael's Mount caught on the causeway by the sea. The village made a useful turn from the ones stranded overnight, or charged a ransom to row them ashore, when the time allowed for their almshouse meal had overrun. Thomas found some pity for these bewildered mariners stranded on the beach, their backs to the encroaching waves. Not so much pilgrims, he reflected, more like young lambs on market day in Helston.

"Who is in charge here?" Thomas scanned the foreign faces, as he tried his Latin pronunciation - it was several years since he had last needed it in court. His manner demanded a response and Alvares stepped forward instinctively.

"Here!" he replied and rapidly proceeded to recite a prayer of thanks to St Michael, words in Latin he knew by heart.

During this incantation, Thomas dismounted again and handed the mare to Moyle. He pointed to the sheaf of papers Alvares was clutching in his hand. Nervously, the Factor passed him the manifest – glad to be relieved of his precious possession by such an imposing and learned gentleman. Thomas read carefully. The Portuguese meant nothing to him, but the fantastic figure totalling the value of the cargo was clear enough.

"Crowns?" he asked, stabbing a finger at the page. Nineteen thousand crowns would be worth nearly five thousand pounds – a record value for a wreck – but then this was no ordinary cargo.

15

The Portuguese shook his head.

"Ducats, then?" Thomas raised his voice, partly in excitement, partly in astonishment. Shaking his head again, Alvares mumbled something through his chattering teeth which sounded like "*livres*" and Thomas drew a deep breath. As a lawyer, he had an intuition when not to press a point to its conclusion. There was now a crowd gathering round and if they gained an inkling of the true value of the wreck, there would be complete mayhem.

"But where?" Thomas spoke softly this time, as he levelled his eyes at Alvares and gestured slightly with his hands. There was no way nineteen thousand pounds worth of cargo was scattered along the beach.

"*Em navio.*" Alvares lowered his head as he shifted his eyes towards the wreck, so only Thomas could understand.

Thomas deliberately turned the other way and fixed his gaze on some large chests he spied half way up the shore, before turning back to Alvares and giving a discreet nod.

This was enough. The crowd took the hint and charged off on the false trail. They trampled over half a dozen corpses already washed up by the tide, leaving Thomas and John Moyle alone with the survivors.

"John, listen to me carefully. Send for ten of our men and together help these wretches protect their possessions. Do not let them into harm's way, nor let them out of your command. I'm off to see Mr Godolphin and obtain his assistance."

"But Mr Thomas," Moyle replied, "what abou' Captain Millaton's men? Some of them are here already – Pengersick Castle is only a few miles away. Who's to stop them spoiling the party? Not to mention Chynoweth!"

Thomas paused. James Chynoweth had no idea of the value of the hoard and there was a fair chance he would not show up for another day in any case. Millaton was another matter. He was captain of the Mount, but his own home, Pengersick, was nearer the cove than any of theirs. Thomas made a cold calculation.

16

"Tell Captain Millaton's band that the Penwith Justices are taking charge here together. So they must take their orders from you. They can send a messenger to confirm it with the captain on the Mount if they wish – you can be sure I will make it my business to reach him first."

Moyle grimaced in sympathy, as he handed back the mare's reins. Seyntaubin and Millaton were not nature's bedfellows and any bargain with the captain would prove a hard one. Still clutching the manifest, Thomas shook Alvares firmly by the hand, motioned to put him and his crew in the care of Moyle, remounted and was gone.

Thomas glanced at the mob surrounding the large chests as he rode up the beach. They were open now. He saw a succession of copper barber's basins appear. There must be over a thousand of them, he calculated, enough to hold the attention of the rabble away from the wreck itself. The ship's secret cargo would remain hidden for a fair while yet. Given a calm sea, its weight on the rocks would prove an anchor.

Thomas now had a plan, one which could save his birthright from Arundell's clutches and make his partners rich beyond their dreams. But he had barely twelve hours to make it happen.

****

As Thomas Seyntaubin was grudgingly composing his letter to him, John Millaton was deeply engrossed in a journey of discovery with his Irish sorceress. His rapid appointment to Justice of the Peace and Captain of St Michael's Mount may well have aroused the envy of his neighbours, but the arousal Millaton cared for at this moment was being provided by the red-haired nineteen-year-old, whose arching body he caressed with his tongue.

Millaton usually liked to dominate his women. But as she gently coaxed him, this Irish beauty had tempted him with lilting tones to her way of doing things. With the girl leading him,

Millaton was momentarily able to obliterate any thought of the demons which possessed him at Pengersick Castle.

They were in the captain's quarters, a light south-facing bedroom looking out across the bay. The ceiling was decorated with a plaster pattern with gilded corners, an extravagance added by Millaton to mark his appointment. In one corner, the dark wall panelling gave way to a small fireplace, which vied with the sunlight to fill the room with warmth this morning.

Millaton had been determined to obtain the Mount's captaincy. His success had taken many by surprise, but it was not hard to see why the Crown had preferred him as an outsider, to control the staging post of so many Cornish revolts. Then a series of casual women had started to appear, much to the amusement of the local gossips, whose explanations for his absence from his marital home quickly became common currency. But the truth was slightly different. The dark secrets of Pengersick Castle were starting to drive Millaton to distraction. Here at the Mount, he could leave behind the domestic quarrels, the haunted room in the tower, the unbidden guest behind the wainscot. So long, that is, as he had some way to occupy the long night hours of watchful duty.

Then there was the sense of kinship with his garrison. Millaton soon realised that they too had demons on the mainland which they had come to escape. Their solution was alcohol, readily available as in any port. He preferred young women, loose vulnerable girls, willing to please.

The sun was now beaming through the narrow window, bathing the body of his Irish conquest, as she continued to stroke him on the soft feather bed. She was teasing him to provide her with more pleasure, artfully rubbing her buttocks against his side. Millaton's lustful energies had begun to stir again, when a loud knocking at the door suddenly interrupted.

"What in the name of St Michael do you want?" he cursed through the timber partition, reluctantly pulling some clothing towards him as the girl slinked behind the screen to perform her ablutions.

"'Tis a message, Cap'ain, urgent mind, from that Mr Seyntaubin."

Millaton groaned inwardly. Godolphin he could stomach, but towards Thomas Seyntaubin he felt an instinctive hostility. Some tiresome magistrate's duty was no doubt about to prevent him from enjoying that one final burst of activity with his wench.

****

Thomas Seyntaubin had never been the most diligent law student. Even now, he and his friend Vyvian were steeped in trouble with the Inns of Court for failing to attend the Inner Temple's Christmas Feast.

But shipwrecks being such a feature of life along the coast where he grew up, he had studied the law governing the salvage of their cargo with a passion. As he cantered towards Godolphin House, the home of William, his good friend and fellow Justice of the Peace, Thomas turned over in his mind the legal conundrum which now presented itself.

William Godolphin was fond of Thomas. At first, he read the look of deep concern on his face, as he hastily arrived at Godolphin House, as a portent of bad news. But it did not take long for the sheer excitement of the events Thomas unfolded to capture his imagination.

"The wreckers on the shore are totally outside the law and their thieving risks the death penalty," Thomas was saying.

"But arresting them would be a fool's errand!"

"Too true. For the Right of Wreck means all goods recovered to land can be claimed by Sir John Arundell, while any recovered in the sea are the Crown's. We would take the pain, before one of them took the prize."

"Meanwhile, cannot the ship's surviving crew demand the

19

return of all the goods, just by paying the costs of recovery to whoever had helped them?"

"That's just why it suits Chynoweth to let the wreckers have a go first. They will leave the shipwrecks with nothing in hand to make such an offer."

"And what of the near twenty thousand pounds in treasure you reckon is still concealed on the ship, Thomas?"

Thomas concluded with a wry smile, "Seeing how the ship is stuck between the water marks, at low tide 'tis Sir John's for the taking and at high tide the King's!"

Sir John was married to Mary Seyntaubin's much older sister. It was an uneasy connection, even without the dire business of the mortgage, and for sure the ties of marriage would carry no weight if a Queen's dowry was at stake. Should a rival claim to the treasure come from London, on the other hand, Thomas might garner Sir John's support in any dispute.

"It makes more sense to my mind, William, to prise the bounty at high tide, when the shipwreck is in the water. Being the King's Justices of the Peace, after all, we'd have a cast-iron defence for our actions, should we be spotted. Then, once aboard our own ship, the hoard can be brought ashore at the point of our own choosing and avoid any confrontation with Chynoweth."

"That's acting within the law," William replied. "But surely that would only entitle us to some payment from the true owners, for the costs of recovering their cargo?"

It was no part of Thomas' plan to part with the vast fortune hidden in those chests for a bill of service, he explained. He had to persuade the Portuguese survivors to pass on ownership in a binding contract. But as Thomas started to outline the details of this legal position, William could contain his enthusiasm no longer.

"Cousin, your barrister's brain runs ahead of me. You must take such matters at a snail's pace if you want your point to stick."

"There's time enough to explain the detail," Thomas replied,

20

"so long as the Godolphin snail has strength enough to complete the course."

They both laughed at this. They were standing in the very garden where one afternoon their fathers had staked their farms on the outcome of a snails' race. As the Seyntaubin snail raced ahead, Godolphin senior had vented his frustration with his own champion by pricking it with a pin. At this, the mollusc expired, leaving his rival a clear run to the finishing line.

The two families had stood side by side for generations. There was no question of the bet being literally enforced. But every spring, Thomas still sent his bailiff round to Godolphin House to collect the token rent of half a crown.

"The problem is Millaton. It's impossible to deal with him, but the whole plan is doomed without him."

Thomas looked pleadingly at his cousin. He couldn't stand the captain. But William was a diplomat by nature and besides, there was a budding romance between their children. Just then, William's daughter Honour strode into view. She was, as her father knew, a difficult proposition, but despite her mean streak and her haughty airs, somehow she had captured the attention of Millaton's son. To Godolphin's way of mind, they were well suited.

"You've sent him a note already, you say," William replied. "I will send him one of my own, with a proposal the rascal is bound to accept."

The two friends got to work. One team was sent to the beach, to keep some semblance of order amongst the wreckers, while making sure that the Portuguese were surrounded by a phalanx both to protect and constrain them. Another team, a list of the most capable and loyal followers of their two families, was assembled for the coming night.

Godolphin set off to meet Millaton near the cove, confident he could convince the captain to join their plan, while Seyntaubin went to secure a ship for the night's work. The tide would reach the wreck around seven o'clock. They would have about four hours to complete their haul of the chests onto the boat and set course for Pengersick. Six miles along the shoreline, the castle would provide the ideal staging post for their booty, while negotiations with the Portuguese commenced.

Thomas calculated that lightening the load on the wreck would cast it adrift from the rocks. With the outgoing tide and a fair wind to pull it to sea, the *Santo Antonio* would conveniently sink into the depths, along with all knowledge of the remaining cargo.

It was a excellent plan, fraught with risk. There was not much he could do about the weather, while Millaton was now for Godolphin to handle. But there was one other problem he had to contain first.

Chapter Three

*...one of them being inhabitant of the county of
Cornwall then and there was piteously drowned and
perished*

Pessoa's Petition to Star Chamber

James Chynoweth paced the floor, fox-like in his lair. It was
strange for Justices to appear at the scene of a wreck, let alone on
the first day. As for the latest lunchtime reports, that they had
brought forty men with them, there was even less sense in it.
Chynoweth's anxieties were stirred and finally he made for the
door. But at just that moment, a visitor appeared.

"Mr James, I count myself lucky to find you here. Are you not
needed in Gunwalloe?"

"Not at all, Sir. As you should know only too well, 't would
never do for the law to be acted on in haste. 'sides, I gather we be
dealin' with Portuguese gentlemen at the cove. So tomorro' I'll be
taking Mr Beauchamp at my side to do some translatin'."

"Is that so? You must think it a matter of some to do, to be
fetching a Penzance man along on a Sunday."

"This is no fifty ducat wreck, to be sure." He lowered his voice
and looked at Thomas intently. "I've recommended to Sir John
that we go to eighty."

"Well, I'm not to know about that," said Thomas Seyntaubin.
"But 'tis always some effort to prise the goods from the wreckers.
Don't go totting up the value of the cargo and not allowing for the
costs of collection."

"Then perhaps you can help me, Sir. Because I'm damn'd if I
know why your fellow Justices have turned up, with their men
an' all. You can't be expecting your brother-in law Sir John to be
paying wreckers' money to thee, surely?"

"Not at all, Mr James. But while you've been waiting for things
to go quiet, there's been riot afoot in that cove today. Justices have

23

to keep the peace. So if you don't mind, we'll continue to make sure that the poor beggars who've survived the wreck, survive the wreckers too."

Chynoweth gave an involuntary laugh. He was not a murderer and the wicked treatment of survivors by some of his countrymen was hardly a matter for Cornish pride, as far as he was concerned.

"So you'll not be planning to pocket their possessions for the Crown, I take it? After all, I hear they be corralled below the high-water mark."

"You have my word, Mr James, so far as it is in my power and the other Justices' too, every single piece from that ship shall be kept for the good of the county."

Chynoweth's face relaxed into a knowing smile. He wouldn't have taken it so easily from Millaton, but Thomas Seyntaubin was a Cornishman through and through. He could tell from his eyes that he meant every word he spoke.

"You hardly need my advice," Thomas concluded. "Just bring your Mr Beauchamp to the cove tomorrow and stick to your price."

Highly satisfied with this exchange, if for differing reasons, both made their way. Chynoweth saw to the arrangements for James Beauchamp to join him the following day, while Thomas sped on to Helston to secure the use of a small ship now awaiting the tide by the river bank.

Chynoweth was no longer a risk, provided that the chests and the wreck could be gone by the morning. Thomas would advise Godolphin to draw over a hundred ducats, or fifty pounds, so he could be sure to trump any offer on Sir John Arundell's behalf for the visible cargo.

****

Helston was served by the Cober, a navigable river which over three hundred years had allowed the town to develop into a thriving centre for the export of Cornish tin. It would be an easy matter for Thomas to engage one of the tin shippers to take his heavy load from the wreck and sail it to Pengersick. But he must do so without his purpose being revealed.

Thomas rode into the market square, left his fresh horse with the innkeeper at the newly built Angel Hotel, and went inside. The gentleman who soon joined him was only too eager to please. Master Pengelly was a shipping agent. He was also the younger son of a farmer on the Clowance estate. Thomas' brother had paid for his training and his unswerving loyalty could be relied upon, even were he to be put before the Star Chamber itself.

"Master Pengelly," Thomas spoke softly, but with an inquisitive look.

"It is done, Sir. The ship's captain will hand over to Moyle's men at six this evening, just above the river mouth. He will quit with all his crew. Surety has been given and all he requires is the ship's safe return by dawn the day after t'morrow."

"Does he know our purpose?"

"I'm sure he don't, Sir. And everything is done to disguise your part. Besides, he's a Frenchman, so of course he hates the Spanish and their Portuguese cousins for locking up his King. He has no cause to tell against us."

"Well done. This is a deep affair and I could not find a more trustworthy servant to play the part."

"To be certain, Mr Thomas, 'tis a double pleasure, not only to serve thee, but to prevent God's grace from being wasted on a Welshman."

Thomas smiled broadly. There were still many Cornishmen who despised the Welsh antecedents of their Tudor king. Some families – like Pengelly's – had suffered at first hand the brutality with which Henry's father had suppressed the Cornish rebellion thirty years ago. He brushed aside any lingering doubts. The essential details of this scheme were safe in the hands of the devoted agent smiling back across the table.

The two left separately, Thomas paying the innkeeper as he

collected his horse. The winter light was fading and he felt a breeze blowing in from the north. Everything now depended on the weather holding for a few more hours. A light northerly breeze would ensure that the tinner's ship sailed on time; a gale would turn the night's excursion into a nightmare. Spurring on his mount, he determined to cover the four miles to Gunwalloe before nightfall. He must check the position in the cove with Godolphin before joining John Moyle.

****

Moyle had led Alvares and his men to a shelf of rock well above the wreck, for at Gunwalloe the tide rises up to cover the shingle. There the Portuguese found that they and their possessions were safe from the tide and the wreckers, but also trapped in a way that left Alvares deeply uneasy.

All the while, Millaton and Godolphin's men went along the shore to restore a sense of order, carefully noting which of the local farmers and tinners were taking part in the fray. For most wreckers, the day had both exhilarated and now exhausted them. They had salvaged as much as they could handle and were ready to head for home.

The Officer of Wreck would be there in the morning and their chance was over. In fact, it was a mystery why the Justices' men had turned up at all. Some said it was because it was a King's ship; others, because Chynoweth was frit to come himself. But a few hung back, eager to plunder the wreck's remaining secrets before another storm came and the sea took it away.

This was the scene which Thomas surveyed approvingly. Moyle had the Portuguese in hand. Whatever suspicions were aroused during the coming night, the foreigners were now rendered impotent. Meanwhile, as his fellow Justices' men stood their ground, the dwindling mob showed little spirit for a fight.

They knew William Godolphin to be as tough a man as Millaton. Their followers would run a sword through any wrecker who crossed their path.

"Gentlemen, our men have done well. The ship is arranged. With God's speed, our plan is afoot." Thomas shook both Millaton and Godolphin warmly by the hand. This was the greatest test of their lives and past differences must be sunk.

"Once this rabble is dispersed," Thomas continued, "we need some of the ablest men to share guard duty on the Portuguese. Seafarers under Moyle's command will collect the ship. Others will haul the chests on board here, then take themselves to Pengersick to help unload later."

"Captain Jack," he continued, turning directly to Millaton, "you and I should both go with the ship and crew. Mr William here can oversee matters in the cove."

"'Tis agreed, Mr Thomas. But you'll find plenty of my men to help unload at Pengersick. There's no need to leave Mr William short-handed."

Thomas nodded his consent, but he knew he needed to stay one step ahead of Millaton. That was why he had not yet revealed the full truth about the cargo. He still half suspected the man of plotting to take it all.

It was now evening and the sun's reflection was disappearing from the side of the new moon. Led by Moyle, the two Justices and the crew found their way to the mouth of the Cober. There, as arranged by Pengelly, they boarded ship in pitch darkness.

****

Never had Alvares uttered so many prayers to the saints. The discovery that Antonio Paciecho, the fleet commander, had perished on board had completely unnerved the ship's master,

27

Diogo Vaz. As for Jeremy de Corfe, the one Gentleman of the King's Chamber to survive the wreck, Alvares was sorely tempted to assist in his dispatch.

It was now ten hours since he had sent the bosun to fetch help and Alvares' hopes of rescue were fading with the light. Regarding the learned gentleman on the horse, he dared not admit to himself that handing over the ship's manifest might have been a foolish error.

Suddenly, several thick-set men appeared. Knowing the sight of a tinner's vessel was bound to stir the suspicions of the Portuguese, Godolphin had arranged for one of his servants, John Wylliam, to take a couple of Millaton's men to pay Alvares and his compatriots a visit, sword and shield in hand.

"Now listen 'ere!" Wylliam shouted. "You can't be staying all night on this godforsaken spot. 'Tis not right. We're to bring you an' your goods an' all an' we're to take you to Chinal's house."

The Portuguese simply stared at Wylliam, too exhausted to make any effort to comprehend what he said, let alone argue with it.

"What's the matter? 'Tis only half a mile. Don't you mind Trehannick an' Geyge here, they're to help you with the cargo."

These last words were spoken even louder, with a menacing smile which quickly persuaded Alvares to corral his troupe into following. They walked painfully up the coastal path and the half-mile inland to Chinal's, in a tiny hamlet from where the *Santo Antonio* was completely out of view. On their way, Alvares felt too weak to protest, even when he saw some of their most precious artefacts being loaded by Geyge onto a wagon, before slowly disappearing in another direction.

The northerly breeze was stirring the waves as the tinner's ship made its way along Gunwalloe towards the wreck. Parts of a corpse floated on the surface and half-submerged effects knocked the prow as they drifted past. Moyle keenly felt the dangers of the night all about them. He was relieved when they reached their destination, ordering the ship face to wind and the sails down as he dropped anchor.

Ropes were thrown and the crew waiting on the wreck pulled it alongside, as the ten-inch thick anchor holds were eased. Godolphin already had several chests ready to put across and the men, well honed by their passion for Cornish wrestling, made light work of them.

Moyle's family were fishermen on his mother's side, so as a boy he had learnt the essential skills of seamanship and every detail of the coast. The sea was reaching high tide and he was only too aware of the danger of being left on the rocks with the wreck, once it turned.

Four of the heaviest chests were saved for last. They had been discovered deep inside the wreck, part of the ballast which had kept it steady through the day. There was no doubting their importance – the massive brass locks and hinges hinted at the value of the contents. But Moyle saw that the moment they were transferred, the wreck would start to move, while their own ship became trapped by the extra weight.

"We have to pull away," he barked. "Lower the plank – we'll walk the chests over!"

Greed overcoming fear, the crew dutifully loosened the ties to the wreck and pulled the ship seaward on the anchor holding. A gangplank was fastened at both ends and the first of the four chests slowly ferried across by two of the well-muscled crew.

The strengthening breeze and the turning tide were making for choppy waters. With the second chest, the next two crew members lurched and nearly lost their balance. The wreck was becoming lively, as its weight lifted.

All tides and winds come in phases and as the third chest was about to cross, there was a sudden lull. The men lost no time in making their way over to safety, looking behind expecting to see the last one follow.

But the lull had presaged a larger wave, one which stretched the plank's ties to breaking point. The two crewmen, caught midway between, pitched left, then right, before losing their balance as the weight of the chest plunged them into the freezing water.

The sea was a fathom deep. One of them, who could swim, broke the surface. He grabbed a line and was hauled on board, his body tortured by the cold.

All waited for the other. They could see a hand reaching up from the deep. A rope was thrown. But a piece of wreckage, loose in the water, chose this moment to waft by and hit something below with a dull thud. The rescued crewman gave a desperate cry but the other men stayed rooted to the spot. Then a voice broke the deathly silence: "That poor lad's drunk his fill."

31

Overleaf

St Michael's Mount

32

Chapter Four

On the morrow, being Sunday, there came to the Portuguese Chynoweth and in his company one James Beauchamp...

Pessoa's Petition to Star Chamber

At Oxford University, John Arscott's absorption in the writings of Roger Bacon, his medieval hero, had aroused deep suspicions. Bacon had been a genius before his time. He had discovered gunpowder and found a way to magnify distant objects. But his novel experiments with alchemy and magic earned him many enemies. The brilliant Oxford Friar had ended his years in prison, accused of necromancy. Fearful of his own predicament, Arscott had accepted his appointment as archpriest on St Michael's Mount as a welcome sanctuary in his native Cornwall. Here he could pursue his study of Bacon's works, safe from the prying of superstitious minds.

When the night sky was darkest, Arscott liked to gaze at the stars and planets, rendered so visible by the clarity of the air on the Cornish peninsula. All alone, Arscott would bring out the spyglass he had developed secretly in his Oxford days, drawing on Bacon's writings: a tube with a lens at one end and a hole at the other. He had perfected the strength of the lens and the length of tube which, thanks to his long-sighted vision, enabled him to see far further than with the naked eye.

Long after his sacristan, clerk and porter had retired, he would climb to the top of the chapel tower and look out from a height two hundred and thirty feet above sea level. Or if a strong south-westerly gale blew up, as it had that evening, he might divert his star-gazing to the parapet below, which ran in front of the entrance to the Lady Chapel.

Here, Arscott felt the rush of freedom as he stepped out and was hit by the fierce winter cold. The sky was clear and his sense of wonder kept him enthralled for many minutes' study, before his attention was drawn to the ships' lanterns out to sea and the darkened scene along the shoreline.

He could make out a tin-bearing ship entering the Mount's harbour mouth. Coming from the Lizard, it was lucky to drop anchor before the tide had retreated too far. Strangely for a French ship, some of the men then found their way to the harbour front and making for the causeway, which was just parting, they walked ashore.

The crew would not know a soul on the mainland, Arscott thought to himself, so perhaps they planned to raid a local house. Mildly curious, he waited for the signs of a scuffle in Marazion, yet there was none. The men had simply vanished into the dark.

Then a voice from the ship reached his ears. He squinted through his device. Not a Frenchman, as he would have expected, but a Cornishman with a vaguely familiar face. Then he saw another, voice raised in anger, someone he recognised instantly. It was Arscott's cue to go inside before either he or his device was noticed.

The next day being a Sunday, matins was a busy time for the archpriest and his assistants. Arscott led his congregation in the familiar Latin verses. As he did so, he was pleased to note that the weekly communion had drawn a respectable throng of pilgrims. It helped that the causeway had parted that morning just before the Chapel bell had begun to toll. John Millaton's appearance in his pew, however, aroused Arscott's curiosity about the French ship with a renewed intensity. He resolved to find time after the service to walk to the harbour and make a discreet inspection.

But the ship had already slipped anchor. By the time Arscott emerged from his clerical duties, she was no longer visible to the naked eye. As for his device, it was not an instrument to brandish in broad daylight.

****

Dead bodies. If there was one aspect of his job which James Chynoweth found distasteful, it was the evidence of human destruction at the scene of a wreck.

"'Tis not that I think them wreckers wrong," he was explaining to Beauchamp, his Portuguese-speaking companion that morning, "to refuse to bury the bodies. I'm with them on that – I mean, why take the risk if 'tis true what they say?"

"It be no more than an excuse, Mr Chynoweth, as you know well. Where in the Bible does it say that you pay with your life, if you bury a man drowned off a ship? 'Tis nothing more than superstition dressed up as reason, so as these fellows can go about their lootin' without bothering their conscience. That's if they have one, mind, which I doubt."

Beauchamp halted. They had just reached Gunwalloe and the sight along the cove could not fail to sicken even two hardened Cornishmen.

The change in the wind to a strong sou'westerly had left many more body parts scattered along the shoreline, as the tide receded that Sunday morning. Forty souls had been claimed by the sinking of the *Santo Antonio.* The sea had now chosen to give up her dead and the stench was drifting inshore.

Strewn amongst the human wreckage, one battered corpse demanded their attention above all others. But first they passed the Gentleman of the King's Chamber, who had evidently dozed off on the night of the disaster still dressed in his Court finery, now forever stained by blood and salt water. Chynoweth noticed that two of the fingers of his left hand had been snapped off, no doubt to remove his rings. Disgusted, they hurried past the headless corpses and the skeletal remains of the other Portuguese mariners. But then in front of them, freshly served up by the spewing sea, was the body of a young Cornish boy.

"I was at school with his father," said Chynoweth, shaking his head. "Teake was his name. An' 'e's been long gone. They're a

Marazion family – what's to become of his mother, I've no idea. But that lad was always one of Millaton's lot, when he'd need 'im."

"'Tis a shame," agreed Beauchamp, "and for what? As you told it, Mr Chynoweth, I was expectin' we'd find a King's ransom here today. But I see no wreck, let alone anythin' priceless like, in fact nothing but these damn'd corpses."

He was right. Only the barest remnants of the ship's cargo were still to be seen. The riches of which Chynoweth's informants had spoken were gone.

"Where's them Portuguese? And where's that wreck?" Chynoweth's voice could not help betraying the first signs of panic. Sir John Arundell was not the forgiving sort.

"Mr Chynoweth!"

The two men on the beach turned, both surprised and relieved by the sight of John Moyle walking towards them.

"A terrible business, an' him bein' one of the strongest wrestlers in your village team an' all. They've been and told his mother already. And the captain's promised help, which is more than he needed to, to be fair. I don't mind telling thee, even them wreckers were spooked when they saw this boy washed ashore. 'Tis wrong, but there's nought we can do about it."

"Are they going to leave him here?" Beauchamp demanded. "'Tis one thing to have these foreigners on the beach, but surely the Teake lad deserves a burial?"

"I'm all for you on that," agreed Moyle, "but who's to be doin' it, that's been the question. I've just heard it from a mouth, though, that Millaton's priest at Pengersick will step for'ard. What with tales of ghosts at the castle an' what have you, he's had it with our superstitions in these parts. So he's declared there's to be a proper funeral an' all."

"Well, thank God for that," chimed in Chynoweth. "Now tell us, Moyle, it looks as if there's been hell'up 'ere. Where's our cargo to? An' where's our ship?"

"Your ship, you say? No one told me it was a Cornish craft that went on the rocks t'other night."

"Now you look see, my good fellow, my Sir John Arundell will not be having any nonsense. 'Tis his wreck and I'm just here to do my job. You know that as well as I do."

"All I know," replied Moyle cautiously, "is that the Portuguese gentlemen who came off that ship be lodging at Chinal's place, which you will be pleased to recall is an Arundell tenancy any how's. 'Tis just half a mile from 'ere, as you would know. Seein' as you've brought your Mr Beauchamp, 'twould be a good idea for him to speak to 'em, 'cause no one else can make sense of their tongue, that be for sure."

"All in good time, Moyle. But what I want to know is this. How come the wreck has disappeared? As I was told, it was lodged between them rocks and was good for several days yet. And where's its load? We was told not all the wreckers in Penwith and Kerrier could have carted it off in one day."

"As I'm sure you've noticed," Moyle answered, "what we have now is a sou'westerly, leavin' the wreckage on the shore as the tide goes down. But the wind changed direction during the night. Before then, the spring tide yesterday was taking the flotsam out to sea and what wind we had was helping."

"That's not what I know," replied Chynoweth suspiciously. "I heard, from a good source, how this cove was littered with stuff, far more than the wreckers knew what to do with. An' the ship was stuck, as like she had plenty more on board. So this change in the wind you mention should only have helped us."

"Like I say," Moyle replied slowly, "those Portuguese gen'lemen be at Chinal's. They was here all day long. You'd best be asking them."

Chynoweth was beginning to doubt that the Portuguese would be any use to him, but he could see he had no choice but to follow Moyle's advice. One thing he knew was that the Justices' men had been there. Perhaps they had made the recovery for him. If so, they would not want to be falling out with Sir John, not over the few pounds due to them for their trouble. And he had Mr Thomas' assurance. It was just a matter of patience and negotiation.

"Very well," he sighed. "If you would be good enough to show us the way."

The path inland to Chinal's house took only a short while, the south-westerly wind behind them. At the door, Beauchamp found one of the Portuguese, who had evidently taken charge of his motley band.

"Greetings, we have come to help you. Our master is Sir John Arundell, the Lord of this place. His rights in this matter derive from the King of England."

These words were spoken by Beauchamp in Portuguese. Alvares found himself instantly wishing that he had waited to put his manifest into these hands. Although their owner lacked the demeanour of the man on horseback, the sound of his own tongue being spoken at once lifted Alvares' spirits and then unleashed the floodgates of his despair.

"My good and honest friend, we had given up all hope of finding mercy in this place. For certain, the people of this house have provided shelter this past night and the man besides you protected us from the villains on the shore. But where are our possessions? What is become of our ship?"

Beauchamp looked unnerved by this outburst. Before he could translate, Alvares thought to add: "But pray forgive me, *Senhores,* I am being most impolite. Let me begin again and first allow me the pleasure to introduce our distinguished company."

With this, Alvares produced Vaz and de Corfe for Beauchamp's inspection, with as much ceremony as he could muster in the damp confines of a Cornish farmhouse. But if he thought that meeting a member of the Royal Court of João the Third would impress their hosts, Alvares was soon disabused.

"This is all very well," Beauchamp said with a smile, "but our business is really quite simple. We will purchase the ship, goods and merchandise, and with our money you and your fellows can make safe return to your country. No doubt one of your ships in the Fal will be only too pleased to bring home such an illustrious band and company."

Alvares sensed a trap. It was all too easy for these men to claim they were acting as the King's representative, but he could not afford to be tricked a second time.

"The ship and the goods are all only the King of Portugal's and so it does not appear upon our charter party which of us left alive has the power to make a sale to you.

"In any case, first we have charges to be heard, for we have been robbed and spoiled during the night. Before we discuss the sale of the cargo, or any other business, who is the law in these parts? Who can we see to make complaint and seek proper remedy?"

Beauchamp translated this to Chynoweth, who smiled discreetly.

"If one or two of you will go with me to certain gentlemen, being Justices of the Peace, I think that they will cause you to have restitution of your goods again."

After Beauchamp translated this reply, an animated discussion broke out between the Portuguese as to whom to send. Alvares prevailed, his sense of purpose restored by the prospect. He had no doubts about who had proved the villains of the piece. He now relished the chance to see law and order finally brought to bear for the horrors inflicted on them during the past day and more.

"'Tis fortunate," Chynoweth was explaining through Beauchamp, "that two of our Justices lie within a few miles of this point. We'll be getting you there as soon as we have word that they are ready to receive us. They would not sit on a Sunday, as a rule, but seeing as how you come from the King of Portugal an'all, there seems every reason to make exception."

The truth was that Chynoweth himself wished to waste no

more time in reaching the bottom of this mystery. He expected the Justices to have the answers.

****

As soon as the service in the Mount chapel was ended, Millaton went ashore to seek out William Godolphin and apprise him of the situation. They had agreed to meet at the Angel Hotel in Helston, which had become a popular place to retire after a day's sitting on the bench.

"So let me understand," Godolphin spoke carefully. "Our fellow magistrate is now, as we speak, afloat somewhere in the middle of Mount's Bay. He's laden with cargo, awaiting nightfall to come into Pengersick."

"That's right," Millaton replied. "The death of the boy and the sudden change in the wind – they unnerved us all. 'Twas always going to be a risky business, putting into Pengersick last night, but in a sou'westerly…"

"For certain," Godolphin nodded. Many were the ships ruined by a southwesterly gale, turning the south Cornish coast into a leeward shore. In such weather, Mount's Bay had a crab-like ability to ensnare a ship, as she tacked vainly from side to side heading helplessly for the rocks. The previous night's plan had all hinged on the breeze coming from a northerly direction. That fatal lull and the change in the wind had forced Moyle to alter course.

"So you made for the Mount harbour, then?

"Well, there was no other choice. We knew we had just time enough to make it before the tide turned. Wait any longer, and we could have been caught in the bay by a gale even more dangerous than the one that took the carrack. None of us was for risking that."

"So you and Mr Thomas must have made fast friends in the night, if you trusted him to take the ship away on his own, Captain John."

40

Millaton scowled.

"It is true that the two of us make awkward allies. In fact, we almost had a falling-out when we reached safe harbour. My idea being, unload it there and then. But he was right not to and besides, he's not going anywhere with that ship. As he said to me, it's his man that's given surety for the vessel. And you and I know he's not one to leave his family, even for all the riches of a Queen's dowry."

"Of course he's not. So what's the plan tonight, then?"

"We have to do it on a turning tide. It's the only way not to leave the ship stranded on the beach. First, as the tide's still coming in, we bring the ship right close to shore, anchored in the water. She's not too deep in the hull, which is lucky, while the sand at Pengersick falls away gently. So in the shallow waters, our men will unload the cargo. The tide and the loss of weight then lifts her off the sand and she sets out to sea as the tide turns in her favour. Come the dawn, that ship will be back at the mouth of the Cober, just as we agreed with the French."

"You will have wagons on the shore to take the load then?"

"That's right. By midnight, the King of Portugal's treasure will be safely hidden in the castle."

The two continued to go over every detail of the plan, they could not afford another mishap that evening. As they did so, Richard Borno, one of Godolphin's men, approached their table with a couple of his friends.

"Richard," Godolphin beamed, "I see you keep good company. Captain Millaton, allow me to introduce young Lower here, one of my cousin John's men, and here's John Polgrene, he works for Mr Vyvian."

"You have an excellent memory, Sir," remarked Lower, as they all shook hands.

"So tell me, Richard, how goes it? Has Moyle met up with Sir John's men?"

"To be sure, Sir. That Beauchamp fellow, he is a master of them

41

foreign fellows' way of speakin' and that Mr Chynoweth, he's impressed them no end."

"I'm glad of it. So are they ready to agree a sale?"

"Well, that's just it, Sir. They will be having nothing to do with a sale, at least not until they can make proper complaint like, for their treatment."

"I see. So who do they wish to see, to make this complaint?" Godolphin asked with some unease. They could do without Sir John Arundell, the senior Justice of the Peace, becoming involved at this stage.

"Well, Sir, seeing as you and Mr Millaton here are nearest, that Mr Chynoweth was wondering if you would be prepared to hear them. He'd not want to be bothering his master t'other side of Truro, any more than we do."

"Of course not. Besides, Sir John is a highly religious gentleman and I do not suppose he would relish a hearing on a Sunday, even one pertaining to his Right of Wreck."

"'Tis true, Sir. So what to do with this Portuguese fellow, who Mr Beauchamp tells us be their Factor or some such? Could he be brought to meet you two Justices today, here in Helston?"

Godolphin and Millaton looked at each other and nodded agreement. The town hall where they met was across the road. It was nearly noon and now that Sunday observances were complete, daily routine was returning for all but the strictest believers.

****

The dutiful Catholic in Alvares was certainly troubled to be going about this business on a Sunday. But as the biting cold invaded his senses, he fought to keep his mind on the vital task of presenting his case to the Justices. He had hoped that a second member of the crew might accompany him, as Chynoweth had at first suggested. But the other one, the tall fellow who had kept guard over them the day before, would not allow it. Perhaps he had guessed Alvares' plan to slip word at last to the Portuguese ships anchored up the Fal.

They arrived in the central square. Pinched between the heavy bulk of Moyle and Chynoweth, Alvares walked cautiously into the Helston town hall.

It was an elegant room, with raised windows towards the high ceiling and oak panelling around the sides. A fire had been started but had yet to generate any warmth from the grate. The noontime winter light poured into the room, casting a shadow across the figures of the two Justices.

Alvares was asked to sit down. He felt a moment of calm. Then, for the third time in less than two days, fear entered the pit of his stomach. When the two Justices in front of him began to speak, he recognised them as the very men he had been about to denounce. They had orchestrated the wreckers on the beach, he was sure of it. As his mind raced furiously over the words he had prepared, Beauchamp broke his concentration.

"Mr Alvares! The Justices have asked me to explain your basic rights..."

There followed several minutes of hesitant Portuguese – legal phrasing was evidently not often deployed when Beauchamp handled wreckage claims. Then Alvares was invited to make his case and after some preliminary remarks, he came to the heart of his complaint.

"When we came ashore, we had managed to salvage upwards of a thousand ducats from the wreck. But the robbing and the spoiling, especially during the night just past, have deprived my good King João of much valuable property. I am certain that you Gentlemen do not wish to anger my King, or see your own King Henry embroiled in such a matter as this. Seeing as you are the law in these parts, then surely you can restore our rightful property."

"Your rightful property, as you say, is for you to dispose of.

Our laws grant you possession, as the survivors of the wreck. But as to recovery, that is a cost for which you must pay. Perhaps it would help to agree such a cost, if you told us more about the extent of the goods you have lost."

"I had a complete manifest of the ship's cargo, but this gentleman and his friend came and took it from me." Alvares pointed at Moyle.

"Mr Moyle, do you have possession of the ship's manifest?"

"If it pleases your Justices, no I do not, nor can I tell this court where or what it is."

"I see," murmured Millaton, with which both he and Chynoweth looked at Godolphin enquiringly. William simply shrugged his shoulders.

"Without evidence of this so-called manifest, we must ignore it" he declared. "But as you have already told us, you recovered one thousand ducats on the shore, is that correct?"

"Yes."

"And this amount was robbed from you on the shore, you say, even as Mr Moyle here was guarding you?"

"Yes."

"Well, there is no remedy therein, for it is the custom of the county."

"But if you and your fellows will sell us the ship and the goods," Chynoweth interjected, "we shall give you well therefore and furthermore we will do the best for you that lies in our powers."

"But neither I nor none other being here present has power to make sale thereof, for it is all only for the King of Portugal. I am just the Factor on this ship. The person in whose name the charter party was made is now drowned."

The Justices discussed this point for a moment and then spoke again through Beauchamp.

"You and your fellows are subject to our laws now. Our statutes provide that the salvage from any wreck belongs to the survivors, if any there be." He paused, to make sure Alvares understood exactly what he said.

"But if there be none, then all goods recovered become the property of the Lord of the Manor. In these parts, that would be Sir John Arundell. He has the Right of Wreck."

Alvares looked at them all. He had been saved only to make a bargain. If he did not, then he and his compatriots were worth a great deal more dead than alive. As for the manifest, were this Lord of the Manor to discover the value it placed on the cargo, it would surely prove their death warrant.

Pengersick Castle

(Grose, *Antiquities of Cornwall*)

Chapter Five

On the first floor some of the wainscot is remaining, on which are diverse verses and moral sentences written in the ancient black letter, one comparing a miser to an ass loaded with riches...
Pengersick Castle, Grose, *Antiquities of Cornwall*

The break in the clouds had continued, as if the rain knew it had done enough to destroy farms and families up and down the land. But while the sun blazed unawares, desperate folk began to take full measure of the damage to their stock. A landlubber, the thought merely added to the gruelling ordeal facing Thomas Seyntaubin.

Adrift at sea, his every nerve was now tested, concealing this priceless hoard on the fringes of the drama. He fretted whether Godolphin had grasped the finer legal points, or if Moyle's powers of persuasion would suffer, after the shock of the boy's death. Above all, he feared that in his absence, Chynoweth might have the wit to strike his own bargain with the Portuguese. Then all this effort would have been for nought, while his role in the episode would leave him exposed to the mercy of the Arundell estate and his aloof brother-in-law.

In formulating his plan, Thomas had known he could not allow for every contingency. He had run with the main chance, counting on his understanding of each player. Godolphin, for example, liked to act the goodly fellow. Underneath, he was as sharp as a knife, even ruthless. Thomas was just glad to be close to such a kinsman. Moyle might be counted on to carry Chynoweth and Beauchamp with him. But how the Portuguese Factor would react to seeing him again was anyone's guess.

Then there was Millaton. Not a Cornishman, he had suddenly appeared twelve years ago, with his castle on the coast and, all too soon, his appointment to the Mount and now picked as the latest Justice of the Peace. There were families, Thomas reflected, who had waited a hundred years to achieve the same position in society, as Millaton had stormed to in barely a decade. This was the King's way, of course. Men like Wolsey, rising from nowhere, running the country as if they owned it. Not that Millaton had a hope, in Thomas' view, of going any further. He was too rash, too opinionated and – judging by last night – strange in device and mind.

They had all been shocked by the boy's death. For all the gravity of their scheme, in so many ways the evening had been one big adventure, with a fairytale prize at the end of it. The boy's death changed all that. It was one thing to have the corpses of strangers floating along the shore, their presence utterly divorced from the lives of friends and neighbours. It was quite another to imagine the cold white face of a boy they had all known since a child, watched as he made his first communion, cheered as he won his first wrestling contest. Thomas felt the burden of blame for the Teake boy's being there on the night and shared the guilt at his death.

Yet for Millaton, it had mattered not at all. Thomas had lost count of the time spent in that ship, remonstrating with Millaton to provide for Mrs Teake in Marazion, who faced starvation without her son to support her. Millaton was solely driven by money and position, he concluded, with all the sense and charm of an ox.

So here he was. Someone had had to stay with the ship and its precious cargo. Millaton could not be trusted and Moyle had a better chance of stringing Chynoweth along than Thomas. Besides, his absence meant some awkward questions over the manifest could be avoided. The wreck had been successfully dragged out to sea and sunk that night. In a day or two, the heavy cargo would be safely buried in the vaults at Godolphin, Clowance and Pengersick. Lose the trail of the manifest and nothing beyond the recovered wreckage would be left to argue the ship's true value.

"Mr Seyntaubin – the bosun's asked me to tell you, we're heading back towards the coast!"

Thomas gave a smile and looked out to sea. The evening was closing in. It had been one of those dry, cold January days when the wind bore down without threatening a real gale, yet with enough strength to clear the mist and keep the shoreline in view. The distant sound of waves lashing the rocks had acquired a reassuring rhythm. Tonight they could be certain of a steady beacon from the Mount, as they guided the ship towards the beach at Pengersick. The last act in their escapade was about to commence.

****

Jeremy de Corfe, Gentleman of the King's Chamber, was fidgeting. He loosened the salt-encrusted garter on his left stocking. He discreetly adjusted his damp-bottomed breeches. He quietly cursed his Lisbon tailor, as he eyed the ashen-faced Factor of the *Santo Antonio,* standing before the modest hearth in Chinal's house.

"My dear *camarada,* you want me to believe that the very scoundrels who have robbed us of the King's fortune are the officers of the law in this place?"

"Yes, your honour."

"And this other one – this Chynoweth, you say – he thinks he can buy everything we have for his own master for just fifty ducats?"

"Yes, your honour," Alvares replied wearily, "though I think I could raise him to eighty."

"Idiot! Can you imagine what our King John will say to me, if I inform him that his beautiful wife's dowry, which has been so kindly donated by her royal brother, Charles of Spain, the Holy Roman Emperor himself…"

"Yes, your honour."

"Of course we cannot sell the King's *tesouros*, not even for a thousand ducats."

"No, your honour."

"But what is our choice?" The ship's master, Diogo Vaz, stirred himself. "Whatever we do, we have to escape from here alive, or soon the treasure will belong to them anyway."

"Can that be right, Alvares?" de Corfe looked hard at the ship's Factor. "I am no lawyer, but surely such theft is forbidden by the Rules of Oleron."

"Yes, your honour. In fact, *Senhor* Fernandes taught me the Rule Twenty-six by heart, before we left Flanders."

"Ah yes, Roderick, the King's Consul – remind us what he taught you again?"

"*If the Lord of any Place be so barbarous as to assist in such villainies, that he may have a share in such wrecks,*" Alvares recited, "*the said Lord shall be apprehended, and all his goods confiscated and sold, in order to make restitution to whoever as of right it belongs.*"

"Very good, Alvares. So did you tell this Sir John Arundell's friend – this Chynoweth – about Rule twenty-six?"

"Yes, your honour. And even more, I warned him of the Punishment of Oleron!"

"The Punishment?"

"Yes, your honour. The Rules of Oleron, they say that any Lord of the Place doing these things, he shall be fastened to a post in the midst of his own mansion house, and all shall be burnt. *The walls shall be demolished, the stones pulled down, and the place turned into a market where they sell only pigs, unto all posterity!*"

"Very good, Alvares," de Corfe beamed. "So this Sir Arundell, how can his man still think to insult us with his offer?"

"Well, your honour, I do not understand. When I get to the part about posterity," Alvares replied, "this translator, he gave out a little laugh. Then he turns to the Chynoweth fellow, I think to explain it in their tongue, and they both start to laugh rather louder. Soon the whole room is pointing the finger, roaring with laughter – all of them joining in the joke!"

"Let them enjoy their little joke," de Corfe sneered, angry now at the blatant offence to his countrymen. "Do they really think the Kings of Europe will allow such an insult?"

"You are right, your honour," interjected Diogo Vaz. "Has not their own King Henry been called the "Defender of the Faith", by none other than our Holy Father in Rome?"

"And is not his Queen Katherine the aunt of our King John, now that he has married her niece?"

"By the priests of Portugal, surely you are right again, your honour."

"And does not his Cardinal Wolsey care to be the next Pope?"

"Your honour excels himself. He cannot rule Rome, who fails to observe the Rules of Oleron!"

"So, gentlemen, our first aim must be to escape from this mad place. Then we must look to their King and his Cardinal!"

"To defend the law of our Holy Catholic faith!"

"To return the property of their Brother in Christ!"

This animated discussion would have continued long after darkness had fallen and the new moon was gone. But just then reality intruded with a rude knock at the door.

Richard Borno bowled into the room, followed by Lower and Polgrene and a dozen more Cornishmen. As on the night before, they came with shield and sword in hand.

The weightier cargo which the Portuguese had salvaged on the beach had already been lost to the wreckers. But they still clung to a small number of precious stones, chains, brooches and other jewels. The Master carried a silver bowl which his father had given him, along with the chain and whistle which were his marks of office.

Borno wasted no time in explaining his orders.

"There be some wicked people in these parts, you see, an' word of your presence in Mr Chinal's house could provoke a mischief.

'Tis best that you give those things to me now and we'll keep 'em safe an' sound like."

Alvares turned to Borno, whose company stood ready to implement his orders, with as much violence as the occasion demanded. He had understood not a word of Borno's Cornish, but there was no need to guess the meaning. They were being robbed. The Portuguese, belying their reputation as the most hardened sailors on the high seas, meekly handed over the last and most valuable of their belongings. Their remedy must be survival first, retribution later.

"We would speak to your masters – in the morning."

Borno looked at him. He sensed that at last they could be about to capitulate, but he wanted to be sure.

"You're ready to work with our masters – in the morning, yes?"

"*Sim, Senhor.*"

"Come on then, boys," Borno turned to his companions. "We've orders to look after these gentlemen tonight. No harm's to come to 'em, 'specially not afore they meet the Justices again tomorro'. Is that clear?"

Then the Portuguese were left with the room to themselves. Their guard made sure that no one could either enter or leave. Chinal's house had become a fortress.

****

It had been agreed that they would meet at Pengersick Castle. There was no need for Thomas to take the ship back to the river Cober himself – a task best entrusted to Moyle, who took command as soon as she had unloaded her consignment on the beach. The weather behaved. With Godolphin and Millaton both present, to supervise the shore side of the operation, the job was quickly done.

The bleak entry to Pengersick Castle befitted its owner, Thomas thought to himself. Dumb-bell gun ports defended each of the three outer walls of the tower, while above the massive door, he spied a shoot for molten lead. He made his way up the spiral stairway to the generous hall with its large window facing onto the courtyard. Here he found Godolphin and Millaton already installed.

"We have word from Borno," Godolphin announced, delighted at the success of his loyal servant. "The Portuguese are ready to parley."

"Does Chynoweth know it?" Millaton demanded.

"No, but I think he should," Godolphin replied. "We will never satisfy Sir John's curiosity, if we cut him out of the proceedings altogether."

"My cousin William is right, Captain," Seyntaubin said, taking up the theme. "As regards the cargo salvaged on the beach, it is essential that we include Chynoweth in the negotiations, to give Sir John his share."

"So where does that leave the other cargo?" Millaton was confused.

"I have prepared a contract to cover everything that came off the ship. That includes all that they saved on shore, anything collected since and whatever was left, to be found in the water so to speak. The parties are the Portuguese and the three of us."

Thomas looked at them both intently, to make sure they understood exactly what he planned. "Sir John's share is for us to agree with Chynoweth separately. The key is to make that a fixed sum, based on the proven recovery on the shore. Beyond that, he should have no further claim."

"And what amounts exactly do you have in mind, Cousin?"

"Well, the Portuguese fellow spoke of one thousand ducats as the value of the goods they had about them on the beach. But there are the charges we have incurred for protecting them, their lodging expenses, food and drink. Recovery costs for what's been taken could be exorbitant, unless the wreckers prove compliant. Then take whatever's left and divide it in two for Sir John's Right of Wreck. I'd say that leaves about one hundred ducats – or fifty pounds at the most for the foreigners."

"That's very clever but what's to stop Chynoweth coming up with a higher offer?"

"He won't go beyond eighty ducats, he's told me himself. And even that's his record."

Godolphin and Millaton were reassured.

"There's just one other point, Captain," Thomas continued. "Mr William and I have discussed it already. As regards the chests landed tonight, we need our share in our own hands, before the bargain is struck."

Millaton shifted in his chair. "It is all perfectly safe here at the castle."

"We are sure it is," continued Thomas, "but equally it could all disappear by the morning."

Millaton started to become agitated. "Are you saying you do not trust me?"

"Let us simply say this. The value in those chests would pay a prince's ransom. Your ties in the county are rather recent. For all we know, you and the booty could be on your way to Ireland, before we had the chance to follow you."

Millaton's face reddened. Evidently, Seyntaubin had used his night in the Mount harbour to catch up on the local gossip. The captain paused, refusing to react to the taunt.

Millaton really had not thought as far ahead as the man opposite him, being content to see this scheme through and simply take his share. But here was a chance, he now realised, to step into their sphere; to forge a comradeship which, despite their better judgement, they would have to accept. It is human nature to want to share a secret. Millaton felt an impulsive urge to share his.

"Then let me show you," he heard himself saying, "the reason why I cannot leave this place. Come to the room above and all will be clear."

"Is this a trick, Millaton? Because if it is…"

"Why don't you take my sword? There is nothing to fear, unless of course you believe in ghosts."

"What do you mean?"

"This room where I am taking you is haunted. A century ago, Henry Pengersick took his dying wife there, after killing a monk who had raped and stabbed her in the castle grounds. It is said they sometimes still appear."

Thomas laughed. "I don't see how ghosts are going to win our trust, Captain, real or otherwise."

"Of course not," Millaton replied, "but this might." They had climbed the stairs now and he opened the door to the room. Inside, a candle was burning faintly, just enabling them to discern the outline of the figure in the chair by the fire. It was an old man, half asleep.

"Gentlemen," Millaton continued, "meet my father."

"I thought he died twelve years ago," Godolphin said, as his eyes narrowed.

"Middleton!" Thomas' memory was working furiously. "London – 1515 – murder. His name's Middleton."

"What the devil are you talking about?" Godolphin interjected, with a mixture of irritation and curiosity.

"It was twelve years ago, I was still practising at the Inner Temple. A rich client came to see one of my colleagues. He claimed to have been involved in a duel and the other man had died."

"So he was facing a charge of murder?"

"The case looked pretty hopeless. Then we heard that the suspect had disappeared. It was the talk of the City, for a week or more."

"That's right," Millaton said softly. "I had recently inherited the castle from my mother's side. She being a Beville by birth, it was really not so hard to arrange for my father to disappear, by coming down here. He has remained ever since."

"And you changed your name to Millaton, as if you were from the Devonshire family. Very clever, Captain. But would it not have been better for your father to face trial? He might have got off. This is a prison for life."

"My father had many enemies in London. He couldn't trust a jury. Twelve years of Cornish sea air have been a good deal better than the gallows."

They looked closely at Millaton. Even in the weak glow of the candlelight, it was impossible not to share the powerful sense of release he exuded at this moment of truth.

"What is it, Jack?"

The figure in the chair was standing now, his long white hair and thin body making for a convincing apparition. He still wore the clothes of the wealthy merchant he had once been, under a gown made from the finest London russet. He was walking towards them, very slowly, his hands trembling.

****

Thomas had much to think about on his way home that night. He arrived at Clowance utterly exhausted, as much by the mental strain as by the activities of the last two days. Mary knew her husband well enough to tell that he was in no mood to explain his adventures. She simply promised to wake him again at daybreak.

Sleep came fitfully. What had started as an escapade, admittedly one as wild as any of his youth, had now become the challenge of a lifetime. Success would transform the family's fortunes; failure could spell the destruction of all Thomas held dear.

The stakes could not be higher. On one side were the Kings of Spain and Portugal, easily the richest and most powerful men in Europe. On another he faced Sir John Arundell, the foremost man in Cornwall, who guarded his rights to wreckage with as much vigour as he enforced repayment of his loans. Lastly, King Henry would surely seize any opportunity to divert the spoils of the *Santo Antonio* to the royal purse.

At the outset, Thomas had been breezily confident that he could balance these conflicting forces and by dint of his legal knowledge, steer the path to riches. Yet at this moment he could be accused of deliberately concealing a ship's treasure. That was a capital crime. If conviction secured the glittering prize for any one of these mighty figures, then it would surely be obtained – and the legal niceties would go hang along with him.

The extraordinary scene with Millaton and his father had given Thomas fresh worries. Now he and Godolphin were complicit in harbouring a murder suspect. Millaton had skilfully ensnared them in his own predicament.

Perhaps that was why he had relented in the row over how and when to split the treasure. Moyle and Borno had been deputed to stand guard at Pengersick with one of Millaton's men for the rest of the night.

They would meet again in the morning to share the spoils.

Chapter Six

Though youth hath ruled him before this, yet now...
he is well amended and intendeth to be more diligent than
ever he hath been.
Mary Seyntaubin to her sister Honor, *The Lisle Letters*

Monday was another of those crisp winter days which Mary Seyntaubin usually welcomed. Yet this morning, as she bade farewell to Thomas, she found it hard to ignore the worry lines on his forehead and the signs of stress, even as he warmly embraced her and the children.

Mary was relieved that Honor Basset was visiting in a few weeks' time. "Youth has ruled him before," she had written in a letter to her sister, recalling some of Thomas' mad escapades with the Bosworthoggas and the Polgrenes. It had taken her father's intervention to calm his other son-in-law, Sir John Arundell, when Thomas and his associates were caught removing salvage from wrecks along Looe Bar, which Sir John rightfully claimed as his own.

Thomas was older now, Mary told herself, with responsibilities he had never carried before. But if Thomas was in trouble with Sir John again, her father was no longer alive to help. Perhaps Honor could be called upon to keep the peace. At least she was fond of "your old knave", as she liked to call Mary's husband.

On the other hand, Honor was coming to confide in Mary with her own problems. Like all the daughters of Sir Thomas Grenville, Honor had married a much older man, one who admired her beauty rather more than her intelligence. Sir John Basset provided the wealth and security which had turned the raising of her young family into a pleasure, rather than the chore known to nearly every Tudor family. In return, Honor had at last provided him with two sons.

Honor's children were younger than her sister's. She had great ambitions for them, the girls as well as the boys, in contrast to Mary, who simply craved for her brood the same idyllic Cornish life which she enjoyed with Thomas.

They shared an elder sister, Catherine, the one who was married to Sir John Arundell, the grandest of all the family alliances. This gave Honor her opening and before long an invitation to Court for Sir John and Lady Basset arrived. The first building block in her own future and her children's was in place.

Then the Countess of Devonshire died. A Plantagenet daughter, her funeral promised to be a grand affair at Exeter Cathedral, not far from Umberleigh, the large Devon mansion which was the seat of the Basset family. Honor was delighted when her new friends at Court proposed that a tall, handsome courtier, who was representing the King at the funeral, should come to stay with them.

His name was Arthur Plantagenet. As the offspring of Edward IV and a favoured mistress, he was half-brother to the dead Countess. Ennobled and enriched by King Henry as Lord Lisle, he had become a Knight of the Garter and an Admiral of the Fleet. He was about fifty years old and recently widowed. By the end of his stay at Umberleigh, Arthur and Honor had formed an unspoken bond.

****

A very different pairing was being discussed on the way to Pengersick that morning. Thomas met up on horseback with his cousin William at Godolphin Cross and the two of them soon covered the distance to Millaton's castle.

"So tell me, William, have last night's revelations caused a change of heart?"

"How do you mean, Thomas?"

"Well, you told me you were intending to seal our pact with the captain by marrying that troublesome daughter of yours to his son. A neat solution all round, we both thought at the time, but if his father is a murderer..."

"We don't know that," Godolphin responded tartly. "Who's to say he didn't kill the other man in self-defence? Besides, I doubt the evidence is still there to convict him."

"Harbouring a murder suspect is a crime in itself."

"You've spent too long studying the law and not yet long enough imposing it, Cousin!"

"Perhaps, but what kind of a man does all this make the captain? He's no longer your Devonshire squire, is he now?"

"That's true, but he's still the master of Pengersick. And that dying wife he was telling us about, the one who still haunts the place apparently, well she was a Godolphin. The castle should have come into the family years ago; now is the chance to make it happen."

"It would still make a fine addition to your farms, there's no denying it. A castle by the shore has many uses, certainly so long as Portuguese mariners cannot read their charts. But what if history repeats itself – a haunted house and a resident killer hardly make for a happy home."

"Young Honour can take care of herself, have no doubt about that. It's Millaton's lad you should be worried about!"

At this they both laughed. The captain's son had inherited all of his father's gaucheness, but none of his bulk and ferocity. Honour Godolphin would have the upper hand in that marriage and no doubt that was one of its attractions for her.

One facet of the dramatic disclosure the night before had left its mark – Millaton had risked all to protect his father. This unswerving loyalty to family was one trait which Thomas admired. As they pulled up their horses in front of the heavy castle door and dismounted, he determined to keep this thought to the fore, however wary he remained of the captain.

The tower bell sounded the half hour and at that moment the great door started to open, as if both were sprung on the same mechanism.

The two men were ushered through the outer courtyard to the inner court, where Millaton was waiting along with Borno and Moyle. John looked tired but satisfied. Evidently, the return of the ship had gone smoothly. Thomas was pleased to see that all the windows looking into the court had been covered, while in the centre the chests were laid out in three rows, just as he had directed, each one containing a roughly equal number, according to their size and the strength of their seals. Strictly following his instructions, none of the chests had been opened but each had been marked with its weight.

"Thank you, Captain, this is excellent," Thomas began.

"That's all very well, but I still do not see why we cannot open the chests first."

"None of us can lose from this adventure," Thomas reminded them, "so long as we stick to the law. If we enter a bargain with the Portuguese which we know to be false, then it won't take long for them to have it struck out in court. But if we take the risk of buying these chests, contents unknown, then our contract will stand.

"We have all watched these chests from the moment they left the wreck of the carrack. Each of us had the chance to count them and now our men have weighed them too. The differences in types and style are obvious and as far as possible we are each getting the same number of each type."

"How's that, Thomas?" asked Godolphin. "What's with the third row? It looks to have more than the other two."

"There's no trick involved," Thomas replied. "As for each row, to decide who takes which one, I suggest all three of us put in a bid"

"How do you mean?"

"Well, between us we will have to find a good fifty pounds to seal our bargain with the Portuguese. I suggest that whichever of us bids highest gets first choice of which row of chests he takes today. The second highest bidder goes next and the lowest third. And if any of us bids above what we have to pay the Portuguese, then the surplus is split evenly between the other two. "

"Why would anyone do that?" asked Millaton suspiciously.

"Because he believed the longest row was worth that much more," replied Godolphin tersely.

"Gentlemen, here's pen and paper. Let's each write out our bid and put it in the hat."

As a London lawyer, Thomas had enjoyed many an evening playing cards in the taverns around the Inns of Court. He knew how to read a face when he placed a bet. It was excellent practice, he always argued, for reading the mind of a witness or a jury. This well-honed instinct was now put the test. Thomas had no money of his own to spare, but he still wrote out a bid of twenty five pounds, more than half his yearly income. He wished to avert the suspicion that he had nothing to give, or that he thought the chests were worthless. But he was counting on a higher bid from one of the others to bail him out.

The hat was given to Moyle to collect each of their bids and he then passed it to Borno to read them out.

"Captain Millaton's in my hand first," he said, "a bid of ten pounds. Mr Thomas', a bid of twenty-five! Then here's Mr Godolphin, which I read Sir, as fifty!"

"Congratulations," Thomas said immediately.

Godolphin smiled. As Thomas had hoped, beating him was the first thought that entered his cousin's head. By the time he came to ask why Thomas had bid so much less, he would be congratulating himself on having secured a bargain. As for Millaton, his hankering to inspect the cargo seemed tempered by the outcome. His share of the contents would now cost him not a single farthing.

Thomas' ruse had made each of them feel a winner in their own way. His talk of contract law had convinced them. But he was only too aware that, whatever precautions he took to make their contract with the Portuguese binding, in truth they were open to challenge in court at any point. Better to let such things run their course, he thought, than alarm his partners with undue pessimism.

It was now approaching nine o'clock and they were due to meet James Chynoweth in barely an hour's time. The Seyntaubin and Godolphin coaches were loaded, their chests discreetly covered and the courtyard gates opened. Two fortunes surged out of the castle on the few miles' journey to their respective destinations. Thomas had prepared a story for his modest retinue at Clowance. They diligently unloaded the chests into the wine cellar, bemused by the weight of the casks they were carrying. He then sped on to his crucial meeting. Millaton had ridden ahead, to humour Chynoweth with Mount talk, until the other two could arrive.

****

Alvares, de Corfe and Vaz were now lodging with Peter Treneve, a yeoman in the service of William Godolphin. Here they were being well looked after, the food and drink flowing in front of a warm fire. Even the forty- odd ship's company left at Chinal's had noticed an improvement in their victuals. Yet none was allowed to leave. Alvares had no doubt that their fate still hinged on the outcome of the meeting he had requested with the Justices.

James Chynoweth had heard where the Portuguese were now

to be found. It was not far from the Angel Hotel, where he had agreed to meet the three magistrates first. His concern was rising at the way these three had wrested the initiative. He was no longer mollified by that exchange with Thomas on the first day of the wreck. Chynoweth was steeling himself to assert the inviolate rights of his master and the duty of these magistrates to observe the law.

"Good day, Captain," he said. "I expect your fellow Justices will be here shortly?"

"Yes, indeed, Mr James."

"It must be said," he continued, "that the old Justices never took so close an interest in wrecks as you and Mr Thomas have chosen to do, since your recent appointments. I am very grateful, I'm sure, for the assistance, but y'know I have my own methods in these matters. To be frank, Captain, no Cornishman lost his life when I was handling these things by myself."

"We all agree that the loss of the boy was a terrible thing, Mr James. But how often does a ship like the *Santo Antonio* come ashore? It is our belief – and I am sure I speak for Mr William and Mr Thomas too – that the scene on the beach would have ended in a bloodbath if we had not intervened with the full force of the law. His death was the result of an accident, after all, not a fight."

"Which brings me to the next point, Captain. How be so much excitement aroused by this wreck? After all, when I looked around with Mr Beauchamp, there was nothing remarkable on view. We felt somewhat downhearted."

"Perhaps you assessed it right," replied Millaton. "but times are hard an' folks will always find the energy to pick up a free gift. Those gifts are not so easy to recover, mind, once they be at the bottom of the rocks or at the bottom of some wreckers' cellar."

"Aye, so what do you propose? Sir John Arundell is a reasonable man, of course, but he will want his fair share of the spoils."

"You'd best talk to Mr Thomas on that score, Mr James. He understands the ins and outs a good deal better than I."

Chynoweth had no doubt about it. Talk soon turned to wrestling and the chances of Godolphin against Clowance at the Feast of St Pirran, less than two months away. They moved on to John Arscott and whether he would stay another year at the Mount. Millaton had just succeeded in building a certain rapport with Chynoweth, around their shared suspicions of the archpriest, when Seyntaubin and Godolphin arrived.

"Mr Thomas! Just the man. The captain here assures me that you have a handsome proposition for Sir John!"

"Not too fast, Chynoweth," replied the other. "First we must be sure, what right does Sir John have exactly in this matter? After all, there are survivors from the ship. While there may be costs of collection for them to pay, the goods are theirs, are they not?"

"But Mr Thomas, you gave me your word that the riches prized off that ship would remain for the good of the county. Don't tell me you plan to return it all to the King of Portugal – it is not to be borne!"

"To be sure. But there is a proper way to handle these things. My task is to persuade the survivors to make a bargain, so that as much of the bounty sticks to the county and as little as possible to them. But if they chose to pay the costs of collection, then it is out of my hands."

"And what would those costs be, 'cause I'm damned if I know."

"Well, you see Chynoweth, to preserve the peace Mr Godolphin, Captain Millaton and I have incurred some exceptional expenditure. We have also had to let go a great deal of cargo into the hands of the wreckers. We know their names, of course, but getting them to return the stuff will take time and money. The question is, though, not what it will cost us – but what it would cost them, the Portuguese, if they tried to retrieve their treasure."

67

"There's no need to teach me my job, Mr Thomas. I was handling these things a good many years before you came along. And I may say, within my memory, your contribution in a less formal way was not always such a welcome matter…"

"Quite so, Mr James. That is why I am so eager to ensure that this time all is handled in the proper fashion, to give satisfaction to you and Sir John, as well as to Mr William, the captain and me. So let's get to the point. If you had taken on the task from the start, what would you be offering the Portuguese?"

Chynoweth paused. Too high a figure and he would be admitting there was little value left in collecting the cargo from the wreckers. Too low a figure and he would be implying that the wreck was not worth so much after all.

"Like we said the other day, Mr Thomas, she's no twenty-pound wreck. Let's say double that and call it forty."

"Well, Mr James, now we are getting to the heart of the matter. Their leader, that Alvares fellow, spoke of a thousand ducats which he had off the wreck, before it was taken from him…"

"By your men, as I've heard it!" Chynoweth's rejoinder was the cue for some heated haggling with Seyntaubin. After a while, the practised lawyer tried a change of tack.

"You've offered Alvares forty pounds already, Chynoweth, which he rejected. What makes you think he will take it now, when he expects his countrymen to appear any time from the river Fal with helpers to hand?"

"Does he? Where's that idea come from?"

"He was asking Treneve last night how far from here to the Fal. Then it all came out – one of them went on ahead the first day of the wreck." Thomas forbore to mention the man Moyle had come across that first morning, poisoned by a snake and left for dead by the wreckers for his silver.

"So you see," Godolphin weighed in, "this could be even more complicated, if some new Portuguese fellows were to show. What if they came with their King's command and the money to pay all the bills? Then I see very little in it for Sir John."

Chynoweth struggled to take this all in. The discussion was not going as he had planned. He foresaw the entire value of the wreck slipping away. Far worse than a poor bargain would be to report to his master no bargain at all. In Sir John Arundell's eyes, the Right of Wreck must always be asserted, but for a rich man, the precise payment was almost of secondary importance to the principle.

"There's something not quite right here, gentlemen," he resumed. "What you need to understand is that if I come away with too little to show, you will never hear the last of it from Sir John." Chynoweth paused, while he gave Seyntaubin a knowing look. "Mr Thomas, is that really what you want?"

"Not at all, Chynoweth," he replied, trying not to redden at the thought that even Arundell's servant might know his financial predicament. "You tell us what you need and we will see what we can do."

"Very well. She's an important ship, there's no doubting that, one of the most promising wrecks I've seen in all my dozen years on the job. Frankly, I doubt I'll keep my master happy unless I can produce at least three hundred when all is said and done."

"Three hundred pounds? But that leaves nothing for our trouble..." Millaton started to protest.

"Call it two hundred!" Thomas interrupted, determined to control this all-important negotiation, with a sharp look at his colleague.

"Two hundred and fifty."

"Two twenty-five – now that's our final offer. And not a farthing to be paid until we have collected the very last of the loot from the wreckers."

Chynoweth paused. There was still something odd about all this. But two hundred and twenty-five pounds, without any outlay of his own, would satisfy Sir John. Even for the richest man in Cornwall, it was nearly as much as a year's income.

"I'm prepared to sign and seal it, gentlemen, but on one condition." Chynoweth gave them a knowing smile. "Your two twenty-five pounds will buy you whatever has been retrieved from the wreck so far. But half of any treasure brought ashore in future shall still be Sir John's. Otherwise, I can see no end of argument over the stuff found on that beach and what wreck it belongs to."

Thomas had prepared a contract. With this amendment, the business with Chynoweth was swiftly concluded. Godolphin, Millaton and Seyntaubin were now free to strike their own bargain with the Portuguese. Thomas had drafted a second agreement, between the three of them on the one side and Alvares, Vaz and de Corfe on the other. He now handed this to his cousin, bid Godolphin and Millaton on their way and waited at the Angel.

Success was at hand, but Thomas sensed he was best absent from the meeting with Alvares. It would only resurrect his grievance over the manifest. Besides, Godolphin was a skilful negotiator himself and following their arrangement at Pengersick, the payment to settle with the Portuguese would come out of his pocket.

It did not take long for Thomas' partners to return. The Portuguese had sold them all rights in the ship's cargo – found or unfound for fifty pounds. What is more, Godolphin and Millaton had brought Alvares back with them. Part of the bargain was for him to go, house to house, identifying cargo which had been taken and assisting the three Justices in enforcing their right to what was now their lawful property.

Here, the lists of those seen by the Justices' men on the beach played its part. Few were surprised to see them turn up. Most gave readily of their booty in return for paltry sums which to them represented several months' wages. Within just a few days, over a thousand pounds' worth of cargo had been recovered. As a gesture of goodwill, in spite of Millaton's protests, Godolphin and Seyntaubin insisted on returning to the Ship's Master his father's silver bowl, along with the chain and whistle. The Portuguese company were then given safe passage to the Fal, where they met up with their countrymen, to general relief all round.

As they left, Alvares turned to Thomas. He had spent a night at Clowance during the garner of the salvage. Yet the warmth of Thomas' devotion to his own wife and children had left Alvares seething with resentment, not only at his own enforced absence from Marina, but also at the reaction he risked for having agreed the contract at all. Safely surrounded by the Portuguese sailors about to return him home, his parting shot was laced with venom.

"*Senhor* Thomas, we will kindly send you a copy of the *Santo Antonio's* manifest. And then, in the name of His Grace, King João of Portugal, may God have mercy on your soul."

Thomas waived to him cheerily. It was hard to tell who was the greatest threat – the King of Portugal, the English Crown or the Arundell estate. But at this moment, he felt ready to defy them all.

Reasons of State

Letter from Cardinal Wolsey to the English Ambassador Lee:

...it is known by intercepted letters whatever the Emperor pretends, that he aims at obtaining Italy, and becoming monarch of the world; and if he can bring the French King under his power, he will rule all other princes.

Letters and Papers of Henry VIII

𝕿𝖍𝖊 𝕶𝖓𝖎𝖌𝖍𝖙𝖘 𝖔𝖋 𝖙𝖍𝖊 𝕲𝖆𝖗𝖙𝖊𝖗.
Lord Lisle is seventh from the left.

Chapter Seven

He was certain, for he had it from a very good source,
that the greatest part of the money was already lying at
Antwerp...
Cardinal Wolsey to Imperial Ambassador Mendoza,
The Calendar of Spanish Papers

Thomas Wolsey looked out of the window of his palace apartment towards the magnificent herb garden. The fish ponds were frozen over by the bitter winter cold. A songbird caught on the water's edge had turned into a frosted statuette. But within this elegant reception room, the firewood crackled in the grate, radiating Wolsey with the warm glow befitting one of the leading men in Europe.

His gaze alighted once more on the skilfully carved oak panelling, each linenfold discreetly indented with the mark of a bishop's mitre. No Cardinal, he consoled himself, had ever owned such a sumptuous palace as Hampton Court. His recent attempt to become Pope might have failed, but as both Cardinal and Chancellor of England, at once in control of both her Church and her laws, his untrammelled power was eclipsed only by Princes. Even his rival Mercurino Gattinara, the ambitious Grand Chancellor to the Spanish Emperor, was said to be jealous.

Wolsey had been denied the ultimate prize, but he felt no great envy of the new Pope, for whom the Emperor Charles of Spain was proving a constant irritant. Wolsey's influence over Henry, on the other hand, fifteen years after he first seized power in the King's Council, remained all pervasive. Then there was Joan Larke, bearing him another child nearly twenty years after she had first become his mistress. The cosy domesticity which they

77

enjoyed behind the palatial façade at Hampton Court would never be possible in Rome.

Wolsey realised he bore a surprising affinity to the man he was about to see this February morning. Both were in their early fifties; both possessed the easy charm which won favour with the King; both owed their rank and privilege almost entirely to Henry. Yet Arthur Plantagenet, Lord Lisle, Vice Admiral of England, was fortune's favoured son even more than himself, Wolsey reflected. A very different fate could have befallen Lisle, if the battle of Bosworth Field had swung the other way. Whereas a man with Wolsey's capabilities could always rise, whoever wore the crown.

"Lord Chancellor." His visitor had made his way forward with a courtly grace. Not for him the spiral staircase kept for the common caller, but the grand corridor with its lavish suite of guest rooms and gilded hanging tapestries.

"Good morning, my Lord Lisle. Do we have the Spanish documents?"

"They arrived from France two days ago, but their codes have only just been broken. I fear His Grace the King will not be pleased. The new Imperial Ambassador has been here barely a month and already it seems he is trying to deceive us. Mendoza by name, mendacious by nature, it would appear!"

Wolsey smiled, if only to disguise his disappointment. This Mendoza had made him a secret promise to favour the Cardinal with a new Spanish pension.

"Yes, it seems that the money raised by His Imperial Majesty in Antwerp will not be used to discharge his English debts, after all. He's using it to pay for his sister's wedding instead. In fact, the royal groom has already been to collect his dowry. A Portuguese fleet, carrying cargo from Flanders worth a hundred thousand pounds, has sailed for Lisbon."

"And Spain's debt to the English Crown is left at a hundred and fifty thousand! There is no telling what His Grace the King will say about this. You may even be ordered to sail from Portsmouth to intercept this fleet."

"It is too late for that. Besides, our agents in Falmouth inform me that last month's storms have done their own intercepting."

"How so, my Lord?" Wolsey needed some cheering. He had agreed to these massive loans to the Spanish Emperor. So Henry had now forced the Cardinal to pawn some of his own treasured jewels to the King, as security for repayment. Wolsey advanced towards Lisle from behind the lectern where he had been working, all attention.

"It seems that the flagship of the fleet, under Admiral Paciecho, was blown off course near Land's End. The ship foundered on the southern rocks and by all accounts, was stripped bare by the Cornish before it sank."

"Excellent news! So the Crown simply asserts the Right to Wreck and..."

"Not quite, Lord Chancellor. As it happens, the ship was wrecked just a mile into the parish of Winnianton. It's the heel on the foot of Cornwall. As luck would have it, one part of the county where the Crown has passed its Rights to the Lord of the Manor."

"Then let him pass the Rights back, my Lord!"

"Not so easily done, Lord Chancellor. For one thing, the grant goes far back in time, to King Henry II and even before. For another, we are dealing with Cornwall."

Wolsey grimaced. The King had an aversion to the county. As a six-year-old child, the Cornish uprising had forced his mother to take refuge with him in the Tower of London. The Cornish had reached the outskirts of the City, following their surprise victory over the King's cavalry in Guildford. Only his father's brilliantly timed counter-attack at Blackheath had turned the tide on the rebels and crushed their challenge to the Tudor throne.

"I see. So has this Lord of the Manor taken the spoils?"

"That's the curious part. The salvage from the wreck was sold by the Portuguese to three local Justices of the Peace, one of them a captain, appointed by the Crown. It appears that Sir John Arundell, the Lord of the Manor, took no part in the dubious bargain."

"That's cunning." Wolsey smiled. "But leaving aside His Grace the King, I wonder how it will place this Sir John, when the Kings of Spain and Portugal come knocking at his door? Perhaps it would be wise, my Lord, for you to pay a visit to this godforsaken county, before Cornish piracy sours our relations with the most powerful monarchs in Europe."

"My thoughts exactly, Lord Chancellor. In fact, I have prepared for my journey already."

Now it was Lisle's turn to smile. He would not usually involve himself in a dispute so far from his own bailiwick. The roads were treacherous, so he would have to go by ship from Portsmouth to the Fal, then ride the remaining distance. But quite apart from placating the crowned heads of Europe, he relished the pretext to see Honor Basset again.

As soon as he had gone, Wolsey summoned his faithful servant Thomas Cromwell, with whom he shared his thoughts, as they studied the Cornish chart.

"No doubt your Excellency will wish to steer the fruits of this wreck into His Grace, the King's hands," Cromwell remarked.

"At the very least, this affair could release me from the pledge of my jewels, Master Secretary. While, as Cardinal, I am keen not to upset Europe's two leading Catholic Princes. We will need their support in what I am calling The King's Matter. Although remember Master Secretary, that issue is so secret that no one at Court, not even Lisle, yet has a hint of it."

"It all points in one direction, your Excellency, to teach these magistrates, no doubt part of the old regime, a lesson they will not forget - and to ensure that even the furthest parts of the kingdom benefit from your power and influence."

"These old-style Justices seemed to think they can run local affairs as their own fiefdom, Master Secretary. In Cornwall, as elsewhere, it is time to install our own sort, men obedient to the centre. But let the charming Lisle report back diligently, having lulled the senses of his Cornish friends."

"If it would please your Excellency," said Cromwell conspiratorially, "but I cannot help noticing that this shipwreck happened in the corner of Mount's Bay. Now St Michael's Mount may be under the command of this Captain Millaton, but I believe Syon Abbey still maintains a presence on the island."

"So tell me, Master Secretary," the Cardinal enquired with a smile, "are you suggesting it is time that presence proved its worth?"

Both knew that the Cardinal's secret weapon was the eyes and ears of the Church. Where any wrongdoing occurred, a priest's proclivity for gossip coupled with his knowledge of the confessional could be relied on to provide a succinct account of events. Sitting in court as Lord Chancellor, Wolsey's unique ability to draw on such information made a handy contribution to his judgements.

****

Along the Antwerp waterfront, two ships began unloading the day's offering of silks and spices into the massive Portuguese storehouse. Cartloads of pepper and cinnamon were already setting out on their journey through the Low Countries. Roderick Fernandes, striding through the entrance to his emporium, shot one last glance towards the Church of Our Lady, the medieval masterpiece standing proudly on the opposite bank of the river. For fifteen years, he had been inspired by the sight of its new tower, rising stone by stone to dominate Europe's bustling metropolis, in step with his own career.

Fernandes exuded power. As the King's Consul in this commercial epicentre, he combined the roles of businessman, diplomat and spy. No longer an agent in the field himself, who had once risked his life to investigate Brother Luther and the wealth of the German princes, Fernandes today felt angered by the failure of his own agents, just returned from Cornwall. As for the three men he was about to interview, he regarded their story with contempt.

The scale of their loss was enormous. The thieving and hostility of which they told would have been exceptional, had it involved Americans, or even Scots. But to be robbed in England by three magistrates, one a London lawyer, beggared belief. The look on Fernandes' face, as he entered the *sala da diretoria*, was not lost on Diego Alvares. Still yearning for that well-earned rest with his family in Lisbon, still awaiting his commission for a new voyage to the West Indies, Alvares was acutely aware that the mission intended to mark a staging post in his career had instead led him to the brink of disaster. Worse, he remained stuck with Vaz and de Corfe. Their pronouncements on the law of the sea were sounding increasingly desperate, in their efforts to excuse their signatures on that contract with the Cornish.

The last person in the room was a Servant of the King's Chamber, Francisco Pessoa, a lawyer well versed in following his King's instructions in all manner of statecraft. Once he had been Fernandes' mentor in Antwerp, had himself occupied the post of Consul. But personal financial woes at the time of his recall to Lisbon had left the master schemer beholden to his pupil. Now he had his own motives for treating Alvares' story with deep suspicion.

"In the first place, my friends," Pessoa was saying, "England and Portugal have been allies since the Treaty of Windsor nearly a hundred and fifty years ago. So if one of our citizens is robbed, their King has the responsibility to put it right. He is to provide redress within six months. As for the English law, if it states that the salvage from a wreck belongs to the survivors, then it is you three who must seek satisfaction on your King's behalf."

"So we just have to show that we were robbed. The amount that was taken should be clear from the manifest!"

"Go slowly, *Senhor* Vaz. First, you have signed a contract saying that you have sold the goods. Secondly, most of the cargo could still lie in the sea. We have no way to prove otherwise."

"But certainly," protested Alvares. "This wreck was only in one fathom of water, not at the bottom of the sea. The gold and silver treasure could easily have been brought to the beach."

"Quite so. Equally, the English may say that you sold them the treasure in their contract and if they now happen to find it, then that is their good fortune."

"But the contract was forced on us. We were made to sign it by *bandidos* bearing swords and shields!"

Fernandes regarded the trio disparagingly. "No doubt the English magistrates will say they were sent to protect you from the wreckers. As for being forced to sign the contract, my agents have heard a very different story. Is it not true, *Senhor* Alvares, that you even stayed in a magistrate's house? Did you not cooperate with their retinue, as they recovered cargo from the wreckers' homes? It hardly sounds like a forced bargain to me, so how do you think an English court will see it?"

"It is true," Vaz interjected. "We are doomed. King João will never forgive our weakness. May God save our souls!"

"For all I know, you may be telling the truth," Fernandes resumed, while making clear that such a possibility bordered on the absurd. "But consider the matter through the eyes of His Majesty the King. The dowry of his royal bride has been sold for a mere fifty *livres*. That is either a trick or an insult."

Alvares' mind once again began to swim in a sea of worries. That image of Marina and the children, waving at him on the beach, returned to haunt him, as his spirits sank. He began to protest, perhaps too vehemently for his own good, how the law of England had made it imperative to survive at all costs.

"Otherwise," he said, "the cargo belonged to the wreckers. So unless we had agreed the terms offered, there is no doubt we would have died."

Fernandes laughed. "You wish me to believe that these officers of the law – these English gentlemen would commit murder? Kill the men they were charged to protect, by the Rules of Oleron?"

"You are right, *Senhor* Fernandes." Jeremy de Corfe spoke for the first time. All turned to face the Gentleman of the King's Chamber. He had no intention of being dragged down by this pair of bungling ship hands and seeing the tide of the interview turning – chose this moment to break rank. "I never trusted this proposal to sign a contract with the English, *Senhor* Fernandes. Did I not question Alvares when I was trapped in that hovel? Ask yourselves who revealed the manifest, who met with the magistrates and who was guest in the homes of the cunning knaves who have robbed us. Then if there is mischief in this story, you surely know where to find it."

Fernandes smiled. It made his task so much easier when thieves fell out. "Thank you, *Senhor* de Corfe, for a most interesting contribution. But perhaps you can explain one thing to me. How could you, as a Gentleman of the Royal Chamber, dishonour His Majesty by signing the contract at all?"

De Corfe was not the brightest member of João the Third's Court but for this question his answer was ready. "As the ship's Factor, the signature on the contract which counted was Alvares'. Once he and Vaz had sold the pass, my refusing to sign, *Senhor*, would have proved an empty gesture."

"Very well, *Senhor* de Corfe," Fernandes responded. "You are free to return to the Royal Court at Sintra. But keep in touch with my friend Pessoa here, as he pursues his case against the English." De Corfe nodded towards Pessoa and without a glance at his erstwhile allies, promptly departed the *sala da diretoria*, relieved to wash his hands of the entire business.

Alvares turned to Fernandes. He pleaded his innocence. He spoke of his many years' service in the King's commission. In

84

desperation, he begged Fernandes to reunite him with his family. The Consul paused, as if considering whether – despite the damning evidence of his agents – this Factor might be innocent after all. Then he replied: "This is no longer an inquest, *Senhor* Alvares, it is an Inquisition. But this I guarantee. Tell the truth at all times and your family will see you again."

These last words were spoken without a trace of emotion. Then guards were called and Alvares and Vaz were led away. Fernandes allowed silence to descend on the *sala da diretoria*, before he spoke to Pessoa, "This Inquisition must be without mercy, my friend. Alvares' family may see him again, but I do not expect Alvares to see his family"

"My dear *amigo*," the lawyer replied. "Rest assured that our Inquisitors at the Sintra Palace have become most skilled in their use of the *braseiro incandescente*, passed back and forth before the eyes of our culprit. His sight will be burnt slowly by degrees, as the scorching heat of the brazier turns each pupil red and then black. Our search for the truth in this affair shall be relentless."

"Very good, my dear Pessoa. But even if this Alvares confesses to his cooperation with the English, can we ever recover the dowry? Why would the English disown the contract in their own courts?"

"Do not despair, my dear *amigo*," Pessoa resumed. "This Cornish lawyer is a clever fellow, certainly, but he has overlooked an essential detail."

"What is that?"

"In a word, the Cardinal. Lord Wolsey has this Court of Justice, they call it his Star Chamber, where the little people can seek redress against the highest in the land. Dukes are made to pay paupers for their misdeeds. None is above the judgement of the Lord Chancellor. In his Court, he makes the law."

"Could he invoke the Rules of Oleron?"

"Why not? But be in no doubt, *meu amigo*, if the Lord Chancellor favours King João above the subjects of his own King,

85

it will be because the law bows to Reasons of State."

"So you think we have to bribe the English Chancellor?"

"Perhaps. Or else call on the power of the Imperial one."

"Gattinara?"

"Yes, *meu caro amigo*, none other than the High Chancellor to His Imperial Majesty. After all, it is Emperor Charles' sister who has been dishonoured in this matter and his dowry payment which remains to be settled."

Pessoa spoke in a soft, knowing voice. A master of the arts of treachery and corruption, he had no need to elaborate further on these Reasons of State to his former *protegido*. Roderick Fernandes returned his smile.

****

The two letters which the messenger delivered to Clowance from the Helston post boat had not been written to please Thomas Seyntaubin. The first concerned lands seized by the Crown from a renegade on his mother's side. Thomas had reckoned that as the innocent heir, he had the right to recover his forebear's lands, if not his honour. Now he learnt they were to be granted to some favourite at Court, who was certain never to set foot in Cornwall. The second letter, from the Chief Steward at the Inner Temple, made him even more incensed.

"Ten pounds!"

"What, beloved?"

"They want to fine me ten pounds, just for missing a dinner in Hall. Surely my absence meant more wine for the rest of them..."

"Yes, beloved. What did you say the Steward's name was?"

"Anthony Wayte. He's always been so kind to me in the past. I know – I'll send a note to John Vyvian, he was supposed to be there too, perhaps we can claim the Cornish weather defeated us. Truly, I am sure that the rain made the roads impassable."

"Anthony Wayte, you say? Well, I've a better idea. He has a

86

cousin who is paying us a visit next month, there's no one better placed to put in a good word for you."

"A cousin – are you sure, Mary? I thought it was your sister and her family who were coming to see us again."

"He's coming with them, Thomas. A delightful man, so my sister tells me. Lord Lisle's his name. He's not only the learned Mr Wayte's cousin, he's the Vice Admiral of the Fleet. Come to Cornwall about that wreck in Gunwalloe, she tells me."

Thomas' face paled. He had heard of Lisle. He knew there were some rumblings from January's adventure, the detail of which he not entirely revealed to Mary. But the speed and scale of this development were disconcerting.

"And why would he be staying with the Bassets? I would have thought that your sister Catherine, Lady Arundell, would be the obvious choice."

"My sister Honor tells me it's because Tehidy is so much nearer the scene of the wreck. But the truth, Thomas, is that Honor and this Lord Lisle have taken a liking to each other."

"I'm not sure I follow you, beloved. Your sister is one of the most respectable women I know. I cannot think for one moment she would do anything to taint the good name of the Basset family."

"To be sure, my beloved. On the other hand, she has every reason to secure her future, before her husband lies on his death bed."

"As she once helped you to do, perhaps?" asked Thomas, now smiling at the memory of their own extended courtship while Mr Bluett, the Devonshire squire who was Mary's first husband, took his time to pass away. "Perhaps I can give this Lord Lisle some assurance that waiting for a Grenville girl is worth every minute."

The two kissed, not the passionate embrace of their courting days, but a loving touch born of two decades of happiness. Then Mary looked straight at him.

"He's not a youth, like you were Thomas. But then we are all older now. Honor has her children. Now she sees the chance of a life at Court for them, as well as her."

"But does she at least find him attractive? He must be twenty years older than her…"

"Not all women go for younger men, Thomas! Honor says he is utterly charming, by which I think she means he treats her thoughts and ideas with rather more respect than Sir John Basset. He still sees her as the young thing he married a decade ago."

"As you well know, my beloved, I only want the best for your sister. I've no doubt she would excel at Court and as for her little daughters, I am sure that Anne at least will prove as pretty a jewel as any man at Court could wish for."

"Prettier than your own daughters, beloved?"

"Of course not, but surely not all Cornwall's treasures should leave the county?"

"I can agree to that. Besides, none of them would welcome the thought of living in London again. We are all so happy here."

This went some way to comfort Thomas. So did the interest of Lord Lisle in his sister-in-law. If his investigation of the wreck was a mere pretext – if he truly sought Honor – then Thomas might afford to relax. After all, surely even men at Court were bound by ties of kinship.

Chapter Eight

Among the general customs, we must not forget the manly exercises of wrestling and hurling, the former more generally practised in this county than in any part of England, the latter peculiar to it.

Borlase, *Natural History of Cornwall*

The tempest which had wrecked the *Santo Antonio* proved an end to the drenching rain which had swept through Cornwall that winter. Instead, vanishing storm clouds and the advent of clear skies heralded a nightly freeze, one which yielded some stirring landscapes come the dawn. February gave way to March and St Pirran's Day arrived to a chorus of birdsong. That morning, following the path where he had met Thomas some six weeks earlier, Moyle drank in the view towards the coast. On the one side he saw the waning moon streaked by cloud, on the other the sun rising, bathing the white frosted hedgerows in a pinkish glow.

The Land of Saints, thought John Moyle, as he finished the distance from Looe Bar to Gunwalloe, part of his preparation for the feast day at Clowance. Not for John the drama of the mystery play or the skill of the rower. He was a wrestler. In a few hours' time, he would be pitting his strength and his wits against the men he had worked beside only six weeks before, as they had risked their lives here in the cove. Then, in the afternoon, there would be the hurling match, that ultimate test of skill and teamwork with a silver ball.

After the excitement of the wreck, Moyle had noticed the young men of Penwith falling uncommonly quiet recently. Some feared that the forthcoming enquiry into the actions of the Justices might wreak some punishment on them all. Others shared so much gossip about the sinking of the wreck, they scarce had time left for devilment. Then several of the local loudmouths announced they were planning to dive for the treasure as soon as the sea water lost its icy cold. For sure, they might find something where the young Marazion boy had drowned. But why risk their lives, others asked, when their findings would only belong by rights to the Justices?

Moyle had to admire Mr Seyntaubin. His had been a madcap scheme in many ways, yet it had stopped a riot, staved off the famine and now he had secreted his treasure. A few of those involved were already starting to brag about their role in the escapade, but this loose talk as yet posed no danger. Almost everyone who heard of the fantastic bargain struck between the Justices and the Portuguese rejoiced that such treasure had been kept in the county. Indeed, the payments to the wreckers for recovered goods had spread a wave of relief, a comfort against the coming deprivations of a ruined harvest. As for those involved in the secret deeds of the night, none dared to speak of them. They feared the wrath of the Justices, let alone the outcome of the enquiry. They knew only too well that the fickle mercy of Tudor law was no place for a poor man.

Moyle paused on the beach. He was now standing in front of a makeshift memorial of granite stones to young Teake, the Marazion boy who had drowned. He would be sorely missed this feast day. John prayed to St Pirran for his own strength and survival. Cornwall's patron saint, who had survived crossing the Irish Sea in a small calf-skinned craft, would surely hear him. Then, in a prayer to St Carwenna, the patron saint at Crowan, he confided his secret love, the one he planned to declare today.

****

Thomas had decided to mark St Pirran's Day with a feast as soon as he had inherited the Clowance estate. Now in its third year, it had proved a welcome start to spring. Thomas hoped that in time it would eclipse the other local events culminating in the May

90

celebrations in Helston, which hailed summer's return. The festival at Clowance might never match the fame of Helston's Furry Dance. But the enthusiasm shown by the local youths, for this first chance to display their prowess at wrestling and hurling after the long dark winter, augured well for its future.

Throughout the day, there were dances in front of the house, gig-racing on the lake and stalls set in the park for local traders to sell their wares. At its far end, Thomas had placed a Cornish cross between two tall oak trees, which framed the distant view of Crowan Church. This cross would be the goal for the afternoon's Hurling match. The other goal was two miles away, a granite trough set in the grounds of Godolphin House. The hurling ball, which was made of solid wood, thickly plated in silver and the size of a cooking apple had been placed on a high stand just in front of the cross. It glistened in the sun. As they entered the arena set aside for the Cornish wrestling contest, it caught the eye of opposing team members from Marazion and Camborne. This trial of their individual martial skills in the morning presaged heavy betting on who would emerge as the winning side in the afternoon's all-important rivalry.

A band of minstrels struck up a tune for the first dance of the morning. Just then, the Seyntaubins' breakfast party walked out onto the terrace overlooking the scene. Their distinguished guest stopped and listened.

"Such fine players! Have you hired them from Brittany? The field may be Clowance, but the style is Cloth of Gold."

"You are too kind, my Lord," replied Mary Seyntaubin, beaming at this compliment. "But it is my nephew, Sir Richard Grenville, who deserves your praise. He is one of the few men of the county to maintain his own band. When he heard you were coming, he was more than pleased to lend them for the occasion."

"The tune they are playing brings back so many memories of that meeting. It is odd to reflect, but I doubt His Grace the King has ever been more content, than at that time and place."

91

"One of the Cornish boys who went over to wrestle with the Bretons is here today, Lord Lisle. I wonder if you will recognise him after seven years."

"I hope I will. We all remember the Cornish wrestling, just as" – here, he lowered his voice to a conspiratorial whisper – "we all try to forget the King's."

"So it is true what they say?" enquired Mary's sister Honor. "He really did challenge the French King to a wrestling match?"

"I fear to admit as much, but I saw it myself," replied Lisle. "You see, His Grace is a tall, strong man and it did not cross his mind that the lightweight Francis could beat him."

"There's many bets been lost on that calculation," Honor explained. "Why do Cornish boys so love their wrestling? It is all because speed and skill can so often triumph over strength and weight."

"You surely speak the truth," enjoined Thomas. "Wrestling is as full of manliness as hurling, my Lord, but more delightful and less dangerous."

"Then I am very glad, for the health of the King, there was no Hurling seven years ago!" replied Lisle.

They all laughed. It was impossible not to like this imposing, yet modest man. His early upbringing in Hampshire would not have been so different from his own, Thomas reflected. Then the turn of fate, which had pitch forked Lisle into the cauldron of the royal circle, no less than it might now pitch Thomas and his confederates.

"Please can I dance to this tune, Uncle?"

Thomas looked down at the enchanting face of his six-year-old niece, Anne Basset. Her father, Sir John, already sixty when she was born, had today sent his apologies for his absence.

"But who will dance with you, my little bird?"

"I will, Father," spoke up William, proudly sporting the new breeches which marked a seven-year-old boy's graduation from girlish skirts.

92

"Then you had better ask her mother's permission," Thomas replied with a smile.

William gave a bow so low it seemed impossible he was not about to fall over, before throwing back his head as his face bathed Honor Basset with boyish enthusiasm. This appeal proved hard to resist and the two cousins were let loose, racing to join the children's dancing just as it started.

"I must warn you, my Lord, it is customary for our guests to partake in the last dancing session before lunch. My cousin William Godolphin will be joining us with his party. He's one of the other magistrates, by the way, who can tell you as much about the Gunwalloe affair as I can. He'll be bringing his daughter's betrothed, the young Wil Millaton. His father Jack is the captain at St Michael's Mount. I hear that you dine with him there tomorrow."

"I would be only too glad to join in the dancing myself, if I had a partner," replied Lisle. "Lady Basset, would you be kind enough to give me the pleasure?"

"Only too willingly, my Lord", replied Honor, "so long as you think in terms of rural Hampshire, rather than the Court. I cannot pretend that our country-dancing matches royal standards."

"I am sure it makes up for it with energy, at least judging by the performance of its younger members."

They were now passing the children, turning and swinging at full pelt. William and Anne imbibed the rising cadence of the music, the fastening pace of the fiddle over the eerie melody of the bagpipes. As the Seyntaubin and Basset children stood around voicing encouragement from the sidelines, the dancers felt themselves drawn into a pattern of primitive intensity. Just then, a loud shout from the far end of the lake announced the start of a rival attraction. Spectators had gathered for the wrestling. Thomas' party made their way across, as he explained the finer details of the contest.

"So who are those three men with poles in their hands?" Lisle was enquiring.

"They're the Sticklers, my Lord," Thomas explained. "They keep a strict eye on the detailed rules of the contest, awarding points for each throw. It's the points, you see, that give a man victory."

"Then tell me how was it that contest in France – the one I mentioned earlier ended so quickly? Surely our champion could not have lost on just the one throw?"

"My guess is that his opponent tricked him with a Flying Mare. That's where your man is turned over and landed full on his backside, both shoulders and a hip touching the ground at once. That's a three-point throw – we call it a 'back' and it gives outright victory."

John Moyle had just entered the ring. He shook hands with his opponent, as each reached behind the other's shoulder, to grab their wrestling jacket at the back of the neck in a "hitch." A slow dance then ensued, as each sought to catch the other unawares and toss him over leg or arm. But any manoeuvre risked opening up to the other fellow and being unbalanced oneself. Lisle could see that this was a game of bluff and guile, as much as brute strength.

"As in any game of skill," Thomas was explaining, "the art is to know your opponent. If you can predict his moves, then you can stay one step ahead. If not, you will be the one to be tripped."

"So tell me, Thomas," Lisle replied quietly. "In the game you are playing, are you sure you know your opponent?"

"I think I know the Sticklers," Thomas replied with a smile. "The three members of the Board of Enquiry are due to be named shortly."

"Then you must hope that the game will be played on your terms. But what if the other side are not happy to see this contest settled on Cornish soil? You're an Inner Temple man, I hear. Surely you realise that the odds could be very different if the match goes to London?"

94

"If you are right, my Lord," replied Thomas, as he looked at Lisle intently, "then I have no doubt we will need all the friends we can find."

"Perhaps," Lisle answered guardedly. "But no one at Court can save you. It's having the right man in court that counts."

Lisle paused. He could not explain why he felt an urge to help Thomas. Maybe it was the hope of impressing his sister-in-law; or a kindred feeling for an outsider; or an impulsive desire to let the Cornish enjoy this one stroke of good fortune. For beneath the brave festive spirit, he could not fail to notice the dire poverty in this far-flung corner of the kingdom.

Moyle had just moved his right leg around his opponent's, lifting it to the rear high enough to overbalance him. A sharp pull on the jacket brought him to the ground with a cheer from the crowd. The Sticklers conferred before awarding two points. The bout continued.

"There's no disputing the Sticklers' decision," Thomas was explaining. "And if they disagree among themselves, then two out of three carry the day."

"In your contest," Lisle responded, "there is only going to be one Stickler and his name is Cardinal Wolsey. So as I say, you need a man on your side who knows his rules of play. Have you ever met Densell?"

"John Densell, my Lord – the Lincoln's Inn lawyer?"

"The very same. He's a Cornishman, so he's more likely to take your point of view. Even more important, he cannot be bribed. There are four leading counsel who specialise in Star Chamber work, but there's only one you can truly trust."

"No doubt that makes him a very busy man. He'd hardly look at our suit."

"Densell is an old friend. When you meet, mention my name." As he said this, Lisle took Thomas by the collar and gave him a friendly hitch.

"Don't let my sister's bedfellow fool you, my Lord," Honor

Basset interrupted genially. "He can pull a Flying Mare in a trice, you know."

"I've no doubt," he replied, "there are a good many things our host could teach me. But he seems to know what he is doing. Now tell me more about the dancing, Lady Basset. If we are to be as sprightly as the children, I at least will need some practice."

Lisle took Honor's arm and started to lead her back towards the music. Some of Thomas' party followed. The children were finished now and the minstrels had begun to play a more formal tune. "The choice of dancing partner at the spring feast," someone was remarking, "can lead to far more serious propositions in these parts." Wondering if her suitor had overheard, Honor looked at Lisle with a gentle smile which lit up her face.

Thomas stayed with the wrestling. John Moyle had won his match and now he was facing Trehannick, one of Millaton's men on the beach that night. A brute of a man, he attempted to lift John clear off the ground. But the latter managed to entwine their legs and could not be pulled up further. Instead, Moyle hurled his full weight into his opponent. Trehannick lost his balance and toppled backwards, crashing to the ground with John falling on top of him.

The Camborne crowd raised another cheer as the Sticklers awarded a "back". John Moyle was through to the finals. As Thomas joined in the applause, he caught sight of his own daughter Ann, just turned sixteen. She had also forsaken the dancing and did nothing to hide her pleasure at witnessing John's victory. Trehannick, on the other hand, took his defeat badly.

"I may not be the only one about to lose a daughter, Thomas. But I'd wait until young Moyle there has faced up to my John Wylliam." It was William Godolphin, Cornish leader of the wrestlers and archers, who drew their strength from the sport.

"I dare say they will meet in the final round," Thomas replied. "But just because Wylliam beat the French, I'll wager he won't find a Clowance boy quite so easy."

"You have your bet, Cousin. Shall we make it ten pounds?"

"Your man is still the favourite, William. Let's call it ten pounds to me if Moyle wins – and half a crown a year to you if he loses."

"That's a clever offer. But as your last one seems to have worked out so well for me, I'll take it gladly."

"So you know that for a fact, do you, William? I'm bound to say, I've treated my treasure chests like vintage wines, not to be opened until fully matured."

"I've not opened mine yet. But surely the game is won now. With two brothers-in-law and a nephew about to be put on the Board of Enquiry, can even your cautious legal brain doubt a favourable outcome?"

"If it stopped there, I would agree with you. But as the presence of our distinguished visitor today makes clear, our little adventure has caught the attention of the highest in the land."

"And what of it? We have a contract, do we not?"

"It's a good start. But we won't be safe unless it can be made to stand up in the Star Chamber."

"That surely puts us in the hands of the Cardinal? I wouldn't like to..."

"I know. His punishments are increasingly severe. One man had his ear nailed to the Westminster pillory in the morning, then pulled away at nightfall, before the unfortunate wretch was banished from the realm. Wolsey's even forced men onto the cucking-stool."

"But that sort of treatment's for vagabonds, surely not for men of rank?"

"Who's to say, if a man is found guilty of perjury, even more if he's a magistrate? You see, William, our problem is how to deal with those hidden treasure chests. If we admit to them, Wolsey will have the three most powerful Kings in Europe clamouring for their return. If we deny them, we commit perjury in the Star Chamber."

Godolphin paused for thought. "So you think that if we keep it hid, all these people will simply forget about the treasure? Isn't that just wishful thinking?"

"In my experience, Cousin, it's best to take the law one step at a time. Let's see if we can get through this local enquiry without the missing treasure being raised at all. To be sure, I'll be handy with some fine legal arguments to prevent it. So please, make my task easier by keeping your bounty firmly under lock and key – and do all you can to ensure Captain Millaton keeps his tongue tied as firmly as his treasure!"

William and Thomas had left the wrestling while they were talking and soon found themselves back at the dancing. The sun which had risen so brilliantly along the sea shore that morning had now banished the chill, so that discarded garments from the more energetic dancing partners were scattered round the edge. Honor had evidently found her pupil a fast learner. She and Lisle were now joining in the dance ahead of the guest party's turn, to the delight of the crowd.

"It's not often that Cornwall plays host to a Knight of the Garter and the Vice Admiral of the Fleet," Godolphin observed. "But then he's not your usual sort of courtier, that's for sure."

"He's no fool either," Thomas responded defensively. "He's been more than friendly to me, for which I should thank my Lady Basset. But he'll be on the lookout tomorrow, when the captain takes him round the Mount."

It was time for the last dance of the morning. Thomas and Mary led the way, as the minstrels started playing the King's own ballad, *Pastime With Good Companie*. The Vyvians and the Millatons came next, then the older Godolphin and the Basset children, lastly the Seyntaubin children, the slow dignified pace of the music drawing the morning's excitements to a stately close. At that moment, a huge roar was heard from the wrestling crowd. Thomas divined that he had won his bet. He glanced round to see the reaction of his daughter Ann, only to realise she was not there. He smiled. Perhaps young Moyle had been spurred on by an even greater prize this morning.

The Great Hall at Clowance had barely altered in all the time William Godolphin had known it. So today, the difference was glaring. Along one wall, for all Thomas' talk of discretion, the Seyntaubins had hung three large Arras tapestries depicting hunting scenes woven in flamboyant colour. Lord Lisle had appeared too polite to comment, until Thomas launched into the tale of how they had come from the recent wreck in Gunwalloe. It was an account which involved a highly partial explanation of the agreement struck with the Portuguese.

"I can't help wondering," said Lord Lisle after an awkward pause, "what happened to the rest of the cargo. I mean, if I understand correctly, about a thousand pounds were recovered on the shore, one way or another. This presumably included these fine tapestries, which as you say, you purchased from the survivors. But what about the chests filled with precious stones, let alone the gold and silver coins on board, of which we hear tell?"

The entire Hall fell into a nervous silence at this point. It was the question on everyone's lips, but which none had dared to put to the master of the household.

"I know!" A young voice spoke from the other end of the table, where the children were seated. "Uncle Thomas dug a big hole in the sand and he's buried the treasure!"

Anne Basset's spirited interjection defused the tension and laughter broke out all round.

"I certainly wish I had," Thomas responded quickly. "But truth to tell, I am quite certain that none of the treasure you speak of ever came ashore at Gunwalloe. As for the ship herself, I'll wager anyone in this room that she's still lying somewhere in the bay."

William Godolphin chose not to look at Thomas at this point. His expression might give too much away. But glancing down the table, he caught the eye of John Moyle, who gave him a wink.

"I've already lost one wager to you today, Cousin," said

Godolphin, keen to change the subject. "But given the success of Mr Moyle here in the wrestling, no doubt you all rate Clowance favourites for the Hurling match this afternoon. What do you say to taking me on a straight bet Godolphin House to win – double or quits?"

This prompted a fierce debate throughout the Hall on prospects for the afternoon's match, while Thomas ruminated on risking the ten pounds he had now banked to pay his fine to the Inner Temple. Clowance had the superior speed, there was no doubt of it. But Hurling was a sport where force counted too – and the Godolphin team had corralled both Millaton and Chynoweth men from Marazion to their side.

"Are you familiar with the game, my Lord?" Honor asked Lisle, realising that this debate might be leaving him confused.

"I've seen the game played at a wedding once."

"That would be Hurling to Goal, my Lord. In these parts, we regard that as the tame version. What you will see this afternoon is the game Hurling to Country."

"But I saw one of the goals by the wrestling, did I not?"

"There are still two goals – and the winning side simply has to touch their opponents' goal once with the ball. But instead of being a few hundred yards apart, they're set a few miles apart. In these matches, the hurlers find their way over hills, dales, hedges and ditches, even the streams running between Clowance and Godolphin. There'll be upwards of twenty men tugging each other in the water at times, scrambling and scratching for the ball."

"So to win, does a man simply have to run faster than the crowd?"

"He can try. But as like as not, he'll be met by some fox at a cross lane or corner who will throw him to the ground, when he must release the ball."

"The ball in play," Thomas continued at this point, "is like some infernal spirit. Whoever catches it forges ahead like a madman,

100

struggling and fighting with those that try to hold him. Then the moment he has relinquished the ball, the fury seems to subside and he becomes as peaceable as a lamb."

"It sounds an excellent sport," Lisle observed, "to make men hard and nimble."

"That's true," enjoined Godolphin. "It puts the courage in their heart to meet an enemy in the face. But it can also leave them sorely wounded. There will be plenty of bloody noses and broken bones to be mended tonight."

"So tell me, gentlemen," Lisle enquired, "are there many rules to this game? Do your Sticklers make an appearance?"

"There are customs, certainly," Thomas replied. "The ball itself is inscribed: 'Guare wheag yu guare teag' – *Fair play is good play.* So a man touched by an opponent, for example, will be given the chance to deal, or throw the ball, before he's tackled to the ground."

"Then in our game," Godolphin continued, "we respect the rule that a player throwing the ball cannot pass it forward, as that makes it all too easy for one side to play the advantage of possession."

"Another tradition, my Lord," said Thomas, "is that the match is started by a visitor to the parish. Standing at a point roughly mid-way between the goals, he throws the ball high in the air before a scrum of the opposing teams. We trust, my Lord, that you might pay us the compliment of performing that role today."

"The Basset family have already warned me that I may have to work for my day's pleasure" Lisle replied, as he turned to Honor. "I would hate to disappoint them."

"I can assure you, my Lord, there is no chance of that," Honor replied coyly. "But you may be certain there will be some very disappointed faces this evening. Many believe that good fortune goes with the side which wins the game, as they retain the ball throughout the ensuing year. And great is the glory of the player who secures the victory."

"I noticed the silver ball on display by the wrestling," Lisle responded. "Do I take it that Clowance were the winners last year?"

"That's right," said Thomas. "It seems Godolphin have suborned some Marazion men to their side today. On the other hand, the Vyvians here have lent us a few from Trellowarren. So I'd judge the outcome still to be finely balanced."

The lunch party over, the Seyntaubins and their guests observed some final gig races on the lake, before moving on to collect the silver hurling ball with much ceremony. It was shared around members of the Clowance team, in the hope of imbuing them with its good fortune, then passed amongst their womenfolk and some old stalwarts of the game. Finally it would fall to John Moyle, as the day's wrestling champion, to present the ball to Lord Lisle and for the match to start.

They had now reached Drym, a farm roughly half way between the two estates, which was the starting point. A loading wagon had been decked out as a suitable platform for their distinguished visitor and wheeled into the front field. The observers now moved apart, as more than fifty players on each side gathered round a central scrum.

A few wise heads had held back along the way, a few more now pealed off towards Godolphin House to stop any quick breakaway by the Clowance boys. Thomas observed wryly that it was his own daughter Ann who finally gave John Moyle the ball from the crowd, their hands pressing tightly as she did so.

Taking the silver ball from him, Lisle waited for John Moyle to resume his position in the Clowance team. Lisle's tall, imposing figure on the wagon held the crowd in sway, as he lightly rocked his arm. Then, with a massive effort, he heaved the gleaming globe high into the air, the sun giving it a momentary magical quality, before it started to hurtle towards the eager players below.

Overleaf

Clowance

(Borlaise, *Natural History of Cornwall*)

Chapter Nine

It is doubtful when this Mount was first appropriated to religious uses; it is however certain it was deemed a holy place as early as the 5th Century...

Grose, *Antiquities of Cornwall*

"On the instructions of His Excellency, the Cardinal..." As he read the missive from his Abbot one more time, John Arscott realised that his hand was shaking. The archpriest at St Michael's Mount had spent his life avoiding confrontation. Yet the situation now before him could not be more invidious.

Arscott was seated in his rooms, next to the side entrance to the chapel. He looked out to sea, clouds gathering on the skyline as the sun made its afternoon descent. A few fishermen in the bay were taking advantage of the clement weather, forsaking the chance to enjoy the feast day at Clowance to keep their families from starving. A gull landed on his windowsill, demanding attention. He meekly acceded by sharing the stale bread left on his plate, as he contemplated his choices.

He could reveal what he had seen in the harbour on the night the *Santo Antonio* had disappeared, with untold consequences at the hands of Captain Millaton and his garrison of murderous thugs. Or he could hold his peace until a more propitious time, as he had originally planned. This would now incur the wrath of the most powerful man in the Church, for withholding information when he needed it.

Arscott could simply forget his night-time excursion to the chapel balcony and the scene he had witnessed. This was the safest course. It would also avoid any awkward explanations about his secret spyglass. But Arscott quietly relished the deadly information with which he hoped to hold sway over the unpredictable Millaton. He was loath to waste his best lever for avenging the many slights and humiliations which the military commander heaped on him and his assistants.

"Arscott!" The familiar, harsh voice was at his door.

"Yes, Captain, what can we do for you today?"

"I've a most important visitor tomorrow. His name is Lord Lisle and he's the Vice Admiral of the Fleet. I'm giving him the tour of the island defences. I'm counting on you to show him round the chapel. Is that clear?"

"But of course, Captain. Is his Lordship coming by sea?"

"No, he wouldn't chance the Lizard Point. He'll be coming from Tehidy, as the guest of Sir John and Lady Basset."

Arscott did not require divine assistance to deduce the reason for this illustrious visit. He felt a weight lifting from his shoulders, as an opportunity opened up to resolve his problem. Millaton failed to notice any change in the other's expression, as he was in a foul mood. His Irish playmate had tired of the winter's bitter cold and the barren isolation of the Mount. He doubted her promise to return in a few months' time. The captain would gladly have raided one of the treasure chests buried at Pengersick to persuade her to stay, but he had made a promise to Godolphin, on pain of breaking the betrothal of their two children, not to touch the chests until they had word from Seyntaubin.

The thought of the forthcoming wedding did nothing to alleviate his gloom. His son's passion for Honour Godolphin appeared to have cooled almost exactly from the moment that her hand was assured. As for his future daughter-in-law, Millaton realised that her sole interest lay in becoming chatelaine of Pengersick; on the other hand, his own thoughts were how this alliance with Godolphin might advance his position in the county, rather than his son's happiness at home.

The captain undertook a final inspection of the castle. The garrison had been made to work, despite their protests at missing the Clowance feast day. He would not allow the Vice Admiral of the Fleet to leave Cornwall doubting his competence in charge of the Crown's strategic outpost. Every sword was polished, every gun cleaned, every cannon oiled. He had persuaded the archdeacon to produce the Abbey's finest silver for lunch in the Chevy Chase dining hall and he had put a young trooper to work until it shone with a mirror finish.

Millaton had decided that questions concerning the wreck were best approached directly. With this in mind, he placed a set of gold vessels, purloined from the Portuguese as part of their bargain, at the centre of the table. Likewise, he had asked Chynoweth to join their lunch party. He could be relied upon to corroborate the ostensible details of the story.

Yet still Millaton scowled. He should have been in the Great Hall at Clowance today, not left here to arrange tomorrow's side event. He was tired of Godolphin and Seyntaubin's failure to recognise him as their equal.

****

He had lost them. Ahead stood the bridge over the river into the Park. The Godolphin goal was now barely five hundred yards away. As the confused cries of the scrum hollered in the distance, John Moyle knew he was on the threshold of victory. His lungs were bursting now. But the thought of the girl he loved expelled the pain as he drove himself forward.

No wonder he was oblivious to the shadows cast by the lowering sun. Too late he realised they hid two men. Geyge and Trehannick emerged suddenly from the sides of the bridge. They blocked his way and now they were starting towards him. Moyle decided to dart for the water and swim. The river was fast but with luck it would wash him to the other side. He gambled that Millaton's men would fear to follow him into the swell.

Only Millaton's two henchmen had anticipated his plan and reached the river bank first. Suddenly, the immense effort expended in losing the scrum and taking the lead with the ball started to tell on Moyle. Sensing defeat, he wearily hurled the ball back towards the sound of the other players, expecting the two opponents before him to race after it. But they just stood their ground.

"What's up men? You're not still sore about this morning, surely?"

"We're not here 'bout t'morning. We're here about t'boy."

"What boy?"

"Don't you go foolin' with us, Moyle. You know 'xactly. Young Teake, that's who. If it weren't for you, he'd be here now and we'd be winning this hurling match fair and square."

"You were the ones who brought him on the night. And what happened was an accident, you know that as well as I do."

"Mrs Teake don't see it that way, I can tell you. And she and I, well since her husband died, we've been pretty close, if you see what I mean. So I can tell you for nowt, she blames you for what happened – and 'tis not for me to disagree with 'er. The truth is - that boy should never have been put to a man's job. An' heaving those chests across a plank like that was a ludicrous plan. That was your doing, Moyle. You were in charge – no doubt you was hopin' somehow to impress that fancy Seyntaubin girl. Well, now it's time for you to pay."

As Trehannick spoke these words to Moyle, he realised that the other villain had come behind him. Geyge punched him in the back.

"There'll be no Sticklers to observe this one," he whispered. Moyle gasped as his arms were caught in a vice-like grip.

Then the man John had defeated in the morning squared up to him. Trehannick began with a sudden blow to the solar plexus. Moyle was still unprepared and started to retch in agony. Then a second blow cracked a rib. His nose started to bleed. A bloodshot eye turned blind. Pain darted up from his groin. Now he was hurling through the air, until his flight path plunged abruptly into the rapid flow of the river. His mind slowly started escaping into dreams – here was Ann, bedecked in jewels; here was Thomas, smiling; here was a silver ball shining – as Moyle's soon unconscious body began a steep descent, ever deeper into the flowing water.

Geyge and Trehannick moved away slowly. They found where Moyle had chucked the hurling ball and tossed it some fifty yards further towards the trees. It caught the branches and the clatter of its fall was heard by the scrum advancing on the far side. Millaton's men were pleased to see that they had caused a scramble and they soon heard the game was afoot once more.

The two retired into the shadows.

****

The fire in the Great Hall at Clowance crackled and spat as a roasting pig was turned in readiness for the evening feast. Torches along the walls flickered, while ceiling lanterns gently swayed as they were caught by the draught. Minstrels played in the gallery. Guests offered their condolences. Thomas was taking news of Clowance's defeat in the hurling match, with no more stoicism than one of his daughters.

"No sign of young Moyle yet," he commiserated with Ann. "Since the match finished, he seems to have hidden his face and figure. There's really no cause for that– his was a true and valiant effort. They say he nearly beat the entire field at one point."

"I don't know why you are telling me, Father'" Ann replied, blushing. "But I'm sure he must have had some important business. It's not like Master Moyle to hide from anything."

Ann's words revealed a note of concern. Just then, her little brother, William, and their cousin, Anne Basset, appeared at the door looking like a couple of vagrants. Covered in mud, they scampered upstairs to escape the rising call of their parents, part in jest, part in fury. Ann decided to follow them and avoid further interrogation.

Thomas turned to John Vyvian. "I'm afraid that today's defeat hurts our pockets as well as our pride, John. If I'd won my bet with William Godolphin, I'd planned to pay both our fines to the Inner Temple."

"I'm not sure my men would have deserved the spoils and the glory, Thomas. But you've had that letter too, have you? Ten pounds for missing a dinner – Master Wayte must be short of legal work, to demand such sums from us country fellows!"

This exchange was spoken loud enough to catch the attention of Lord Lisle, who joined them.

"Do you speak of Master Anthony Wayte? He's a cousin of mine, one of the most fair and generous of men. At least, as far as lawyers can ever be so"

Vyvian seized this opening and Thomas was content to let his good friend make the running. Lisle began to explain his connection to the Senior Bencher at Inner Temple and as they sat down for the evening meal, they soon found themselves hearing all about his Hampshire family. It was a remarkable story, clearly intended for Honor Basset's benefit as well as their own.

"My mother was a great beauty," he began, "called Elizabeth Wayte." She had caught the eye of Edward IV and some years later Arthur appeared, where the King was holding court at the time, in Calais. At the King's insistence, all his children – in or out of wedloc had taken their father's surname and so he was christened Arthur Plantagenet. In the final throes of the Wars of the Roses, there was no telling what the future held.

"While my mother returned to Hampshire, I stayed with the royal nursery, playing younger brother to my father Edward's two royal princes," he went on. "Then the old King died and soon the unlucky princes were trapped in the Tower by their uncle Richard.

"I was just eight years old," Lisle explained, "and I was allowed to escape to Hampshire. The new King did not even care his own offspring, so he was hardly prone to dwell on me."

110

"If you don't mind my asking, my Lord," Honor interjected, "did the late King Richard really have any offspring?"

"A natural son. I met him once, my Lady Basset, a man old before his years, working as a farmhand. He hardly knew who he was himself by then, poor fellow."

But for Lisle, the Battle of Bosworth had changed all. Henry Tudor wanted his victory over Richard to mark the end of the bitter rivalry between the Houses of York and Lancaster. He married Elizabeth, Arthur's legitimate half-sister. To heal wounds, he gathered all around him and so two years after he left, Arthur Plantagenet found himself summoned back to Court.

"I hardly knew the late King Henry's eldest son, another Arthur being groomed for kinghood, but the arrival of a younger son brought me a little companion," Lisle explained. "I was fifteen years old by then, of course."

Honor imagined how the young Henry must have quickly grown to trust the older boy's good nature, to learn from his charm, to rely on his loyalty. She had heard speak of Henry's intense jealousy and deep resentment of his own brother. The growing Prince would have found nothing to envy in Lisle and much to admire.

"Then the Prince's elder brother, Arthur, died," Lisle continued. The Henry who unexpectedly ascended the throne at the age of eighteen found a crafty way to elevate his childhood playfellow. One of the least popular men in the kingdom was Edmund Dudley, his father's tax collector. Henry had him summarily executed. This left a widow, whom Henry gave in marriage to Arthur, along with her dead husband's attainted fortune.

"Some call His Grace the King despotic, but to me he has always been generous," Lisle commented with only a hint of irony.

He was now sent on a dangerous mission, during war with France. "We launched an attack on the French fleet in harbour,

111

but my ship hit a rock at the entrance and began to sink. As the waves swept over the deck, I was convinced I was about to die."

Lisle had reached the crux of his story. The entire room was listening. At this moment, six-year-old Anne Basset stormed into the Hall, unabashed at making her second grand foray of the day.

"It's true, mother, I promise you," she pleaded.

"What's true, Anne?"

Lisle looked on ruefully for a moment. Queen Katharine would scorn the indulgence being shown, even to such a pretty little girl. Yet he could not hear the devotion in Honor's reply without a pang of envy. His own childhood had been robbed of any such feeling.

"William and I found him, we really did!"

"Found whom, Anne?" Thomas asked gently.

"John Moyle, of course, Uncle!"

"I see, little Anne. But what's to worry? John Moyle's bigger and bolder than you and not afraid to take care of himself."

"He's in the river, Father!" Anne's cousin William had run down after her, determined not to miss his own chance to shine. "But my sister won't believe us – she says we're just teasing her. But it's true I tell you, he's there!"

Thomas looked at his son. William was not a boy to go telling lies. There was guilt in his expression, that was for sure, but Thomas could quickly account for it. The children should never have been at the scene in the first place.

"Now listen to me, William. I'm not going to scold you. But we need to know what you are talking about. Tell me now, where is Master Moyle?"

There was a pause and then the story spilled out between the two children. They had followed the hurling match at a close distance, cheering John Moyle when they saw him steal ahead with the ball. Then they lost him, just like the scrum. But William knew the bridge into Godolphin Park and guessed that was where he would be headed. They ran to the spot, arriving just in time to see two villains lay into him. William and Anne had crouched behind a tree.

After they were sure the two villains were gone, William and Anne made their way to the river bank. Moyle was nowhere to be found. The two started to follow the river and that was when they saw him, his body cast on a mud bank, half in the water, half out.

The river was shallow here, so the two children had crept down and rolled his body over away from the water. Then they heard a groan, looked at each other and fled. William and Anne were now lost. It took them until dusk to find their way back to Clowance. Muddied and exhausted, they had crept into the house, not daring to say a word.

Thomas gave his boy a hug, rose from his chair and ordered horses and torches. John Vyvian and a couple of retainers joined him, while men drawn from the feast day helpers' party, then in full swing in the Clowance kitchens, were dispatched on foot. Ann Seyntaubin begged to join, but her mother Mary said she needed her help to prepare a room. She left her sister Honor in charge of entertaining Lisle and the other guests in the Hall.

As they left Clowance, Thomas noticed the waning moon beginning to rise in a clear night sky. He could find his way to Godolphin blindfold, but this additional light would make the task of locating Moyle much easier. Thomas cursed himself for treating his disappearance so lightly. He had forgotten that the feast day might be taken as an opportunity to settle scores. He felt angry and insulted, as well as puzzled as to who could possibly bear a grudge against John Moyle. It made no sense.

It took twenty minutes to locate the body. Moyle was motionless. As Thomas approached him, his mind was filled with dread at the thought of how to tell his daughter. Just then John Polgrene, one of Vyvian's men, stepped forward.

"If you don't mind, Mr Thomas, I have a little practice at this sort of thing, men caught off the Lizard and so forth."

"Go ahead, Polgrene, there's nothing I can do."

John Polgrene stooped down and lifted Moyle's neck from behind. Then putting his hand on Moyle's chest and his ear to his mouth, Polgrene demanded complete silence.

There was a pause, before Polgrene stood up slowly and turned to Thomas.

Chapter Ten

Arthur Plantagenet... being in great peril of shipwreck, called upon Our Lady of Walsingham for help, and vowed that if it pleased God and her to deliver him, that he would not eat flesh or fish till he had seen her.

Cottonian Library Manuscripts

Arthur Lisle had fought hard to rescue the crew from his shipwreck and after they were saved, he undertook a pilgrimage of thanks to Walsingham. Now he was on another pilgrimage, to St Michael's Mount, in the aftermath of another shipwreck. This morning, his reason for giving thanks was at his side. On their way from Clowance to lunch with Captain Millaton, as Honor Basset began to explain what to expect when they arrived, Lisle realised he had never felt happier.

"In ancient times, the Mount was known as *Carrack Looz en Cooz*, or the Grey Rock in the Wood. Then the water flooded into the bay, so now the Mount becomes cut off as the sea ebbs and flows with the tide. Otherwise, men may come from Marazion to the Mount on foot, as we will do this morning."

"The flood, you say, my Lady? When would that have been?"

"Well, my Lord, no one knows for sure, but it may have been in the time of your namesake, King Arthur, that the Mount finally became an island. The truth is that even now, the sea is ravaging the coast of the bay and land can often simply disappear after a heavy storm. In diverse places, at the low-water mark, you can still find the roots of trees, as a token of the ground wasted.

"The Mount, being made of granite, stands firm in all weathers. At its foot, I would reckon its compass to be a mile round. The south-east part is pasturable and breeds some fine rabbits. The residue is high and rocky. On the north-east, you may notice a garden with certain houses and shops for the fishermen. Below, there is a pier for boats and ships."

"To reach the chapel, will it be a steep climb up the hill?"

"There will be no cause to exchange your horse for a mule, my Lord. The way to the church ascends by broad steps. They start by the houses at the bottom, curving up towards a strongly walled courtyard. The chapel of St Michael is in front of you, the chapel of our Lady is to your left. The captain's and the priest's lodgings are behind, facing the south side."

Their road had now reached the headland above Marazion. The view across the bay towards Penzance was still obscured by the morning mist, a carpet of cloud which hid the foot of the island entirely. The Mount Church rose above, as if floating on air.

"I have rarely seen a sight so magical and mystical," said Lisle. "Nor could I wish to do so in the company of a more fair and gentle lady."

Honor blushed. "My Lord must forgive me, but he appears far more used to the customs of courtly love than I will ever be."

"Courtly love is truly just a façade, Lady Basset. But sometimes it serves the purpose of hiding an honest disposition."

Honor laughed nervously at this artful piece of flattery and rapidly changed the subject. She began to speak of Captain Millaton and the guests they would soon be meeting for lunch. It was evident that she shared her brother-in-law's caution towards the captain, even if he was the coming man in their midst, making evident her preference for the coarse frankness of a true Cornishman like James Chynoweth.

"Now tell me about the archpriest, John Arscott. His Excellency the Cardinal has sent me a note to make a point of speaking to him directly," Lisle enquired.

"I hardly know him, my Lord. But whether or not it is merely the prejudice of the place, I'm told he is more loathed than liked by the islanders." She paused, before adding, "It's said that if his coat and his hood be sewed together, they are not to be trusted."

Honor now amused Lisle with the scandal which had forced the Church to dismiss the Gilbertians, the holy order which had run

116

the Mount in the days before the garrison. Believing that a monk's vow of chastity signified little unless he was daily tempted by women, they had invited an order of Carmelite nuns to join them in the island monastery.

"In such an outpost," Lisle commented with a wistful smile, "one can imagine the forces of nature soon overcoming the strictures of religion."

"The surprise in Marazion, my Lord, was that the nocturnal communion between the monks and the nuns escaped censure for so long," Honor replied with a knowing look.

Arscott was third in the line of secular priests, who had replaced the disgraced monks, along with the garrison, she explained. He survived on a modest stipend of six pounds a year, while his distant masters at Syon Abbey still collected their valuable feudal rents from the Mount lands.

They had now reached the centre of the town, where the Mayor headed a welcoming party for the honoured guests. Arthur Lisle was as close to royalty as any of them would ever see. It was market day. Invited to meet the stallholders, Arthur and Honor caused a stir as they made their way through the bustling crowd.

Arthur was all of six foot four, as tall as his father had been, with the same powerful features. He also shared the late King Edward's easy faculty for mixing with people. He welcomed this opportunity to josh with the tradesmen and flatter the young girls, soon drawn to their imposing visitor like moths to a candle. Honor gleaned that her watchful eye might be all that was preventing Arthur's flirtatious inclinations from leading him astray.

"Good morning, my Lord," came an unmistakable voice. "I'm Chynoweth, Sir John Arundell's Officer of Wreck, instructed to take you over to the Mount. We must be moving now, or the sea may defeat us."

This was not quite true, but like many living by the island, Chynoweth found that talk of tides was a useful way of getting pilgrims to do one's bidding : however high and mighty they appeared. So the lunch party made their way across the sand, as the mist cleared to reveal the island looming ahead in all its splendour. They passed Chapel rock, so called for the staging post it offered pilgrims who took the boat to the island when the tide was in. Chynoweth regaled Lisle with the legend of the wicked Cormoran, said to have buried his wife under this rock, before he was tricked down a well and drowned by Jack the Giantkiller.

The land of saints is also the haunt of sinners, Lisle reminded himself. It would be easy to be beguiled by these people, loyalty to the King notwithstanding.

****

John Arscott retreated down the tower, nearly slipping on the narrow spiral staircase as he went. With the aid of his spyglass, he had stood on the turret and observed Millaton's illustrious lunch guests from the moment they had appeared at the top of the town. He had admired the sensation they had caused in the market and smiled at their patience while James Chynoweth told his stories on the way across.

Arscott had regretfully declined the invitation to join Millaton's lunch party, citing the importance of preparing for his role in showing the chapel and its relics. The truth was that he was an intensely shy man and he wanted to save his courage for imparting to Lisle his vital evidence. He was confident that he could persuade Lisle to climb the tower alone. He felt sure that Lady Basset would decline the opportunity, along with the others who had been there before.

This was where he had now left his spyglass, having carried it up in a large wooden box with painstaking care. Arscott harboured ambition, like most men of his time. He knew that if he could persuade Lisle that his device worked, certainly he would be thanked for his information about the night the wreck disappeared. But surely the Vice Admiral of the Fleet would also grasp the tactical advantage of his invention and reward him accordingly.

Arscott reached the north courtyard from the chapel, just as the voices of the lunch party warned of their imminent arrival. It appeared that Chynoweth had overreached himself during their lunch, his fiercely protective loyalty to his master Sir John playing into the hands of Millaton.

"I should be careful," the captain was saying to him, "or the Vice Admiral here may recommend a review of Sir John's privileges. Is that not so, my Lord?"

"Sir John certainly enjoys a unique position," Lisle replied carefully. "Along the south coast, where I exercise the Right, it is merely on behalf of the Crown. I may allow for my costs and expenses, but the proceeds of a wreck belong solely to the King, if not to the survivors."

"Then you will be aware, my Lord," Chynoweth rejoined, "how hard it often is to recover any proceeds or profit, once expenses have been paid. At least, 'tis so in these parts."

"That may be true of your normal wreck, but a really valuable load presents a different case. Suppose, for example, that the *Santo Antonio* carried the priceless load of which we hear the saying and rumour. Then I wager His Grace the King would take a very different view – and your Sir John would be a fool to stand in his way."

Chynoweth took these words to heart. There was no benefit to his master in delving into the disappearance of the Portuguese treasure and all stood to lose if his Right to Wreck were revoked entirely. Millaton saw this and could not help smiling. The enquiry, which everyone expected Sir John to chair, now looked certain to provide a favourable outcome. A sense of relief pervaded Millaton as, unsuspecting, he handed his guests into the care of the devious archpriest.

Chapter Eleven

... should six or seven thousand men land on the coast
of Cornwall to espouse the cause of both mother and daughter,
forty thousand Englishmen would at once join them.
The Imperial Ambassador Mendoza to his Emperor,
The Calendar of Spanish Papers

Mary Seyntaubin rarely scolded her daughter but this business
with John Moyle had unnerved her. Mary had been sixteen when
she first married and could only remember how little she had
known her own mind at the time. Roger Bluett had not wooed
her. He had spoken exclusively with her father, who had then
presented his marriage proposal to her as some kind of birthday
present. It was one which he had made clear she could not
possibly refuse. Thomas was a different man from her father and
times had changed, so it had not been hard to persuade him that
their girls should be allowed a wider berth, when it came to
finding a husband, one who brought a chance of the happiness
that the two of them had realised.

Yet she was bound to resist the idea of their daughter's union
with a man like Moyle, whatever vital service he had recently
performed. Thomas had been surprisingly vague about the
details. Now Moyle had been set upon by rogues and was lying at
death's door. It was enough to start Mary worrying that her
husband was himself involved in some new devilment.

Moyle had survived his attack. His lungs were half full of bilge
and his body was bruised and broken. But his strength and vigour
had saved him. So it was decided to bring him to Godolphin
House, rather than take the much longer route to Clowance. Here
he had been made instantly welcome and was now being eagerly
attended by Honour Godolphin. This was a situation which

120

evidently tormented Ann Seyntaubin, despite Honour's betrothal. Ann did not trust the girl and was searching for excuses to go to Godolphin House herself. Mary and Ann were exchanging heated words on the propriety of a visit to their neighbour, when Thomas appeared.

"Your face is nothing but vexation and trouble," his wife remarked. "Young Moyle is found, so what can concern you now, beloved?"

"It turns out that his assailants were two of Millaton's men. The captain's entertaining our guests today," Thomas replied, "so cannot be enforcing their arrest. But they shall have the devil to pay for what they have done to our man. On our feast day, of all things."

Mary found it difficult to discern which had upset Thomas more – the injury to Moyle or the insult to Clowance. This was as he wished it. For Thomas also worried that the affray brought fresh dangers, raising questions about their actions on the night after the wreck, just when he felt Lisle's view of the affair had been squared. He needed to see Godolphin, as much for his counsel as for his henchmen, although their help would surely be needed to track the two villains down.

"I am going to see my cousin, beloved. Would Ann like to ride with me? I could do with some company to lighten the journey."

This neatly resolved the difference between mother and daughter and soon they were on their way. Ann was a skilful rider and had no difficulty in keeping up with her father. Both proved preoccupied with their own thoughts and the time it took to arrive at Godolphin House sped by. Ann soon pressed herself into service alongside Honour, at the bedside of the wounded warrior, while her father retired to the library with William Godolphin.

"It is a foul business, Thomas. Godolphin House can hardly claim to have won the hurling match fair and square. Here, take

121

back the ball – it's only right for Clowance to hold it until next year's game."

"No one's died, William," Thomas replied, wondering if his cousin's generous gesture might extend to their bet as well as to the ball. It appeared not. "But those two rogues have opened up a Pandora's box. We can't let them get away with it, but we can't chance the matter in court either."

"Bring the matter to court, Thomas – are you mazed, as my tin workers say? There can be no question of a remedy at law. Besides, it would only be Moyle's word against theirs. So I've instructed my man John Wylliam. After all, the assault happened on my land. He knows how to deal with those two – he was with them on the night, you may remember. They're to be given a fair taste of their own medicine, then put to a year's hard labour with the tinners."

Thomas nodded his appreciation. It was far less than the hanging they deserved, but a harsh enough punishment to keep other troublemakers at bay. Godolphin Hill, barely a mile from the main house, was Helston's most valuable source of tin. But extraction of the ore was back-breaking work and those employed there were a violent lot. Many of them would have been wreckers on the beach. They were not the type to give Millaton's two villains an easy ride.

"What I still find hard to explain," Thomas continued, "is why Geyge and Trehannick attacked young Moyle in the first place. Was it the wrestling match?"

"Not at all, Cousin. It was that Mrs Teake in Marazion."

"You mean the dead boy's mother? Tell me, do you happen to know if the captain has made arrangements for her, as I advised?"

"No, he has not, Thomas, but I think there is something about Mrs Teake that you should know. She's the town whore. Millaton was embarrassed to pay her, in case people thought that he used her himself."

122

"I'm beginning to see the captain's parsimony in a different light."

"Quite so. But like many a tawdry tart, she likes to have a favourite at her beck and call. Trehannick's the lucky man these days and now she's provoked him to exact her revenge on Master Moyle."

It was all beginning to make sense to Thomas now. But his opinion of Millaton remained suspended. "Now John Moyle has taken a beating, I suppose Millaton will feel justified not to pay her a farthing. It doesn't seem right, somehow."

"Life isn't fair, Thomas," Godolphin replied. "You and I both know that, as you reminded me only yesterday."

"I fail to follow you, Cousin."

"I mean this business of the wreck. When the Portuguese want to break their word and you tell me the law of England may be bent to their purpose, it's enough to turn a man's mind to mutiny!"

"My family's paid a high enough price for sedition already, Cousin," Thomas replied, recalling the disastrous support his brother Peter had given claimants to the throne. It had been the start of the family's descent into debt.

"I was sorry for your brother's troubles, Thomas. But we were never taxed as hard by the Plantagenet kings as we are today. Imagine if your Lord Lisle were to raise his standard at the Mount. With our treasure behind him, he could take the Crown in weeks. In truth, I said as much to your Lady Basset last night."

"Take the Crown? Now I think you are the one to be mazed, Cousin."

An offer of lunch was accepted, where Thomas managed to steer the conversation back to local matters and the forthcoming enquiry. Later, Thomas visited Moyle upstairs, before taking his daughter Ann home with him. But his mind kept returning to Godolphin's remarks.

****

This twelfth-century tower was not designed for tall men, Lisle reflected as he eased himself onto the chapel turret. While the others had declined the assiduous climb to the highest point on St Michael's Mount, Lisle was as eager as Arscott to have a private word.

"Have you heard from His Excellency?"

"I have a letter here from my Abbot, my Lord, instructing me to assist Cardinal Wolsey in any way I can."

"I can tell you have some information, man. So make speed with it." Already, Lisle was beginning to side with Honor's view of this shifty-looking individual.

"It is true that I can help the Cardinal, my Lord. But to explain how I came by the information, there is something I must show you first. Do you see the market square where you were this morning?" Arscott pointed towards the Marazion mainland, the heart of the town no more than the size of a horse cart from this height. "As you passed the stalls, a pretty woman in a purple dress smiled as she took your arm and gave you a bawdy look."

"Who told you that?" Lisle looked surprised. To his amusement, the naughty wench had scurried away when she caught a scornful glance from Lady Basset. Had this archpriest spoken to Honor?

"No one told me, my Lord. I saw it myself, standing here."

"But that's impossible. It's too far to see."

"Not with this, my Lord." Arscott had produced his spyglass from its box, and was gingerly setting it up. There was now a marked tension between them. Sensing Lisle's mistrust, the archpriest was rapidly reduced to a bundle of nerves. The tube slipped out of his hand. But he caught it again, just as his precious lens was about to smash onto the stone parapet.

This hardly convinced Lisle of his firmness of purpose. But now

124

Arscott had the device set up and was checking it himself. He had the lens fixed on the market square, where the same woman was now luring one of the town boatmen. He invited Lisle to look for himself.

"What am I supposed to see? Through this tube, there is only a blur." Lisle found it hard to disguise his rising irritation.

"On the contrary, my Lord, look carefully and I swear on my oath, you will see right into the town centre. A man and woman are talking outside the Ship's Inn."

Lisle looked up at Arscott, as if he were mad. "Archpriest, that's what men and women do outside an inn on a sunny day. Just as ladies of a certain kind make passes at strangers."

Arscott was puzzled by Lisle's reaction. Under an oath of secrecy, he had allowed his sacristan to try out his device to make sure it worked for both of them. He had not seen quite as clearly as Arscott, it was true, but he had been convinced of its viewing power. The reason was that both of them were long-sighted. The lens in their eye refracted the object in their sight and gave it focus. Lisle, on the other hand, had normal vision, never having spoilt his eyes by poring over manuscripts. Without a second lens at the near end, to refract the beam to the back of his retina, Arscott's device was useless to him.

"Master Arscott, let me give you a warning. You are running a terrible risk. Either this business of yours is a trick, or it is sorcery. I should be sending you to the Ecclesiastical Court for this wickedness. There you will surely be condemned, as a blasphemer if not as a heretic."

Arscott looked terrified. "The sentence for either crime is to be burnt at the stake, my Lord."

"Quite so. But perhaps your mind has simply been seduced by the brilliance of your idea. If this tube here could really do what you say, I would take it immediately to His Grace the King. Such a power of sight could turn the tide of a battle. But until any man

125

can make it work, on your life you should hide such a device from all and sundry."

Arscott hesitated. He believed his own eyes had not deceived him. It did cross his mind that he and his sacristan really might possess supernatural powers, just as his medieval scholar, the Oxford Friar Roger Bacon, had once stood accused. But the archpriest was neither scientist nor hero. He had not the courage to die in prison, like Bacon, nor would he risk death at the stake, in order to claim an invention.

"I am ever in your Lordship's debt," he replied. "Confusion comes easily to a lonely priest."

"Let's hear no more about it. But you didn't bring me up here just to show me this device, did you, Master Arscott?" Lisle continued. "You said you can help the Cardinal. Now is your chance to redeem yourself."

So Arscott told Lisle what he had seen on the night the shipwreck disappeared, how a tin ship had sailed into the Mount harbour, with Thomas Seyntaubin and John Millaton on board. Arscott deftly moved his own watch post on that night, from the chapel parapet to the island harbour, by making up a story about a late-night stroll.

"Do you usually walk about the island, on a moonless night, when a storm is brewing?" Lisle asked sceptically. There was something false about Arscott's account and yet again his reply failed to convince. Honor's distrust of the man was well judged. All the more reason, Lisle reflected, to give Cardinal Wolsey a report in person. Just then, the door from the tower swung open to reveal the petite figure of Honor Basset.

"Master Arscott, you are wanted by the captain," she announced, shooting a curious glance at the contraption he was carrying. "Something to do with arranging a boat to take us ashore later. Chynoweth went ahead before the tide closed."

The archpriest scuttled past, anxious not to attract more

attention to his device, relieved to escape his interview with the Vice Admiral before his nerves led him to contradict his story. He had no idea why the captain would want to see him about boating, and after failing to find Millaton on the terrace below, he chose to retire to his room.

The sun was now warming the gentle breeze which, as Honor stepped out towards Lisle, billowed in her wisps of blond hair. "How fitting a place to meet a Cornish princess," Lisle said as he reached down a hand to help her into the turret. He noticed her reddened cheeks and shortened breath as he spoke, although whether this was from exhaustion after her climb or excitement at their being alone together, he dare not tell.

"Mind what you say, My Lord," Honor replied. "The last Cornish princess to stand on this spot became betrothed to Perkin Warbeck."

Lisle laughed. "You know, there are those that say Warbeck really was my father's son – and to look at him, I could not deny a likeness."

"You actually met the Pretender?"

"Yes, having grown up with the true royal princes, I was called to testify that he was an impostor, even if he did wear a Plantagenet look. But at least, his uprising forced the King's council to weigh the value of my own loyalty against the risk of my treachery. Thankfully, I was trusted and my good fortune at the hands of His Grace the King has never ceased."

"Warbeck was the pawn of others. But a true contender for the throne would stand a real chance."

"There's many a head rolled, Lady Basset, for the few that have worn the Crown. Even the Battle of Bosworth hung in the balance to the end."

"So I cannot tempt you to join a new Cornish rebellion? Imagine if you could draw on the resources of the most powerful King in Europe!"

"If I had a kingdom in my hands, I would willingly give it to your ladyship. Already I have gladly surrendered my heart. But to betray the kindness of King Henry, who continues to elevate my position..."

"But do you not see, my Lord, why he does so? Your father's rule was loved by all. As for only being his bastard son, the Tudor lineage is hardly pure as snow. His Grace's grandfather was a Welsh farmer!" Honor came closer to whisper to him, as if priestly ears might be lurking in the tower. "Remember the crowd at Clowance and the love they showed you in their faces, or the stall holders in the market this morning? You are a true champion."

The wind assailed the turret and they were now lurking below the battlement for shelter. Honor's belief in him had imbued Lisle with resolve. He said nothing but drew Honor towards him, kissing her gently at first and then more passionately, as his hands began to explore the plump breasts hiding under her matronly robes. Honor slowly pulled herself away.

"I may want to be yours, my Lord, but let us not risk the world seeing us, that at least I owe to my husband. Besides, there is the night here together on the island."

"How so? I thought a boat ashore was being arranged."

"It might have been. But now the tide's closed and the wind is up, where's the point in risking our passage? I'm sure Captain Millaton will be only too pleased to accommodate us."

Honor turned to make her way back, Lisle smiling to himself as her delicate neck preceded him into the tower and down the stairs, the shafts of light from the arrow loops playing on her figure. But long before they had reached the bottom, Honor stopped by a door to the side.

"Would you like to see the belfry, my Lord?" she asked with an innocent smile, as she quietly opened the door, the church bells looming in the darkness beyond. They stepped inside and Lisle closed the door behind, reaching out as Honor turned to face him.

Her mouth yielded softly to his lips and then his tongue, as his hands once again began to explore her breasts, before moving down to lift her dress. As Honor gasped with pleasure, Lisle felt himself feeding the aching hunger which she had nursed so long, the thrill giving way to a sense of love he had never known before.

****

Master Pengelly sat in the Angel Hotel, the duties of a shipping clerk cast aside for a moment, listening intently to the bruit and rumour swirling around him. If news was a currency, to be bartered and exchanged by word of mouth, then the Angel was its hub. The usual banter – a scandal about a girl with child, a change in the price of tin, a dearth of cattle in the auction – was seasoned today with talk of the Clowance feast day. No detail of the event had escaped the attention of the Angel's customers. As his mother was fond of saying, "If you sneeze in Helston, they'll ask how your fever's runnin' when you reach Marazion."

Pengelly was not strongly built like Moyle or Treneve. While they had entered the St Pirran's Day wrestling contest, he had gone to the Feast for the dancing. At the hurling match, he had been one of the milling crowd of Clowance supporters, eager to touch the silver ball for good luck, on its way to the start of the match. There was no Mistress Seyntaubin to impress in his life, he reflected. But he had wished Moyle well in his quest, for he had come to admire the man's proficiency and purpose, not least his firm command of the tin ship on that cold January night.

When word of the brutal attack on Moyle reached Pengelly, his feelings of sympathy were mixed with fear. He had no idea why Moyle had been set upon, but he was sure it was connected to their escapade. Listening to rumours flying around the Angel, as they multiplied with Cornish inventiveness, the shipping clerk readily convinced himself that his part in the affair would emerge. Then whoever was planning these attacks would come after him, demanding the information which he had sworn to secrecy with Mr Thomas, or even exacting further revenge.

Cut off from the close embrace of the Clowance estate, Pengelly had few friends to whom he might turn for advice and comfort here in the town. But as a child, his guide and mentor had been the priest at Crowan Church, Father Trelobys. He had spotted the boy's talent and persuaded Thomas Seyntaubin's father to provide for his education and training as a clerk. Pengelly was not to know that in their youth, the Seyntaubin sons had been the bane of Fr Trelobys' life. Nor could he know that the crusty priest still bore a deep grudge against Mr Thomas. He had consorted with the village troublemakers in his youth and the priest felt he ill deserved to inherit the family estate. As for the March festivities at Clowance, in the eyes of Fr Trelobys they were an insult to his parish saint, St Carwenna, whose own feast day took place barely a month before. Thomas' use of a Cornish cross, as the goal in his hurling match, was nothing less than sacrilege and idolatry. Such a list, once started, is easily continued.

It was the Abbot at Tewkesbury who had the living at Crowan and who had appointed Fr Trelobys many years before. It was through this Order that he had continued to fulfil his lifelong devotion to the Church. Now into his retirement in Helston, he still maintained regular contact. Only this morning, the Abbot had sent him an urgent enquiry on behalf of Cardinal Wolsey. Then he had received Pengelly's message, asking to see him on an important matter. Fr Trelobys was only too alive to the rumours circulating around the town and had little trouble trying to connect the interest of the Cardinal with skulduggery at Clowance. Never one to believe in coincidence or superstition, Fr Trelobys could tell when the hand of God was working to help him.

As he entered the Angel, none could guess these thoughts from the affable smile which the old priest gave Pengelly. He had quickly spied him across the room and made his way accordingly. Soon the shipping clerk was relaxing in the presence of his childhood mentor. Moving to a table where they could not be overheard, Pengelly unburdened his soul to the kindly cleric. Assuming him to be bound by the confessional vow, Pengelly spared no detail of his part in the hire of the tin ship that fateful January night. Fr Trelobys heard few confessions these days, but his sharp mind still caught every salient detail of this story, as he beguiled Pengelly with a practised ear. What he heard truly shocked him.

Fr Trelobys did not share the common view of shipwrecks. Far from thinking them "God's grace", he saw only the devil at work in the scavenging on the beach and the callous disregard for life which so often followed such disasters. He gave no credit to Thomas Seyntaubin for having saved the survivors' lives by his actions at Gunwalloe. That was his duty as a magistrate. What he saw as the robbing of the ship, on the other hand, was all the more damnable by a man of law. He would never be able to explain how old Mr Thomas could have sired such a wicked son.

Fr Trelobys added the words "haste-haste-haste – on your life!" for the messenger, before he sealed the letter which he carefully crafted that evening to the Abbot of Tewkesbury. Then he retired to bed. To fashion so sharp a weapon with so clear a conscience, the elderly priest told himself, was a rare pleasure.

Chapter Twelve

*His Majesty writes to the King, to ask restitution of
copper and other goods from a Portuguese ship which was
wrecked on the coast of England, Antonio Paciecho and forty men
perishing.*
King João III of Portugal to Cardinal Wolsey,
Letters and Papers of Henry VIII

The May sun shone into the central courtyard at the Royal Palace of
Sintra, as an Atlantic breeze wafted through the mullioned
windows. Smoke billowed out of the conical chimneys which
overshadowed the city skyline, while the oven furnaces in the
Palace kitchens were stoked in readiness for yet another royal
banquet. A gastronomic army was at work roasting twenty-five
plump chickens, some with salt, some with sugar, while five dozen
eggs were turned into omelettes stuffed with pigeon or beef. Oyster
dishes garnished with pepper were placed on tables inlaid with
silver and ivory, spring flowers were arranged in extravagant
turquoise bowls.

Above the cavernous kitchens, members of the Royal Household
bustled and jostled in the Palace courtyard, idly exchanging gossip
as they sought out information on the latest Crown appointments.
The Cortes could complain about the waste they incurred, but
more than two thousand noblemen now gorged on their
misbegotten sinecures.

The King's receipts from Portugal's seafaring empire, from
Indian spices and Brazilian gold, from Japanese silks and African
slaves, now approached a million pounds a year. Even the loss of
ten ships every year to French pirates did little to dent his fortune.
There was still plenty from Portugal's lucrative spice routes to
shower generosity on his favoured courtiers.

King João alternated the opulence of his banquets with days of fasting, religious observance of saints' days and Fridays, when fish was served plain. The giving and withholding of food, like the place settings at his dining tables, were all part of the protocol which reminded each courtier how a career could be made or broken on a capricious royal whim.

This morning Jeremy de Corfe, Gentleman of the Royal Chamber, strode across the courtyard sporting an oversized codpiece, one of those extravagant fashions which his Lisbon tailor loved to promote. De Corfe no longer felt one of the chosen few, in fact he was a deeply troubled man as he made his way to discuss the latest report in the ongoing saga of the *Santo Antonio*. He could not understand why King João was so obsessed by the wreck of this one ship on the English coast.

He knew that his King was a pious man, with little imagination. The King was capable of believing any number of wild stories about the mysterious loss of his treasure, fed to him by devious members of the Court, no doubt seeking to discredit de Corfe's standing in the race to win new royal favours. The man entrusted to guard the royal dowry, Admiral Paciecho, had drowned with the ship and the salvage had been sold for a song. As the only survivor of noble rank, de Corfe was uncomfortably aware that a finger of suspicion still hung over his role in the affair.

He felt many eyes following him, as he left the courtyard and disappeared into the *Sala das Pegas*. The Magpies' Room was an apt choice for this meeting. It had been so named by King João the First. He had been caught there by his Queen, Philippa of Lancaster, stealing a kiss from one of her ladies-in-waiting. The King then covered the ceiling with as many magpies as there were ladies at Court, as if to say to his English Queen that there was only one bird of royal plumage in their midst. Now a tiding of magpies had stolen from a Portuguese King. The English alliance, cemented by João and Philippa, was facing its first test in over a hundred years.

Francisco Pessoa, the King's wily legal operator, had arrived in the chamber before de Corfe and was already conversing with His Majesty. To the nobleman's concern, the domineering Queen Catherine was also at her husband's side. His fashionable accoutrement earned her instant disapproval.

"Fernandes' agents may have returned to Antwerp empty handed," the King was asking Pessoa, "but what news is there of the Commission of Enquiry promised by my Brother in Faith King Henry?"

"The details have just been received, Your Grace. If I may say so, they are an affront to Your Majesty's intelligence!"

"Greetings, Your Majesties," de Corfe interjected with a graceful bow. "But may it please *Senhor* Pessoa to explain why this investigation offends him – surely it shows that our friends at Court have the ear of the English King?"

"My dear Sir, we may have the ear of the King, but these Cornish *pegas* have the ear of their enquiry. According to our London ambassador, one of the Commissioners to be appointed is called *Senhor* Chamond. He is the first cousin to *Capitão* Millaton and the brother-in-law of *Senhor* Seyntaubin, two of the principal accused in our claim."

"How many Commissioners are there?"

"Only three. Another is called *Senhor* Lower. Alvares' testimony named a Lower as one of the *bandidos* who robbed him on the night! The Commissioner's own brother actually stole the most precious treasure which the crew had salvaged."

"Is this true?" King João III glared at his nobleman in sudden earnest.

"Yes, Your Grace, *Senhor* Pessoa is quite correct. But he told me that the matter was to be raised with His Excellency Cardinal Wolsey, at his Star Chamber, not with another den of these Cornish *bandidos*."

"This Mount's Bay is like Castelo Rodrigo, Your Royal

Highnesses, only with St Michael and the sea rather than St Francis and Spain to contend with. Of course, Your Grace must seek justice in London," Pessoa interrupted.

"Quite so, Pessoa. After all, if the case were reversed, would not his Majesty King Henry seek justice in Lisbon? But until this moment, my good friend here seems to have overlooked these things." De Corfe gave a gentle smile to Pessoa, sensing that for once he had bested the lawyer.

"It is not for me to question the great knowledge of a Gentleman of the King's Chamber," Pessoa responded sarcastically, "but I am sure Your Highnesses understand that the English law must be allowed to wind its course, before it reaches the Court that counts."

"Certainly, Pessoa," King João replied. "But how long could that take?"

"It could take more than a year, Your Grace. Meanwhile, we cannot afford to rely on our ally's goodwill. My sources tell me that the English have been offered the rights to Spanish discoveries in the spice routes. Two large English vessels are about to challenge our monopoly."

This news touched a raw nerve in King João, who guarded his precious spice routes as a lioness guards her cubs. He took a fierce interest in managing their tiniest detail. The unexpected threat to his spice fiefdom set the hairs prickling on the back of his neck.

Jeremy de Corfe sensed the change in mood. He saw the chance to build on his momentary advantage over Pessoa. He also preened with news he had secretly acquired and longed to share. Fatefully, he said, "Your Grace need not fear this alliance between England and Spain lasting too much longer. My own sources at the English Court tell me that King Henry will soon divorce his Queen Katharine"

Too late, de Corfe realised that the news he had so wantonly discharged was having precisely the opposite effect to the one intended. The colour in King João's cheeks now began to drain, as

135

he looked towards his unfortunate courtier as if an untrained puppy was standing on his finest Persian carpet.

"Do you refer to the aunt of Her Majesty our Queen, de Corfe?" It was Pessoa who posed the next question with rapier skill. "With what heinous offence against the Church could King Henry, the 'Defender of the Faith', possibly accuse his Spanish Queen?"

De Corfe failed to see the noose which he was unwittingly about to tie around his own neck. "In London, they are calling it The King's Matter. This Defender of the Faith married his brother's widow. According to the Book of Leviticus, this offends against God. So their marriage is unlawful."

How strangely silent the King had fallen, de Corfe thought to himself, as Pessoa pursued his point remorselessly. "So are you saying, my dear Sir, that the Princess Mary, the offspring of the English Crown and the cousin of our own dear Queen Catherine, is a *bastarda*?"

Jeremy de Corfe was not the sort to recognise his hand on the lever of his own trap door. "*Bastarda*, Your Majesties," he replied without falter; and his royal audience blanched.

João the Third seemed now poised to say something, but his Queen intervened. "So, *Senhor* de Corfe, you claim this Book of Leviticus bans a widow from marrying her dead husband's brother. Does it also ban a widower from marrying his dead wife's sister?"

To say that Jeremy de Corfe was one of those quick-witted courtiers used to saving a situation with a dazzling turn of phrase would be wrong. He was more the predictable sort, guessing which answer was expected to be supplied with an abundance of flattery. "Her Majesty has yet again shown her remarkable grasp of the Holy Scriptures," he opined.

"Traitor!" King João's colour had returned, his face now a picture of incandescent rage. Silence had fallen among the courtiers outside, as all strained to hear these exchanges unfolding behind the closed doors of the *Sala das Pegas*. The King sought to contain his anger, while only Pessoa and de Corfe could hear Queen Catherine, as she quietly resumed with measured fury: "Has it not crossed your stupid brain that the late King Manuel, the father of His Grace the King, married his dead wife's sister?" There was a regal pause, before she added: "First you insult our honour by selling our marriage portion for a pittance. Now you attack the honour of our husband – by suggesting that the King of Portugal is a *bastardo*. Dom Juaõ, by the Grace of God, think how your grandfather would have dealt with such a man!"

"My dear Queen Catherine," João replied, "I believe he once stabbed eighty nobles with a dagger, just to settle a dispute. Perhaps we should…"

But the King's train of thought was interrupted. A man's chilling cry, which usually would have been drowned out by courtly chatter, emanated from the dungeon windows several floors below. The royal couple turned to Pessoa for some explanation while de Corfe, stricken with guilt, recognised in the cries of the torture victim a voice he knew only too well.

Pessoa's thin lips revealed a ghostly pleasure at this well-timed intervention. "Your Graces will forgive me, but I have found it necessary to test certain elements of our seafarers' testimony – and so to test various parts of their bodies with the *braseiro incandescente*. There are so many inconsistencies…"

"Inconsistencies?"

"Yes, inconsistencies in their telling. For example, they say that the most they recovered from the wreck was three thousand ducats. Yet the *Santo Antonio* sunk in one fathom of water! They say that attempts to seek Portuguese help failed. Yet it was no more than four leagues to our vessels in the Fal! They say they were robbed and pillaged in the night. Yet before he collapsed, Vaz confessed to us how Alvares had been fêted as a guest in the mansion of that rascal Seyntaubin. To Vaz himself they gave back a chain and silver bowl!"

"Before his collapse?"

"Yes, before Vaz collapsed." Pessoa looked knowingly at de Corfe. "I have instructed the Inquisition to spare no effort in order to discover the truth and unmask the accomplices in this affair. As Your Majesty Queen Catherine has so wisely remarked, it was a monstrous dishonour to our kingdom to sell such a priceless royal marriage portion for merely fifty *livres*."

"Tell me, Pessoa," Queen Catherine asked earnestly, as she looked hard at de Corfe. "As well as hot irons for the feet, maybe the *Corregedor,* he uses hot bricks for the buttocks? And rather than the *garrotilhos* to break the bones or the *trampa* to tear the legs, my brother Charles, he always says the *bostezo* to distend the mouth is best."

De Corfe stared, his head shaking as he heard this, his mouth dry, his tongue the texture of parchment. "But English law..." he managed to start saying, before Pessoa smoothly interrupted once again.

"Yes, indeed. Your Majesties, I fear we have one slight obstacle in our path, which is the law of England. If there are no survivors, there is no claim! This Gentleman of the King's Chamber, he is barely fit to become one of the butchers in your Majesty's kitchens, stigmatised by the blood and smell of the meat he touches. But I regret his life must be spared as a witness."

No one in the room doubted his royal forebears would at least have struck the dishonoured Gentleman of his Chamber, but King João still hesitated, while Jeremy de Corfe continued to stammer and stutter, shaking his head. He mouthed apologies to his Queen but mortal terror prevented words from coming forth. Weakly, he began to beat a retreat from the *Sala das Pegas*, every step in fear of his life.

King João, at last regaining his air of supreme piety, was relieved to avoid the need to add anything at all. The Gentleman of the

King's Chamber had banished himself from Court. To be implicated in the loss of a Queen's dowry was already odious; to import the slightest doubt as to the legitimacy of the Crown – in front of his King and Queen, was an atrocity.

Pessoa's face wore a look of shock and concern, masking his inner glee with the cunning of a weasel. The downfall of one of the legion of nobles who festered around João the Third was never a sadness to Pessoa. He would enjoy the rewards of advising the King, as to where to reassign de Corfe's sinecures amongst his greedy Court rivals. A banished de Corfe would provide a useful scapegoat, if Pessoa's plan to recover the King's treasure should fail. Above all, he anticipated many years' pleasure in taking grovelling bribes from de Corfe, to obtain some fresh commission. Pessoa was quite certain that none would ever be granted, unless perhaps it was in those kitchens.

"Tell me, Pessoa, has His Imperial Majesty, my brother Charles, been informed of these developments?" Queen Catherine gave him a jolting stare.

"Certainly, Your Majesty, I wrote to his Grand Chancellor, Mercurino Gattinara, three months ago."

"Very good, Pessoa." The Queen placed great faith in Gattinara and his bold design for a universal monarchy.

"But I gather that there is a slight difficulty, Your Majesty." Pessoa almost winced as he produced these words, painfully aware of the unwelcome news he must impart.

"Difficulty, Pessoa? When has my brother Charles ever been defeated by difficulty?"

"Do not misunderstand me, Your Majesty, but I have learnt that the English King Henry was due some payment from His Imperial Majesty out of Antwerp. It appears the English are aggrieved that the funds in hand were used to pay your dowry rather than their debt. So Mendoza, the Spanish Ambassador, finds it hard to raise this matter at all."

139

Queen Catherine's eyes lit up like a tiger's. "This English King is a monster! First he disowns his own daughter. Now he expects my brother the Emperor to rank his tawdry debt ahead of the sacred marriage portion due to my beloved husband."

At this, King João smiled benignly at his wife. He loved these Castilian fireworks, even if he had no idea how to light Catherine's fuse himself. Just then, a young courtier bore a message. Tactfully, the Queen handed it to her husband to read.

King João beamed uncertainly. He was deeply disturbed by what he read, even more so when he saw the joy it brought to his wife. "The Imperial troops have taken Rome," he announced. "The Pope is their captive."

Pessoa had no wish to become the lightning rod of their latent discontents.

"It must be said, Your Majesties, that His Magnificence Chancellor Gattinara has shown great wisdom, to place his overwhelming desire for a universal peace above pride in his native Italy. And now that Rome is tamed, why not England?"

"But who would lead such a campaign, Pessoa?" asked the Queen, warming to the theme. "It is thirty years since the Flanders boy staked his claim."

"Forgive me for reminding Your Majesties," Pessoa replied cautiously, "but while Warbeck's claim was bogus, he was carried by his Cornish followers with a courage that still nearly crushed the upstart Tudors."

"Yes, of course, Pessoa – and it is these same demon Cornish who now have our gold and silver. Tell me, Your Grace," Queen Catherine asked, turning to her husband, "would it not be a noble sacrifice – to forgo my dowry in order to place our niece on the English throne?"

"I'm not sure I follow you, my dear," King João replied. "But would it put paid to this *bastardo* business?"

Queen Catherine smiled. Where family honour was concerned,

her husband was easily persuaded. Soon it was agreed that these Cornish *bandidos*, who only moments before had been the objects of their fury, would be hailed in Lisbon as heroes if they marched for Princess Mary. The Imperial debt would be cancelled. Then a grateful Emperor would repay the Portuguese King for his support and reaffirm those vital spice routes into the bargain.

"But these English like to be ruled by Kings, Pessoa," the Queen added thoughtfully. "This rebellion will need a leader and the Princess will need a consort."

"There is one of the Plantagenet line," Pessoa said as he entered his stride, "whose claim to the throne is in many ways stronger than his King's, Your Majesties. This man is recently widowed. What is more, our agents in Antwerp report that he has just been to Cornwall – to stay with the very *bandidos* of whom we speak."

"What is his name?" Queen Catherine asked, yearning for the boldness of another Gattinara.

"He's called Lord Lisle, Your Majesties." Pessoa paused, regretfully adding, "There is just one problem."

"Yes, Pessoa?"

"He is another *bastardo*."

****

The Lord Chancellor walked through his gardens at Hampton Court, enjoying the glow of mid-morning sunshine, the scent of late-spring lavender easing his troubled mind. For the first time in his long and glittering career, Cardinal Wolsey felt the tide of fortune turning against him. The King's Matter, so clever in conception, was proving dangerous in execution. He had fired Henry's hopes by devising a means of divorce from his now barren first wife, Katharine of Aragon. He had planned a new royal marriage to the King of France's beautiful sister, a strategic alliance to counter the Spanish. But all this required Henry's release from

Queen Katharine by the Pope, a step blocked by the latest news.

A languid figure was walking towards him. Wolsey had acceded to Lord Lisle's request to see him this morning, anxious to discuss his recent errand to Cornwall. Here was an affair where the Cardinal felt in easy command. He welcomed these diversions from statecraft, albeit ever mindful that the pawns on a chessboard can tilt the outcome of the game.

"The sack of Rome shocks us all, Lord Chancellor," Lisle commiserated, after they had exchanged the usual formalities. "For once, you must be glad that it is Clement and not you who became the Vicar of Rome."

"But the Pope's misfortune is also mine, my Lord, where His Majesty's divorce is concerned. As the King wisely observed, I have been trying to move a stone which was already lying in its place. Now the most powerful man in Christendom rests his foot on it."

"Even the Imperialists cannot hold the Pope captive for ever, Lord Chancellor. His Grace King Henry need only remain patient for a while. In time, His Holiness will be even more willing to grant his divorce, given his antipathy to the Emperor."

"That might have been true, my Lord, if The King's Matter had been kept secret until the time was ripe. But now the affair is abroad, we can be sure the Pope will not be granted his freedom without first ruling in this matter as Charles of Spain dictates."

"All the more reason, Lord Chancellor, to ensure that the Pope regains his freedom, in spite of the Emperor and not because of him."

"Quite so, my Lord. I can tell you, in the utmost confidence, that already I have a meeting arranged with the French King, to begin war against Spain, while the Italian League prepares to take back Rome."

"But there can be no marriage to confirm this alliance before a divorce is granted," Lisle commented.

"So His Grace the King, as a token of their newfound friendship, intends to anoint Francis the First as a Knight of the Garter. Perhaps, as one of the Order who is fluent in the French tongue, you might be sent with that commission on the King's behalf?"

"It would be the highest honour, Lord Chancellor. Meanwhile, if the policy is to fight the Spanish throne, what is the policy towards the Spanish dowry? I presume we have no interest now in restoring this lost Cornish treasure to our King's enemies."

"On the contrary, my Lord Lisle. As you may know, His Majesty has debts owing from the Spanish Crown. The King is highly vexed that funds in Antwerp, which the Spanish should have used to repay his loans, were sent to Portugal instead. He sees that treasure as his own. What is more, we may only surmise how that fortune might be misused, should it fall into the wrong hands."

"So if the Court finds that the treasure should be returned, you will seize it as surety, I suppose. But will that simply not aggravate the Portuguese, who after all are the actual claimants? I wonder if all this can be worth it, Lord Chancellor, for a few thousand ducats."

"If that were all at stake, I would agree with you. But the Portuguese have sent a copy of their manifest. It values the missing cargo at nearly twenty thousand pounds. So the question for now, my Lord, is where lies the treasure? Tell me, has it sunk off the rocks, or have Cornish renegades spirited it ashore?"

Lisle responded with a detailed account of his journey and all he had gathered from his Cornish hosts. Then he paused.

"So as far as these Cornish defendants are concerned, the bulk of the cargo has simply sunk without trace?" Wolsey asked. When Lisle indicated his assent, he continued. "But what of the others you spoke to – such as the archpriest I mentioned, before you left?"

Lisle proceeded to recount his meeting with John Arscott at the top of the Mount tower, adding, "The truth is that he proved an unreliable fellow. There were parts of his story which made no

143

sense at all. Without other evidence, it would be hard to find against the defendants."

The Cardinal thanked Lisle and privately considered the position for a moment, glancing once more at the reports from the Abbots of Tewkesbury and Syon he discreetly held in his hand. Fr Trelobys had spared no detail in his letter to Tewkesbury.

As well as a thorough account of Pengelly's role in the affair, he had given freely of his opinion of Thomas Seyntaubin, listing his wrecking escapades as a young man for good measure. As for Syon Abbey's contribution, an ideal opportunity had been taken to berate Captain Millaton for a catalogue of errors and omissions. The two Justices emerged from these accounts with little credit to their names. Adding Arscott's information would give the Chancellor ample grounds to find against them in his own Court, as and when he so chose.

Wolsey shared none of these thoughts with Lisle. Instead, he asked: "Tell me, my Lord, could this fortune in gold, silver and jewels have been sent to Cornwall with a purpose?"

Lisle considered for a moment before he replied, "I cannot imagine a shipwreck being wished by anyone, Lord Chancellor. The Admiral of the Fleet perished."

"Quite so, my Lord. You have been more helpful than you can imagine."

Wolsey was left assured of Lisle's loyalty. But as soon as he had gone, his secretary Cromwell appeared at the Cardinal's side.

"A ship sailing from Flanders to Lisbon had no business being so far from its course," Cromwell commented. He had overheard every word of his master's exchanges. "Even if it was blown onto the rocks by chance, the Admiral's ship could still have entered the bay intending to join its fellows waiting in the Fal."

"It is true, Master Cromwell. Gattinara's plans for Imperial domination started well before this quarrel over the King's divorce."

"With both the Pope and the French Crown hostage to the Emperor, His Grace King Henry is surely the next on his list…"

"…while His Majesty's infatuation with the Boleyn maid makes him blind to the virtues of a French alliance! Master Cromwell, I think I should hasten my judgement of the *Santo Antonio* case. It would brighten His Grace, the King and release me from my bond to him."

"On the other hand," Cromwell rejoined warily, conscious of his subservient role, "once our new alliance with France is sealed, Spain will be forced to repay her debts and the threat of Gattinara may go away. Perhaps the wiser course, your Excellency, is to defer the case until the position can be used to even better advantage."

"You mean to maximise the bribe to be extracted from the Portuguese? You learn too fast, young Thomas," Wolsey replied genially. "By the way, what do we know of the Portuguese agent in this matter?*

"I have learnt from my sources in Antwerp," Cromwell replied, "that His Highness King João is placing the matter in the hands of his lawyer, Francisco Pessoa. From my time in Flanders, I can vouch His Excellency will find him a man with dependable instincts and a deep pocket."

"What of the current Portuguese Consul in Antwerp?"

"He is the former spy, Fernandes, Your Excellency. His agents have already visited Cornwall."

The Star Chamber

The Court acts as the curious eye of the State and the King's Council prying into the inconveniences and mischiefs which abound in the Commonwealth...By the arm of sovereignty it punisheth errors creeping into the Commonwealth, which otherwise might prove dangerous and infectious diseases.

William Hudson,
Treatise on the Court of Star Chamber

The Knights' Hall, Inner Temple

(By J. Findlay, published by J.J. Stockdale. *Reproduced by kind permission of the Inner Temple Library*)

149

Chapter Thirteen

John Densell was no corrupt or griping lawyer, for he
made no improvement at all of his estate.
Wood, *Memorials of the Holles Family*

The bell in the Temple Church tolled the half hour. Members of the
choir were completing their rehearsal of the evening's verses and
the sound of chanting began to fade in the rose garden beyond.
The nearby hustle and bustle of Fleet Street mingled in the air with
the sound of barges making their way along the Thames. Young
students fresh from their tutorials sped on their way. A pretty
chambermaid scuttled past with a guilty glance. Thomas
Seyntaubin strolled through the garden, memories returning of his
first visit to the Inner Temple twenty years before.

Then he had been in the company of his new friends Danvers
and Wye, all three sent by their fathers to complete their education
in London. It had been a conscious break with the medieval
pattern, whereby young squires were indentured to the nearest
noble house. Thomas had stayed in London to practise law, while
Danvers and Wye returned to their family homes in Norfolk and
Gloucestershire. By missing last year's Christmas Feast, Thomas
had lost the opportunity to catch up on old times. He hoped to
persuade Anthony Wayte, the Senior Bencher, this was penalty
enough without the burden of the ten-pound fine he had come to
discuss.

Then there were Thomas' sons to consider. The eldest, John, was
going to the Strand Inn, one of ten Inns of Chancery which
prepared boys for study at the Inns of Court. A quiet and sober
child, he would one day prove a safe custodian of Clowance.

The younger boy, William, on the other hand, shared his father's
wild streak; his adventure on St Pirran's Day had not been the first
time he had led his cousin Anne Basset astray. Thomas could see
William in Parliament one day. The first step on such a course

151

would be to make the right connections here. Senior members of the Inns of Court were often made returning officers for their counties. The spare seats were filled with fellow lawyers.

"My dear Thomas, you seem lost in thought." Master Wayte smiled warmly as he took hold of his guest and ushered him towards the Knights' Hall. "We have some excellent beef today and I trust you'll share a tankard from our brewery. Now tell me, how is my cousin, Lord Lisle? He writes to say how much he enjoyed his visit to your county."

Thomas regaled his host with the events of the St Pirran's Day feast and Lisle's role as guest of honour, before conversation turned to other Cornish members of the Inn.

After a while, Wayte asked: "But you haven't mentioned Godolphin. Have not the two of you become involved in some adventure?" An account of the *Santo Antonio* ensued, the Senior Bencher assuming an attitude of intense concentration as he led Thomas on with skilful questioning.

"My cousin tells me that the Lord Chancellor is now involved in the matter. Is this true?" he asked at length. When Thomas nodded, he continued, "Well, it won't be the first time that members of the Inn have been arraigned before the Star Chamber. There's no shame in defending your case, either, as you've told it to me. But I have one piece of advice. You embroider your account at your peril."

"I take your point, Master Wayte."

"I hope you do. Our Lord Chancellor has tentacles which reach into every part of this kingdom. He has the means – I can only guess at them – to find the truth of any matter, if he ever decides to take it in hand. I would not like to be the man found guilty of perjury in his Court. It is, as they say, a cardinal sin."

"I had half believed that the first hearing might settle the matter," Thomas replied. "The case I prepared won the day. The Portuguese affidavit was dismissed out of hand."

"As I say," Wayte replied, "I only know what you and my Lord

Lisle have told me. But the glaring question in this case is the missing treasure. Find it in the bay and it seems to me that your troubles are over. There will be some argument over who is entitled to Right of Wreck and so forth, but at the end of the day all this would be settled out of court. You would still make a handsome profit on your bargain and the Portuguese would go home with their honour restored."

"Sir John Arundell's men are searching the bay as we speak," Thomas replied. "We had a contract with him too, you see – and he stands to gain from any new treasure that's recovered. As I see it, there's too many involved to reach a bargain that would hold fast and true. In fact, the more that's found in the bay, the more men are bound to fall out."

"Then you run the risk, if you're not careful, that the Lord Chancellor will find some grounds to tear up the entire contract and claim it all for the King. But Densell's surely the man to advise you on that, even if he does belong to our rivals at Lincoln's Inn. Now let's resolve this fine of yours."

That afternoon, Thomas was due to visit a goldsmith called Richard Kene, whom William Godolphin had recommended. With some valuables from the wreck stored in his pockets, Thomas entered his negotiation with Wayte in a comfortable frame of mind. It did not take long to settle. Thomas would pay a reduced fine of just four pounds. He would also become Steward for the next Christmas revelries, contributing to the wine on the night. Wayte suggested that he might invite Densell and Lisle as his guests, a show of support before his trial in the Star Chamber. The two parted on friendly terms.

Richard Kene's shop, the Saracen's Head, was a brisk half-mile ride along Fleet Street and into the City. Thomas collected his horse from the Inner Temple stables and set off at a trot. For all its fine shops, Fleet Street was not a safe place. He had no intention of being robbed before he made his appointment and he soon found himself passing St Paul's with time to spare.

The area to the east of St Paul's Churchyard was the home of the goldsmiths, one street alone accounting for fifty-two shops, so rich and full of silver vessels it was said that nothing in Italy could compare for their opulence. A few years before Thomas had come up to London as a student, the sensational Goldsmith's Row had been created – a four-storey terrace of ten houses and fourteen shops. Their fronts were decorated with resplendent goldsmith's arms and richly gilded lead-cast beasts stood guard.

Danvers and Wye used to bring him here when they had money to spare. Thomas had even persuaded his own father, on a rare visit to London, to invest in a beautiful wrought silver bowl. The riches these merchants displayed behind their fortress-like façades would never cease to impress Thomas, even as they reminded him of the enormous gulf between the squire of a Cornish village and the men of real power and wealth in the realm.

Thomas was riding slowly past each shop, hoping to catch a glimpse of the displays beyond as he peered through the high leaded windows, when he was surprised by a familiar figure emerging from the doorway of the Saracen's Head beyond.

"Captain Millaton! No one warned to find you here."

"Mister Thomas, it seems you follow in my footsteps. I hope you find Master Kene as accommodating as I do." As he spoke, Millaton glanced towards the shop entrance and Thomas noticed a pawnbroker's sign hanging next to the goldsmith's.

"I'm not here to borrow, Captain. As it happens, I've decided to sell a few of those pieces I purchased from our Portuguese friend, Master Alvares."

"I'm sure that's wise," Millaton replied, "but my case is rather different." Just then, a young woman with green eyes and reddish hair stepped out behind him.

While only a married woman would cover her chest up to her neck, this one took the licence afforded a pretty Tudor girl to the limit. Her low-cut blouse of fine cambric linen barely disguised the prominent nipples beneath. The chain around her delicate neck dangled a freshly polished emerald on her proud bosom. Thomas sensed immediately she must be the mistress spoken of by the crew on the tin ship that night. Confused, he smiled wanly at them both and hurriedly entered the shop without another word.

Richard Kene beamed with an obsequious smile. "Mr Seyntaubin, I presume. Two friends of Mr Godolphin on the same afternoon – he will be asking me for a commission next!"

Thomas found Kene rather stifling, but he was desperate to know what had passed between Captain Millaton and the jeweller, for he did not feel he could trust either of them. Antony Wayte's words of warning rang in his ears.

"Knowing my Godolphin cousin, Master Kene, I'm surprised he has not done that already. Tell me, did that emerald I just saw on Captain Millaton's companion come from your stock?"

"Yes indeed, Sir. The lady was tired of the jewels they brought with them and wanted something more modern."

"So you agreed an exchange. That's possible, is it?"

"Not exactly, Sir. The jewels I have taken are pawned. Your friend tells me that he expects to come into some more jewellery in the near future – which he will sell to me. I will then return the more traditional items he has handed for safekeeping."

"So Captain Millaton is expecting an inheritance, is he?" Thomas asked, inwardly furious that he found himself trying to dissemble for the rash remarks of his accomplice. No doubt Millaton had pawned his wife's jewels to spoil his mistress and was already banking on his share of the wreck to pay for his extravagance.

"Not quite, Mr Seyntaubin. Although he did not say it in so many words, I rather feel that both of you are due to uncover a Queen's dowry before too long. Is that not the case?"

"Wherever you have heard such rumours," Thomas replied quietly, "I suggest that you cast them aside as infamy and slander."

"Come now, Mr Seyntaubin! The news has spread. You cannot expect some of the finest stones – not to mention chests full of gold and silver bullion – to be sent from Flanders to Lisbon without the knowledge of London's leading goldsmiths. When we hear of such treasure disappearing off the Cornish coast, our first thought is to ask when we might see it here."

Thomas laughed and Kene nervously joined him. "I admire your trust and confidence, Mr Kene," he said at last. "But tell me, it has been many months now since the Flanders ship disappeared. Why have you goldsmiths not put together your own ship and sent it to scour the bay, if you are so convinced of the treasure lying there?"

"We're not in the habit of throwing our savings after seawater, Mr Seyntaubin. Our view is that any treasure has long since left the *Santo Antonio*. Besides, there would be little point, with so many powerful claimants to the profit on such a venture."

As Kene said this, Thomas eagerly moved matters forward by laying on the table the items which he had hidden in his cloak. He hoped they might come to twenty-five pounds. At least a keen negotiation would deflect this jeweller from thoughts of sea treasure. The delicacy of their metalwork soon became the subject of much flattery by Kene. But after a careful pause, he said he very much regretted that the English were proving slow to appreciate these intricate continental designs. While he personally felt embarrassed to offer only fifteen pounds, it was all he could hope to recoup from his clients.

Thomas chose not to be in any hurry to close the discussion. He imagined there would be many more such negotiations to come, as and when they found a way to unlock the riches in those treasure chests. He needed some bearing on the value of different types of jewellery and plate and Richard Kene was only too happy to oblige.

"You drive a hard bargain, Mr Seyntaubin, that's for sure. But seeing as I hope we will be doing business again in the future, I'll make it twenty pounds. Now that's my final offer."

The two shook hands and soon Thomas was leaving with eighty crowns in his pocket. He would deposit half at the Inner Temple for safekeeping, before preparing for the long journey home. It would take at least a week, the persistent rain having made the Cornish moors barely passable.

Meanwhile, the goldsmith retired to his office and started to compose a carefully worded report. Richard Kene was involved in an irksome trade dispute, which was now going through Chancery. A fellow goldsmith, Cornelius Hayes, strongly advised him to find some means to win favour with the Lord Chancellor, before the case was heard. It was he who had then proceeded to tell him about the *Santo Antonio*, knowing full well that Godolphin was one of Kene's clients. As for how Hayes had discovered Kene's relationship with Godolphin, he knew better than to ask. But the information he was about to impart today, concerning Millaton in particular, would no doubt smooth the only court case with which he was concerned.

Chapter Fourteen

...should this King declare war, it might perchance with the Emperor's help break out here...should this King push matters to extremity, it is evidently with these very English, his subjects, that he will have to contend.

The Imperial Ambassador Mendoza to his Emperor,
The Calendar of Spanish Papers

The freakish weather of the last twelve months had brought untold devastation. Beggars appeared on the street corners of Helston, while poor men offered to sell all they owed for a few crusts of bread. An outbreak of thieving gave the Penwith magistrates plenty of work.

The few dry weeks around St Pirran's Day had proved a false hope. Rain had returned to plague the county, every day into the summer. In May, it had rained continuously for thirty hours, causing torrential floods which destroyed the corn yet again. Another failed harvest brought famine to the door. As summer drew into autumn, a scarcity of livestock lifted the prices on market-days. But while farmers could afford to feed their families for the moment, few knew where they would find the money for raising next season's crops and cattle. Fields were being abandoned and short of rent, landlords were calling in their loans wherever they could.

As the evening sun sank below the trees, the fire in the grate at Chinal's house still warmed him and his friend John Moyle against the chill sea air. But no amount of talking could relieve their anxiety as the rent quarter day approached.

"I've known for some time that my livelihood's at risk," Moyle was saying, almost to himself. "To recover from that battering in the hurling match was easy enough, what with the tender ministrations of my Ann. But how can I speak to her father

158

about my rent, when as we all hear he's in no position to pay his own dues?"

"'Tis what they say, John," Chinal replied. "Chynoweth is not known as the mouth of Marazion for nothing, nor's he been too guarded about your Mr Thomas' affairs neither. 'Twas more the pity Chynoweth's scouring of the bay for treasure this summer past proved so fruitless."

"Mr Thomas made a fair bargain with him, that's what Chynoweth can't bear to concede," Moyle replied defensively. "But he was perfectly happy at the time – as I saw it. 'Tis not Mr Thomas' fault if Chynoweth's sea divers daren't go too deep."

"Problem is, John," Chinal replied cautiously, "there be too many that say Mr Thomas and others know more than's bein' told. No one can go blaming the Arundell estate for seekin' a fair share of what's theirs by rights, now can they?"

"And what rights would those be, then? Some'at buried in time, that's to be sure. But in this case, your Officer of Wreck signed a contract."

"An' your Mr Thomas signed another one, for his debt. Now the Arundell estate want their money back, just like he agreed. If one be fair, then so be t'other. And if I be told my rent can wait a while, provided Sir John gets his debts repaid, then speaking frankly, I'd not be too sure you'd find many men siding with Clowance."

"Such men have short memories, that's for certain," Moyle replied. "All were for saying what a fine man Mr Seyntaubin was, when the wreckers were being paid."

"There's another thing, my friend. I don't suppose Chynoweth liked being thought a skinflint, just because Mr Thomas decided to pay out too generous like when 'twere his turn in charge of the reckonin'."

Moyle nodded. Even he had not seen the point of Seyntaubin's generosity to the wreckers, a bunch of ne'er do wells caught in the act of thieving. Ann had spoken of how the price of bread had risen for their families; he had forborne to tell her how much of her father's bounty had fetched into the hands of the Helston inn keepers. Chinal threw another log on the fire and began to stoke the flames, their shadows dancing on the ceiling, before he closed the window shutters and prepared for another cold autumnal night.

"At least Sir John has had his dues from the wreck, not to mention that chest found in the rocks," Moyle continued, after a pause. "Who's to say if it's all he hoped to find, but it must more than cover a quarter's rent from his tenants, surely."

"Well there's another thing, John. That chest in the rocks, it held one ruby the size of a sparrow's egg, they say, and others besides. So Chynoweth'd be thinking there must be more where that came from, and his Master likewise. 'Tis said Sir John's face went white when the Portuguese swore in front of the enquiry how much they'd lost."

"Some men are just plain greedy," Moyle replied. "That Sir John Arundell should be grateful for what he's got. I can't help thinking these demands on Mr Thomas are simply part of a plot, to force him out the picture."

"Or to force him into paintin' the picture, more like. With the Arundell estate, it's all about code and honour, you see – they don't like being hoodwinked, 'specially where their Right of Wreck is concerned. I'm afraid your Mr Seyntaubin's youthful japes are coming back to haunt him on this occasion…"

"Well, 'tis not right. An' if Clowance should have to be sold, God forbid it, don't you try telling me your Sir John would make us all a better landlord…"

"He's not blessed with as pretty a daughter as Miss Ann, that's for sure," Chinal replied. "Nor's he 'xactly been forthcomin' where repairs to this place are concerned, to be honest. Look. John, don't get me wrong, but 'tis only right you should know what our men be sayin' right now."

The friends shook hands and John went outside to find his horse. Storm clouds were gathering in the dusk. It would take half an hour to reach his own farm and he had no wish to be caught in a gale. He picked his way slowly along the path, turning over in his mind how to broach the problem of his rent with Mr Thomas, without spoiling his chances of ever being considered a match for his daughter. As he made his way, a streak of lightning ran ahead. Waiting for the clap of thunder to arrive, he leant forward in the saddle to comfort his mount, stroking her mane as if it were the soft gentle features of the girl he cherished.

****

The subject of their discussion was pacing the Great Hall at Clowance, deep in his own thoughts. Occasionally, he would stop and gaze on the Arras tapestries, hanging as if they had always belonged to the walls they now adorned. One showed a stag at bay in the foreground, proudly refusing to bow his horns, as a knight raised his sword to deliver the fatal blow. On one side were the baying hounds, on the other the followers on foot, staves in hand, eager to witness the slaying of this cornered prince of the forest.

Thomas again read the letter in his hand, written by his brother-in-law, Sir John Arundell, in a tone which left no room for doubt:

My wife and I send regards to you and your good bedfellow and thank her for the kindness shown by her letter and her gift of a dish of puffins.

Concerning the matter of the loan of money which we made to you on Michaelmas last, I require to receive the repayment due before the month end. As your late brother never repaid a penny of my money, I also look to receive the arrears of interest on his loans at that time, as we had agreed.

Lastly, since the storms have wreaked such havoc with the harvest, it is proving ever harder on my tenants to pay their rents. So being, it is only fair to give you notice that I shall require the repayment of all your late brother's loans by Christmas at the latest.

I beg not to require the Cardinal to interfere in such a case.

Thomas searched his mind as to how he could possibly satisfy such demands. The Clowance farms brought in forty pounds a year, not counting the Hall itself and the Park. The whole estate might stand in value at a thousand, although who could tell, as the family had always lived there. His own debt now stood at a hundred, while his brother's had been double that. But the real problem was the interest charges, built up over ten years. All told, he would have to find five hundred pounds by Christmas.

Thomas smiled ruefully at the thought of the treasure in his cellar, possibly worth ten times all that he owed. Yet it was untouchable while the threat of the Cardinal's Court hung over him. Sir John had certainly succeeded in driving his point home.

"Come now, my love, surely you cannot spend the entire evening pacing these boards?" Mary put her arms around her husband, as he passed the letter to her resignedly. She uttered a gasp of horror. "What does this mean, Thomas? How can our brother-in-law write in such terms?"

"He has every right, my love. In fact, you might say he has been far too kind to let my brother's debt run so long."

"I'd like to know where else he'd get such a high return on his surety. No, this is wrong – there's something else I've yet to hear. What has there been between you?"

Thomas led Mary to the library, a small room beyond the Hall, where a couple of spaniels lay waiting for him to light the fire. He sat next to Mary on the hard wooden bench, the last of the sunlight refracting through the leaded lights, as he turned to relate the truth of his entire adventure. In his heart, Thomas had no wish to hide their predicament. No longer shielding her from the dangers he was running, he felt a tide of relief. As he ended, Thomas was surprised that Mary faced him with a smile on her lips.

"My sister's right, my love. You really are an old knave, aren't you? My father would have been quite proud!"

"Knave or not, Mary, where are we to turn? Your nephew Sir Richard keeps telling us how much his place in Parliament is costing – I don't suppose he can spare a farthing. Godolphin has his hands full with tin trading…"

"Aren't you forgetting someone, Thomas – what of your other partner, Captain Millaton?"

"Millaton? I don't know the man, Mary, nor could I like him. After that business with his father, let alone the way he treats his wife…"

"Thomas! Are you going to sit there and tell me that our home and hearth must be forfeit, just because you can't face sharing your problems with the man most likely to help you?"

"How could he help, in any case? He didn't seem too forthcoming when the contract needed paying."

"I can't speak for that," Mary replied. "But his father was a London merchant, you were telling me. Surely men like that have access to money we can only dream about?"

Thomas paused a moment. He had to admit that his wife had a point. He had never considered calling on merchant money, without the running profit from a trade, it was ruinously dear. Yet if he could just buy enough time until the treasure could be sold…

"You do realise, my love, that if this fails, we could lose everything?"

"What is there to lose, Thomas, except an inheritance we never expected, saddled with a debt we could never repay? You have done all you can and more. If we find ourselves back in London, then let's be glad that at least you tried to improve our lot, rather than struggling along for the rest of our lives here as the poor relations."

Not for the first time, Thomas realised that his wife's courage was one of the things he most loved in her. He started to take her in

163

his arms, but she stood up and with a purposeful hold on his hand, led them both upstairs to their bedchamber. It had been far too long since this had happened last.

Much later, with her head resting on his chest and their naked bodies still entwined, Mary imparted the news she had meant to give Thomas when she had found him in the Hall. "My sister Honor is expecting a child at Christmas."

"But I thought Sir John was even more ill."

"Really, Thomas, you are the slowest man in Cornwall sometimes, think who was here six months ago!"

"It's Lisle's child, you mean?" Thomas looked shocked. "But what hope will that leave for her reputation?"

"All the hope in the world, my love. After all, my Lord Lisle is the Plantagenet who can wear no crown. He is the last man in the kingdom to disown his own offspring – on the contrary, he remains my sister's gallant paramour."

"And Sir John Basset – it could still be some time before his coffin is to be measured – what does he make of it all?"

"Honor has already given him two sons, John and George, so the Basset lands and title are secure. If his widow were to become a leading lady at Court, on the other hand, then it would only enhance their prospects. Above all, in his own eyes, it confirms what a brilliant jewel he has enjoyed all these years."

"I don't recall your Mr Bluett being so accommodating," Thomas replied tartly.

"We were both younger then and times have changed." Mary stroked Thomas' leg as she continued, "His Grace the King, planning to marry again himself, is only too pleased to endorse his uncle's intentions towards Honor. It's said Lady Anne Boleyn is to be persuaded to follow Honor's example and put her trust in the King's intentions."

Thomas laughed at this. "There's all the difference between the King and the courtier. I've no doubt Lady Anne would be well advised to tarry. But is your sister sure, where's proof of the King's view of the matter?"

"His Grace has just commissioned Lisle to take the Garter to Paris where he's to grant it to Francis, the French King. Honor tells me that he sails from Dover in a few weeks' time. So you see, Lisle's standing at Court could not be higher."

Thomas pondered this news in silence for a while. He broke it by saying, "I wonder how my father would have taken all this."

"His old world has vanished, my love," Mary replied. "In this new climate, surely we need to look for new alliances."

"You think Millaton will fetch us a fair bargain?" Thomas smiled ruefully. "I have not the means to fortell."

****

The autumn sun filtered through the bay windows at Hampton Court into the private Palace apartments. The last few months had not been kind to Cardinal Wolsey and an evening spent pondering over his chess table provided a welcome distraction.

The ornate pieces, a gift from Italy, glided across the marble surface with an ease which he knew no longer reflected his own command of the English Court. His opponent in the game was his devoted apprentice, the brilliant secretary with a wayward past. For once, the usually compliant Thomas Cromwell was proving his mettle; or else the cares of office were at last taking their toll on the Cardinal's prowess. After careful thought, Wolsey moved his white bishop to check the advance of Cromwell's black pawn, before he rose from the table and walked over to his lectern by the window.

Wolsey stared out fondly towards his gardens. Two labourers were still collecting the last of the rosemary and oregano before the onset of winter. He ordered a sprig of herbs to be brought up to his rooms and waited impatiently for their arrival. Wolsey needed to clear his mind.

On the lectern lay open the latest Spanish missive to have been intercepted by his agents. Encrypted by Don Iñigo de Mendoza, the

Imperial Ambassador, in order to foil the English spies, skilful decoding had nevertheless revealed insidious passages:

> ...*this business of the Queen's has now become public, and should the King proceed with the divorce case, I am convinced that the people's resentment will have no bounds*
>
> *... with the Emperor's assistance, such a flame might be kindled in England that the King would need all his energy to extinguish it, and would have no time left to espouse fresh quarrels.*

Wolsey toyed once more with how to interpret this discovery. "I still hold that the threat to the throne is remote," he concluded at last, more to himself than to Cromwell. "As Mendoza himself has observed, popular favour often fails when put to the test. But I did not become a master of statecraft by remaining a slave to the truth. The question always is how to extract advantage from whatever facts there are to hand."

Cromwell smiled nervously, not sure what response his mentor demanded. "When the information we have is considered in the round, your Excellency, this Cornish escapade appears in a darker and more dangerous light."

"Go on, Master Secretary."

"Well, Spanish gold has landed on the Cornish coast, only to disappear without trace. An illegitimate heir to the English throne has formed a liaison with a Cornish 'princess', even sealing their union – according to the archpriest – in the castle which launched the traitor Warbeck. Now the Hanse merchants, already up in arms over your closure of their trade with Antwerp, advance money to one of the conspirators."

"The London merchants are lending money, are they – to whom?"

"To Seyntaubin. He's borrowed six hundred pounds, my sources tell me. He can have few ways to repay such a sum – rebellion and wrecking being the obvious avenues. But above all, Your Excellency, Chancellor Gattinara is forging his plan to make his Emperor master of the world. The French Princes are held hostage. The Pope is captive in Rome. Now Mendoza's letters prove that the English throne is in their sights."

"I can see the threat, Master Secretary. The danger of Gattinara's creed – that a universal peace requires a universal monarch – is that it sounds so plausible, when the whole of Christendom is facing the Turk."

"The forces of Islam, amassing under Suleiman at Europe's gate..."

"But in the King's eyes, those forces are not a spur but a check on the Imperialists. So merely accusing these plotters is not enough – His Grace will want confessions. Letters can be misread, actions misconstrued and motives mistaken. The King's Council will be quick to trounce on a slipshod case – they know we might try similar methods against them another time. If we could resort to torture, of course, it might be different. But while Lisle remains so powerful, it would be reckless to touch his friends."

"Then let us remove Lisle, Your Excellency. This Spanish threat – if exposed at the right time, could work to our advantage, to fasten His Majesty to the French alliance."

"If we could convince the King that the plot exists – one which casts the dreaded Cornish in the frame, it would certainly put His Majesty in our clutches again, Master Secretary..."

"Not only could Your Excellency fine the London merchants and seize the Cornish treasure, but also shock King Henry out of wasting his suit on that Boleyn girl."

"Too true, Master Secretary, but we still need more evidence. Perhaps extortion could pave the way. Is one of them a weak link in their chain – could we break his bond with the others?"

"Captain Millaton might be our man, seeing as we appointed him. I've learnt that his father, who was once a prominent London

The Star Chamber

merchant, is the one who helped Seyntaubin to raise his loan."

"Where's the weakness in that?"

"Only that he's supposed to have been dead these ten years past and there was talk of a murder he committed in London. So Millaton could be harbouring a fugitive from justice. The problem is, of course, it would take a magistrate's warrant to search his castle..."

"...and his fellow magistrates are his co-conspirators! You raise false hope, Master Secretary, for if one thing is certain, we must take care to observe our own laws in such far-off parts. It is one thing to raise the spectre of Cornish rebels in league with the Spanish Empire. But to send an army into Cornwall against a captain and his garrison, on an island fortress – is not to be countenanced."

"Your caution is wise, Excellency. But in this case, we simply have to wait for our Captain Millaton to come to London. You may recall that letter from Richard Kene, the jeweller, in which he wrote about the Irish wench on the captain's arm..."

"Yes, of course – the one he's in thrall to. On his next visit to London..."

"We separate Millaton from the wench and place her with one of the Southwark bawds. Then we inform Millaton that her body will be debauched by every ribald in London, unless he agrees to a signed confession."

Thomas Cromwell's ruthless side never ceased to impress the Cardinal. "It might work, Master Secretary, although with a man like Millaton, dangling a reward will surely be required as well. In any case, first we must lure the wench here with him, lulling his suspicions." He paused. "Is not our Star Chamber investigation about to begin?"

"Quite so, Your Excellency. But perhaps your new Star Chamber procedures could delay the matter? In fact, they might have been devised for the purpose. If you recall, they usually require a local enquiry first."

"A second Cornish enquiry in this case, don't you mean? Very well, Master Secretary, let it be arranged. Then all we need to do is wait for this pawn on our chessboard to advance into our trap. Rather, as I see, yours has been doing tonight." So saying, the Cardinal's grimace mellowed, as he moved his Queen to declare checkmate.

Chapter Fifteen

We left Dover on 30th October, leaving behind our horses
and baggage for expedition, and arrived that night at Boulogne.
Lord Lisle to Cardinal Wolsey,
Letters and Papers of Henry VIII

The last of the seagulls sang their goodbyes as the white cliffs faded into the distance. The fierce north wind had abated and in the chill dawn air, a gentle Channel breeze ruffled Lisle's thick crop of hair. While his four companions stayed below, he braved the deck of the frigate as he contemplated the journey ahead to meet the French King.

This passage from Dover to Boulogne haunted Lisle with memories of his earlier voyage, as the sea captain of the ill-fated *Nicholas of Hampton*. It never left his mind that the Tudors saw him as much as a threat as an ally. Having blackened King Richard's name with the murder of the Princes, whether true or not, they could scarcely let Arthur disappear. But the news he had survived the loss of his ship had not pleased everyone at Court. More recently, the very warmth of Henry, even appointing Lisle to the King's Chamber, had done nothing to lessen his sense of danger. Wolsey's keenness to send him to Paris, to present the Garter to Francis, merely aroused fresh suspicions.

Lisle looked once again at the secret message he had received, while his mission had been waiting in Dover for the weather to change. *"After Paris, proceed to La Rochelle. We have a message for England's next King."* Enclosed had been a purse of thirty silver coins. They might defray the cost of reaching the southern outpost of the old Plantagenet Empire, but they left Lisle in no doubt as to the purpose of the meeting. One part of him saw the chance to put his fealty to King Henry beyond doubt, by exposing the plot he was to be asked to join. But a greater part thought of Honor's bold words on St Michael's Mount. Her love had awoken an inner faith,

170

kindling his confidence to assert his right to his father's stolen kingdom.

The breeze was quickening now, as the ship reached the mid-Channel, the spray from the waves breaking over her prow. Lisle waived to the bosun at the helm, before joining his companions below. These autumn crossings were never pleasant.

But the next morning, Lisle was being presented with a hogshead of wine by the City burghers, as a peal of guns announced the safe arrival of his party in Boulogne. Then at every town along their way, the diplomats were fêted by the local dignitaries. Paris took all of four days.

It was several more before the French nobility brought the Garter party to the Court. At the stair's foot of the King's chamber, Lisle was met by an inner circle, who led him into the King's presence. Francis was surrounded by the King and Queen of Navarre, two French Cardinals and his Bishops.

Lisle later wrote to Honor with every detail of his audience:

> The great hall of the place was hung with fleurs de lis; the King, in his cloth of estate, in a gown of purple velvet furred with sables, his hose and doublet white, sat in a chair of three stairs high, below which, at each corner, knelt a gentleman usher.
>
> The King of Navarre sat on the King's right in a little chair, while on a stage to the side, three noblemen sat above the heralds bearing their coats of arms. On the King's left sat one Cardinal, the Pope's cousin; nearby sat the Cardinal of Lorraine. A good yard from him, in another chair, sat the Chancellor of France in his bishop's vestments, wearing a hood of black satin. About a yard away, on another stage, sat the Court ambassadors, first the Pope's, then the King of Bohemia's, next the Venetians', and last the duke of Milan's.
>
> We were placed in their midst, opposite the King, about twenty paces away, on a long platform covered with purple velvet. About and behind the King were all the great lords temporal, some leaning on the pommels of their chair, along with the Councillors

of State and the Admirals of the Fleet. The archbishops and bishops were seated in serried rows behind us.

The King talked with them for half an hour. Then he bade them *"bon soir et bonne nuit."*

The next day the King was to take his Oath of the Garter. Lisle and his party were brought once more to the King and followed behind his mule, as he rode towards Notre Dame.

In the choir of the great church, Francis had a little altar dressed for him, to the right of the High Cross. Below was a long stage covered with purple velvet, embroidered with fleurs de lis of gold. The cloth covered both the stage and all the ground within. It was all of the same purple velvet and embroidery of gold. Hard to the wall was set a chair, in which the King sat, covered with the same embroidered cloth.

Beyond sat the King of Navarre, in a chair of crimson velvet, and at his foot was a long stage, right against the King's little altar, covered with purple velvet. This is where we were led. The French Chancellor sat in a chair of black leather; and on the other side of the high altar, in two chairs of crimson velvet, sat the Cardinals. Mass ended with one of them giving his blessing, his back to the High Cross. Then a learned man of Florence made an oration in fluent Latin, lauding the peace and friendship of the two Kingdoms.

Finally, Francis came to the High Cross, made his oath upon the mass book, and kissed it, two notaries sealing his testament. At this trumpets and sackbuts played, and the choir sang the Te Deum.

The ceremony completed, the King's train proceeded to the house of one of the canons, where a sumptuous banquet had been prepared. Lisle wrote to Honor that when the King drank, he was always served by three men.

The first brought only his cup; the second brought a jug of water; and the third brought a flagon of wine from the cellar. After dinner, the King talked with his guests until evensong, when we took our leave.

At the Palace, the following evening, the roof and sides were covered with rich hangings and rolls of green box with garlands of the same; and in the garlands were either the arms of England and France, or else faces drawn from antiquity. Francis and Lisle approached the high dais together, the young lords and gentlemen dancing to the music all the while. After supper, they began to dance again, and the King put on a mask, as did many of the young lords who danced with him.

There were several kinds of masks: two with long gowns and hoods, and great plumes on the head in many colours; and one of coats of white satin with laces and cuts. Two were after the Turkish fashion. There followed a play of shepherds which brought in the Ruin of Rome.

Lastly, two angels appeared, each bearing a wing, one white, one red. One of the angels had a long branch of a rose in his hand; and written in his breast, in great letters, Angleterre, and the other France. And so lovingly held, they joined the two wings together, making their reverences before they departed. The maskers then danced again till two in the morning.

Lisle and his friends took their leave of the King for the last time. They returned to their lodgings, bearing their gifts from the Court. Lisle's was a small crossbow, sprung with a smooth trigger action, its handle inlaid with pearl and silver. It had been engraved with the Plantagenet crest, a falcon perched on an open fetterlock, the ancient symbol of his line's claim to the throne.

****

As Lisle's party had been making their way to Paris, many hundreds of miles southwest a very different scene was being prepared in Castile. Feeding into the Emperor's European territories the wealth of Spain's New World discoveries, the men who ran his Imperial Chancellery had made Valladolid, the ancient Castilian capital, their seat of power. Now Charles' son Philip had been born there, truly a sign that God was pleased with his mortal apostle.

Mercurino di Gattinara, processing across Valladolid's Plaza Mayor this winter morning, noticed the subdued tone of the onlookers, nervously awaiting the ritual executions all were about to witness. The sun appeared behind the Convent of San Francisco, casting the shadow of its towers across the gushing central fountain, as the clock bell sounded the hour. Then the water was stopped and a haunted silence fell.

Three conspirators, heads bowed in guilt, began to troop past the Palacio Real into the main square, their shackle chains scraping the ground behind them. The door to the Palace courtyard swung open and a platoon bearing steel-tipped pikes in hand marched forward and lined up to form two ranks. Their drummer began a slow beat. Once more the heavy figure of the Grand Chancellor loomed into view, now standing at one of the leaded windows overlooking the Plaza from the Camera de Cortes. He smiled with pleasure when he noticed two of the convicted plotters shaking with fear, while the third shivered in the cold. His body had been stripped of clothes, readied for his naked passage through the pikes.

"Welcome, Your Magnificence." It was the Count of Nassau, one of the noble members of the Cortes, who had found Gattinara at his vantage point.

"Greetings, my dear Count," the Grand Chancellor smiled. "I am not a vindictive man, but the brutal punishment to be visited on these Neapolitan traitors this morning is well merited."

"It is certainly a dish well served to the Castilian Cortes, gathered here to hear Your Magnificence. Already, members have filled the balcony below our line of windows to gain their view."

"There are certain precepts," Gattinara explained, "which I hold to be self-evident."

"That is because you are blessed with the fine legal training of an Italian nobleman, Grand Chancellor."

"The need for a universal monarchy is first," Gattinara intoned, more to himself than the Count, "the superiority of the Roman law another; the keeping of good faith a third."

"Those who break any one of these rules surely deserve no mercy," the Count responded, as their gaze fastened on the scene below.

The soldiers now held their pikes erect, softly tapping the ground in rhythm to the drumbeat, as their platoon sergeant prodded the first traitor to the front of the line. The two ranks took a step apart, tempting him to try his luck with a run forward. But their victim only reached the third in the row before their pikes dropped down to block his path, first in front and then behind. There was laughter in the ranks, now closing again, as panic and fear showed in the man's eyes. The first soldier in each line gave a sudden prod to his buttocks, the sharp tips piercing the flesh. He fought the pain, as the blood trickled down his thighs. The next two pikes broke his rib cage and he lurched forward, only to cry in agony as the next shaft penetrated his rectum.

Gattinara turned away. He knew how this finished.

As the rousing glee of the assembled townsmen below intruded, cheering as the first of the culprits met his grisly end, the Count's face betrayed his embarrassment. He turned to flattery.

"To hear you address the Cortes is always a joy, Your Magnificence."

"My dearest Count, at such a propitious moment for his Imperial Majesty, it is my great privilege to do so. We stand on the threshold of events unequalled since the days of ancient Rome."

"You really believe that Christian unity against the Turk is at hand, Chancellor?"

"There is only one Crown left which prevents the Emperor claiming his God sent mastery of Europe."

"You mean the English? But I wager, were it not for the King's divorce, you would hardly be diverting your mind from the Ottoman threat."

"Perhaps not. But Mendoza tells us it is this very divorce which provides our opening. To place Princess Mary on the throne, years before she might otherwise have succeeded her father, is neither a chance to be missed nor God's will to be denied."

Noisy revelling by members of the Cortes, watching the scene in the square, again interrupted their conversation.

Sharing a disdainful look with the Count, Gattinara politely motioned the need to prepare for his speech. He retired to a side chamber to study his notes, ignoring the shoots of pain from the gout in his leg. Eventually the Count returned, to inform the Grand Chancellor that his audience was assembled. As he entered their Hall, the murmuring excited by the morning's spectacle ceased. The most powerful counsellor in Europe commanded reverence and fear in equal measure.

"The universal monarchy of the world, beginning from the east, and so coming to the west, has passed through the hands of the Assyrians, Medes, Persians, Greeks and Romans. Now it has come to his Imperial Majesty, whose seat is here in Spain.

"Why is Spain singled out for such a place?

"Because, after her long slavery and division at the hands of the Moor, this honour is surely conferred by Fate. Conferred with greater splendour than on any of those predecessors; to whom also, according to the vicissitude of human affairs, it did of right belong in their time." Members applauded. But when Gattinara shifted his attention to this new quarrel with England, many showed their puzzlement. Surely there was still a Castilian Queen on that throne?

"The English possess an island well furnished both with shipping and soldiers; and by this means they rob the Emperor and

176

his Spanish kingdoms in all places in the north. These English also wander out abroad, as far as into the New World. By reason of our fortifications along the coast, they cannot lay the foundations of their own kingdom there, yet they do the Spanish no small harm..."

There was much cheering at this point. Valladolid knew well the deprivation of her fishing and merchant fleets at the hands of rogue Englishmen.

"...and now their King insults the honour of Castile with his wicked divorce suit, impugning the virtue of Castile's royal daughters, Queen Katharine and the young Princess Mary..."

"God save Queen Katharine!" rang out from the Hall, echoed by members around the chamber, as Gattinara reached the apogee of his address.

"It is most certain that if the Emperor could but once make himself master of England, as well as the Low Countries, he would truly become Ruler of all Europe and the greater part of the New World. I give you the universal Monarch, uniting all of Christendom under a single shepherd!"

The followers of Gattinara's creed rose to their feet at this point, stirring such feeling that the entire Cortes was soon standing, their ovation lasting several minutes before Gattinara could motion for quiet.

He knew they would be asking how he proposed to achieve the subjugation of England. Gattinara demurred, citing the need for secrecy in all such matters. But he won the confidence of the Cortes, when he said, "There is no man but knows what horrid Civil Wars and what strange alterations and turns have happened several times in England. So that, what I have proposed ought not to appear to any man as things either new or impossible, given God's will on our side."

****

Lisle's companions were bemused at first, when he announced he would not be returning with them to Calais, but rather proceeding to the west coast of France.

"Has our company been so very tiresome, my Lord?" asked Sir Thomas Wriothesley, the Garter King-at-Arms.

"Not at all, Sir Thomas, but I have this great desire to visit the Monastery at Fontevraud."

"Another of your pilgrimages, perhaps, my Lord?" Sir Thomas smiled towards their companions. "After Walsingham and St Michael's Mount, dear Lisle, you are earning quite a reputation as a pilgrim."

"You could say that, Sir Thomas. Fontevraud is the shrine to Queen Eleanor of Aquitaine and many later Plantagenets. King Francis has been kind enough to give me letters of introduction."

So bidding Wriothesley and the others farewell, Lisle took his two servants and arranging a change of horses, easily covered the distance to the Abbey in a single day. Here he was greeted like a King, the first of Eleanor's English descendants to visit the Order in over a hundred years.

He had a few days in hand before his assignation in La Rochelle and Lisle welcomed this period of solitude, where he could consider the most momentous decision of his life, surrounded by his ancestral voices. He wandered the stone-arched cloisters, prayed before the tomb of Richard the Lionheart and confessed his soul to the Abbess. For Fontevraud was a mixed Order, living in harmony, the grace of the nuns prompting many thoughts of the woman he loved.

During the day, Lisle also rode the countryside, tasting the delicate white wines along the Layon river and the deep reds of Saumur, where he was warmly welcomed into the chateau built by his Plantagenet forebears.

Lying hidden amongst Lisle's cases was the wooden box containing Arscott's spyglass. He had insisted on taking this off the archpriest, before he and Honor had left the Mount. Now he took out the spyglass, hid it in his cloak and made his way to the Abbey tower. Reaching the top, he assembled the contraption, as he had seen Arscott do before. After some minutes' wait, one of the monks joined him. He was a small, cheerful man who, like Arscott, wore a pair of glasses to read. His long sight was good.

"Good afternoon, Father. I am glad you could find time to see me here."

"I would not want to disappoint the Abbess, my Lord, who has made me swear an oath of secrecy about this device. To tell the truth, I share your curiosity about it, while having no time at all for talk of supernatural powers."

"All I can tell you, Father, is that a priest not unlike yourself swore by his ability to see far into the distance with this. It just occurred, on my thinking about it, that a man with the same defect in reading his books might also be blessed with the same advantage at longer distances."

"Quite so, my Lord. This spyglass, perhaps, may perform the opposite function to spectacles. No one suggests they are supernatural."

"Indeed not, Father, else the chancelleries of Europe are full of men possessed!"

"That's another matter entirely, my Lord," the Friar replied lightly, before putting his eye to the glass.

There was an awkward silence, as Lisle awaited a response. Eventually, after several minutes, the Friar raised his head and spoke solemnly.

"I can tell you it works."

"Thank you, Father. That is all I require."

The spyglass was put away, Lisle feeling a sense of elation at his discovery. He had decided that if the device was true, it was surely a sign that he should press ahead with this scheme. Not only would this contraption's celestial powers impress the Grand Chancellor, for Gattinara was known to be a keen astronomer himself, but its usefulness in the field of battle or at sea would be immense. Unlike King Henry and his butcher's son of a Cardinal, Lisle believed that the Emperor Charles could be trusted. He lived by the Burgundian chivalric code, had once even felt obliged to let the heretic Luther walk free on the strength of it. As for Gattinara, his attacks on the deceits and broken promises of the King of France were a testament to his own good faith. Whatever people said about the Empire, its principles were set in stone.

Lisle was sorry to leave his monastic haven, but the few days here had strengthened his resolve. The road to La Rochelle proved straight. By early afternoon, he had found the lodgings he had been given, an inn near the waterfront, in full view of the ships resting in the harbour. Gattinara was sending an agent from Flanders, as he explained, to avoid any suspicion falling on Lisle of a Spanish connection. His rooms at the inn were generously provided, Lisle reflected, as he prepared to meet his contact, having let his servants off for the afternoon. Then there was a knock at the door.

"*Entrez!*" Lisle spoke in French, to be sure no English words were overheard.

"*Bon soir*, my Lord, my name is Laurence. I bring greetings from His Imperial Highness." The man bore a sealed letter, but before he would hand it to Lisle, he insisted on asking a few questions.

"Betrayal comes hard to some men, my Lord."

"Few know the ruthless side of His Grace the King as well as I do, Laurence. The bitter cost of his war ventures has been borne by all of us. This latest break with Spain is a reckless risk for our kingdom. In truth, our King has betrayed his subjects."

"They say it is all the Cardinal's doing. Perhaps, like him, you fear the power of our Imperial Majesty?"

"Even if the Emperor does aspire to be Monarch of the world, as we read, he will need Kings and Princes still to rule their own states. Let Spanish gold pay for the wars against Islam, while the people of England and France live in peace!"

"But can this Cornish venture really succeed?"

"I have little doubt, Laurence. We start with a captained

garrison, the leader of Cornwall's archers, their best wrestlers and if rumour be true, nearly twenty thousand in gold and silver."

"I am told that you were in London when the last rebellion marched."

"The old Queen insisted on taking Prince Henry to the Tower for protection. It would have been a close-run thing, had the Cornish rebels not wasted their time gathering Kentish men to their banner."

"You may be sure the Emperor's allies will keep Henry's forces at bay. King James will invade from the north and the Earl of Desmond from Ireland."

"I can count on the men of Hampshire to join us and the Fleet already regards me as the true Admiral of England."

"We are told young Fitzroy, the King's bastard, merely plays at his role." Laurence immediately realised his offence, as he said this. To break the awkward pause, Lisle changed the subject.

"I take it you can read, Laurence?"

"As a former priest, it was part of my training, my Lord. But I use spectacles now."

Lisle unveiled the spyglass, which he had set up before the meeting started. He suggested that Laurence try to spot the ships entering the bay, while he studied his missive from the Emperor. Lisle was a careful reader and he was just reaching the critical passage in the proposal, which came late in the writing, when Laurence cried out.

"It's miraculous, my Lord! It took me some time to screw my eyes to the task, but the distances I can see are not to be believed."

"Just a moment, Laurence. It states here that I am to take the Princess Mary in marriage. Your ambassador Mendoza made no mention of this in London."

Laurence looked surprised. "The young Princess is very beautiful, I am told, my Lord. Slim and elegant..."

"I know how the Princess looks, Laurence. She is merely a child. But that is not the point. I love another."

"Quite so, my Lord, the Lady Basset, I believe. It is said you are to be congratulated on your choice. But do not be alarmed, for the Emperor understands your English ways. You can have your Lady as your mistress, by all means, so long as the Princess remains your wife. It is surely only the Lady Boleyn who takes it upon herself to usurp the royal position… it will be interesting to see how long her devotion will last, once her King Henry has lost his crown!"

"But you do not understand me, Laurence. I have known one loveless marriage already at the English Court. Nor could I ever expect Lady Basset to remain my mistress. I have promised her my hand. Besides, I am not so convinced these Cornish will rise with us, unless I have my Cornish princess at my side."

"Then let the Princess Mary come to Cornwall. Was this not the part played by Warbeck's wife, on that island?"

But Lisle was not to be moved. At length, seeing that the promise of riches had no effect, Laurence tried to threaten him.

"This scheme can succeed well enough without your part, my Lord. Now you will be a marked man when it happens, along with your Cornish mistress."

"In that case, it is the more my duty to make sure you fail, Laurence," Lisle replied, his anger rising.

The Flanders agent began to make for the door, fearing what Lisle meant. As he did so, he reached over to steal the spyglass, so at least his masters would gain something from this encounter. But this gave Lisle all the time he needed to open a drawer and pull out his small crossbow. Its arrow sped across the room. The agent fell, the spyglass dropping from his hand and smashing to the ground. He was dead.

Chapter Sixteen

Today are arrived and now ride in the haven four
Spaniards and Portuguese. Two more have been seen at sea...
The ships came all out of Flanders, they say. Penryn, Friday
Wil Cavarnell to William Godolphin,
Letters and Papers of Henry VIII

Honor Basset may have skirted convention for the sake of love, but nothing would persuade her to defy the rituals of childbirth. Around six weeks before term, her confinement began. Bidding farewell to Lisle, on the point of his mission to France, Honor set off for Clowance and the welcoming arms of her favourite sister. Ann Seyntaubin was deemed old enough to assist her mother, along with Mary's daughter by her first marriage, Philippa, while the younger children were dispatched to Tehidy with their father, where they joined their Basset cousins.

On her first return to Clowance since the St Pirran's Day feast, Honor noticed how resplendent it looked on a clear autumn day. Cracks in the leaded lights had been repaired, long-missing slate roof tiles replaced and the moss-embedded steps to the entrance swept clean. Even the oak panelling in the Great Hall wore a fresh coat of paint. This was more than a tribute to her arrival. Thomas and Mary had determined to make the most of their home for the next year or so, while their future hung in the balance over the Star Chamber case. To this end, Thomas had accepted additional funds from the London merchants, when he had found them willing to lend.

Disruption of their trade with Flanders, it was said, had left them with idle capital. As a result, even their interest charges were not as steep as he had feared. How much this was also due to the influence of Millaton, he could not gauge.

His loan secured, Thomas derived great satisfaction from repaying the Arundell estate ahead of their Christmas deadline. He also won favour with his own tenants by announcing he would forgo the rent due on the September quarter day, until their farms had recovered. Led by John Moyle, they all thanked him personally. But many were the rumours which flew about, as to how Seyntaubin had managed to stave off disaster.

Chynoweth was particularly inventive. Then suddenly he retired, his post was suspended and to the great astonishment of Marazion, Sir John Arundell appointed the three local magistrates – Godolphin, Seyntaubin and Millaton – to act on his behalf. All agreed it was a bold decision. Chynoweth had found it increasingly hard to outwit the resources of the three local squires. But how long this new alliance would last was anyone's guess.

That autumn, Thomas also agreed to assist the stewardship of Tehidy. It was a larger enterprise than Clowance, with its own tinning operations. A disastrous year had brought home to the Bassets that they could no longer manage the estate alone, especially given Honor's increasing commitments at Court. The Seyntaubins were only too glad of the additional income promised to Thomas' new position.

Clowance's finest bedroom was furnished as Honor's retirement chamber. One of the Arras tapestries was brought upstairs from the Hall and hung across the windows to keep out the light. Godolphin lent a set of three extravagant gold plates, the Arundells offered some Italian ceramics and Sir Richard Grenville sent the family's silver christening bowl as a talisman. On the side table lay a string of amulets, a keepsake Honor had clutched while giving birth to each of her children. Seated by the bed, Honor wore a pearl and ruby necklace, her one gift from Lisle.

Thomas had invited Lisle to the Christmas revelries at the Inner Temple. But the failed harvests had caused scarcity of corn in London. The Inns of Court had to cancel their Christmas feasts for lack of bread and the students had been sent home early.

"Wasn't your bedfellow due to be a Master of the Revels this year?" Honor asked her sister one morning, at the start of December.

"Yes, dear sister, but they have promised to renew his appointment. In fact, with so much to do here, he could scarce have afforded the time to travel to London."

"I am sure my Lord Lisle will be disappointed. At the moment, no audience is spared the tale of his mission to present the King of France with the Garter, complete with the dangers of his journey."

Honor's excitement at the world she had entered required no apology, at least as far as Mary was concerned. Cornwall had nothing to compare. Jane, their elder sister, had long treated the Arundells' invitations to Court as the mark of her social distinction, letting drop the odd detail to her siblings as a hallowed favour. For Honor, each letter from her lover, describing the latest episode at Court, was now shared with Mary to their unashamed delight.

Today they enjoyed the black humour with which King Francis had pardoned the shooting in La Rochelle for which one of Lisle's servants stood accused. When he learnt the victim was a Fleming, he wrote saying, *if all the English had killed all the Flemings in like fashion, they would not have much difficulty in getting their pardons.*

Yet Mary could not help ruminating. "We find ourselves in such deep and perilous waters," she remarked, "I thank God you have found such a strong and trusty champion." Honor took her hand and squeezed it with a tender look. Mary's unspoken hopes and fears were understood. "Lisle appears quite capable of getting himself out of trouble, beloved. But how far he can aid and assist your Thomas, I have neither the gift nor means of telling."

Honor let out a sudden gasp of surprise. Ann and Philippa rushed into the room. The perilous journey of another newborn, which Honor had already undergone more than six times, had started. This time, she risked her life for love alone.

185

****

The second enquiry was duly announced and it came as a blow to Thomas. It threatened the truce he had formed with Godolphin and Millaton over their buried treasure. They agreed to confer at Godolphin House, the closest they had to neutral ground, seeing that Thomas knew not which way his cousin William would lean in the matter.

On a sunny winter's day – such a contrast to the rain-sodden year before – he decided to walk past Drym on his way to meet his confederates. Thomas had barely left the confines of Clowance when a familiar face came towards him. It was the fine figure of a young man, as well as any one might find in West Cornwall. But on this occasion, John Moyle also looked more than usually harassed.

"Mr Thomas, we're bein' invaded! Wil Cavarnell's sent message to Mr Godolphin – there's Flanders' ships sailin' up to Penryn!"

"Who's to say they're hostile, John? There's nothing so strange about ships from Flanders, surely?"

"Have you not heard, Mr Thomas? His Grace our King has declared war on the Flemings an' Antwerp be closed to our vessels. So with no storm to push them our way, 'tis only common sense they be up to some mischief. Although I dare say, no one's seen 'em land, like. 'Tis as if they feared what we would be doin' to 'em, I expect!."

"Good enough, John. They're not pirates, we're to assume? Then it reads more like a show of force to me, than a proper threat. Unless they have agents…"

"Agents, Mr Thomas?"

"All right, spies if you like. In fact, it would do no harm to put a rumour about – just to give our countrymen a more vigilant and diligent ear – that a band and company of Flemish spies has actually landed. Meanwhile, I'm on my way to Godolphin House."

Thomas strode purposefully through the park, confident that this new intelligence would sway the other two to his way of thinking. But delayed by his encounter, he reached Godolphin some time after Millaton. It soon became evident that his cousin and the captain already had some other plan afoot. They were sitting in the parlour. Here, William had reused oak salvaged from the cabin of the wreck as wainscoting for the fireplace and walls. Then he had engaged some itinerant plasterers to decorate the ceiling with the motif of a Flanders tulip.

"We agreed nothing is to be touched, until the enquiry in Cornwall is complete and the case transferred to London," Thomas argued. "It will only take a few months, before the legal case shifts from evidence to argument."

"But now there is to be a further chance to present new findings in Cornwall. It could take half a year or more," Godolphin countered.

"To attempt to move the treasure at such a time, let alone to try to sell it, is highly dangerous," Thomas reminded them yet again. But after arranging his recent loan with Middleton's help, Thomas needed to shore up his position. He asked the other two about Cavarnell's message.

"It is fair warning, Thomas," conceded his cousin, who had clearly read the news, "but between these four walls, what if we were to join these Spanish ships?"

Thomas glanced nervously at Millaton, who let Godolphin make the running again. "This new alliance with France sticks in the throat, Thomas, as any of my Cornish archers will tell you. Why, 'tis barely ten years since their ships plundered Penzance."

"Archers will always hate the French, to be sure. But we trade with them well enough."

"That's more with our Breton cousins, Thomas, who would like nothing more than to see this King of France overthrown. He comes from Anjou – by rights, he was born in the territory of the English Crown! To tell the truth, the one fault with this venture is that we took our treasure from Portugal, whereas if it had been a French ship…"

"…your archers would have killed all aboard and we'd have had none to strike a bargain! The real danger, surely, is to be drawn into schemes we do not understand. At least as our matter rests, we have a legal case and a fair chance of winning."

"Fair enough, Thomas. But to our mind, it would be as well to move the treasure now as at any time, especially with Sir John Arundell putting us in charge of his shoreline. Besides, it might be said that the less your Star Chamber has left to retrieve, the less damage it can do."

"That's all very well," Thomas replied, "but the risk you overlook is perjury. If we are forced into any false statement, which is then discovered in the Star Chamber, the penalty will be beyond all reckoning. We should wait for this second enquiry to conclude before we make a move, else evidence of the size of our hoardings will be certain to arise."

"Do we know who has been appointed this time?" Millaton enquired.

"Sir John Arundell will take the chair, I am told, with the help of Robert Vyvian and John Arundell of Trerice. We have different actors, but I think we can expect the same play, if nothing else arises to change their view."

"Why would the Lord Chancellor defer our case by ordering this second hearing, do you think?"

"There's some talk of the new procedures for the Star Chamber, but I would hazard a guess he has made this delay on purpose. I can't say for certain, gentlemen, but the obvious reason would be in the hope of catching us out – which is precisely why this plan of yours is so dangerous."

William went over to a side table, where he poured three measures of Madeira and passed them round. It was clear he and Millaton had been talking for more than a few minutes and he was now entrusted with convincing Thomas. "My dear Cousin, the captain and I will always be in your debt for the bounty you have so brilliantly steered in our direction. But how did you envisage we were going to realise it?"

"Well, I had assumed that once our case was won, we would open discussions with the goldsmiths – your Mr Kene, for example – about a fair price. Not all at once, you understand, but as and when we needed the funds."

"I agree that might work for the odd trinket, Cousin, but we can't be hauling bars of silver up to London by the wagon load. Apart from alerting every robber in the West Country, how would we account for it when we arrived in Cheapside? It would be no good telling the truth, even after we had won our case. You may be certain the Kings of Spain and Portugal will be having us blacklisted. It would surely put Goldsmith's Row's entire trade at risk, to cross their chief source of supply by dealing with us."

"To be fair, William, I hadn't thought of it that way. What's worse, as I'm sure you both know, it's a capital offence to take bullion out of the country, even if the pirates in the Channel were kinder to us than the West Country highwaymen."

"Quite so. But tell me this, Cousin. Since you have assumed the stewardship at Tehidy, no doubt you have attended the washes, where the tinners turn the shoad out of the soil. What happens when they find the odd seam of silver or copper in a lode?"

"Well, when we come to Helston and pay the tin coinage to the Crown, we are bound to declare any other metal separately, for the higher tax. Then we are free to take it to the merchants and negotiate our price as with any other find. Although like as not, it often works better to go easy with them on the price of the bullion in return for a higher price for the tin" As he answered, Thomas' mind was racing ahead to the point of this discussion. He paused a moment, then grasped the essence of Godolphin and Millaton's plan. "Of course, gentlemen, why deal with London goldsmiths, when we have metal traders in our own town, with whom we can strike a bargain stamped with the King's authority!"

"Exactly our way of thinking, Thomas." It was Millaton joining the conversation now.

"Only there would seem no point in taking the metal to Helston, when with less risk and more profit we can load their ships in the Mount harbour. As you know, we often find a tin ship laying up there for the night, when she's left the mouth of the Caber too late in the day and a storm is brewing. It won't be so hard to have included a cake of silver in one of the food wagons heading for the island, while the causeway is open, then pass it on board the ship before she sails in the morning."

"I've only just started dealing with these metal merchants, William. Can we be sure to trust them?"

"There's one or two I've known all my life, Thomas. Godolphin Hill may not rival the Spanish Emperor's gold mines, but we are not a source of tin these fellows would like to lose. Of course, they will want to see a profit in the venture. But the finest grade of German silver is not a commodity that easily comes their way. These are rich merchants and I fancy most of what we have to sell will be for their own safekeeping."

The three began to work out the details of their scheme. According to the *Santo Antonio*'s manifest, there were eighteen cakes of silver bullion, with a total value of two thousand two hundred and fifty pounds. If they shipped one a month, Thomas quickly calculated, his share of the proceeds would repay his debt to the Hanse financiers in time and still leave him well in pocket after all expenses. Even putting aside the precious fripperies saved from the wreck – precious silks and satins, camlets and velvets – their remaining hoard reached another three thousand pounds each, half in jewellery and gold, the other half in copper. Although how to shift eight thousand copper bars was a problem best left for the future.

Godolphin suggested it was time to open the chests and at last find out what their hoards really contained. There was a tension between them as he led the way from the library and down some stone steps to the cellar doors. He turned the great locks to open up a long narrow room with cold granite walls, which he proceeded to light with torches, revealing casks of wine, some booty recouped from the wreckers and a few barrels of mead. There was nothing else to see and both Thomas and Millaton looked towards him enquiringly, as William disappeared round a corner. There they found shelves stacked with copper pots of little value.

William, making sure the main entrance to the room had been closed behind them, leant against the corner of one of the shelf stacks. It began to move, revealing a hidden chamber which it would be impossible to discern from the outside. There within lay the chests his men had ferried from Pengersick a year before. Thomas saw that Godolphin, as good as his word, had left them untouched and unopened since.

"By my reckoning, there's only one type of chest in here that could contain the silver," Godolphin said quietly. As the other two looked on, he displayed his steely calm by taking a hammer and wrench, with which he broke a lock with a single blow. But the lid would not shift. The seawater had had a year to rust the hinges and bow the fittings. Nor could the wrench penetrate the chest, thanks both to its strength and to the solid weight of whatever metal it contained. So Millaton and Thomas came to his aid and after ten minutes, the top was finally loosened. Carefully, they eased it back. The surface they found inside was black and for a moment, they felt like fools. Then Godolphin grabbed a cloth and polished vigorously.

They all stood back and taking the one torch from the wall, held it over the contents. After all the trials and alarms of the last twelve months, the answer to their quest gleamed in the dark.

Chapter Seventeen

...it fareth between thee and me as it doth between a player at the chess and a looker on, for he that looketh on seeth many draughts that the player considereth nothing at all...

Wolsey to the King,
Letters and Papers of Henry VIII

The three figures quietly slipped down the ladder on the side of the Breton sloop and into the gig which would row them to the harbour steps. Francisco Pessoa felt a wave of relief, after the dangers they had run along the Cornish coast. In the end, it had been a simple matter to link up with one of the many neutral ships in the Channel making their way to Plymouth and cajole her captain with a mixture of threats and bribes to see them ashore. Now Fernandes' agents could make their way unseen into Cornwall and keep watch on events in Helston, while he travelled up country to his meeting with the Cardinal's secretary. London would prove a three-day journey.

Nearly twenty years before, Cromwell had been an uncouth young man in Antwerp, while Pessoa had been a leading denizen of the city, the patron of Albrecht Dürer and Consul to his King. Now Cromwell was the disciple of the most powerful Cardinal in Europe and Pessoa, no longer Antwerp's rising star, had become Portugal's Court fixer. He carried a small Dürer etching, a cultured gift for the Cardinal.

This was to be no easy mission, seeing that war had suddenly broken out between England and the Emperor, but Pessoa anticipated that the arts of flattery would soon reveal how much it would cost to secure the return of his Queen's dowry. With Vaz and Alvares finished and de Corfe disgraced, Pessoa was all that stood between her royal fury and the role of Fernandes in the affair, the man who had ordered the *Santo Antonio* on her fateful voyage from Flanders. Success in England would leave many people in his debt, Pessoa deliberated.

After arriving at the Portuguese embassy, a substantial house across the river from the Palace of Westminster, Pessoa arranged for his gift to be delivered to Wolsey. Later, he set off for his meeting with Cromwell. In a determined mood, he crossed the Thames at Lambeth, dodging the street sellers and admiring the first crocuses in bloom on his way to the ferry. At Charing Cross, he overheard a couple of parliamentarians having a discussion about the war with a group of disgruntled merchants, raised voices soon lost in the distance as he turned through the stone archway to York Place. He had been expected and soon found himself ushered into his appointment.

"Good morning, *Senhor* Pessoa," Cromwell said as he came towards him. "If I may say so, you have hardly changed."

"Greetings, Master Secretary, and how pleased I am to see that you have."

They entered the Great Hall, its long leaded windows pouring in light from the gardens, whose arbours and aisles led down to the river. The walls dripped with tapestries sewn in brilliant yellows and blues, in the centre a table was crowned by a solid gold vase, studded with rubies which caught the rays of sunshine. On either side stood a rare medieval bronze. An exquisite Venetian carpet covered the floor, the elaborate pattern interposed with a discreet Cardinal's hat. This could be the home of only one man.

Suddenly, Pessoa's gift felt as small and insignificant as his objective. The contents of the *Santo Antonio*, which on paper dwarfed even the splendours of this chamber, seemed a petty matter on which to trouble so great a figure. That was part of the genius of the Cardinal, who knew how to drive Europe's emissaries to the point of distraction, before outwitting each in turn. Even dealing with his understudy, Pessoa felt unsure of his ground.

"Tell me, Master Secretary, does this war with Spain alter our affair?"

"In practice, not at all, *Senhor*. Your case will not reach the Star Chamber for another six months at least, by which time we fully expect peace to have broken out. As you may have heard, our League with France is rapidly gaining on the Spanish as we speak."

"But once peace is restored?"

"Well, I realise of course, *Senhor* Pessoa, that you claim title to the lost treasure. But I have to tell you, I cannot see His Grace King Henry permitting what is, in effect, a payment to you from Spain leaving our country, so long as the Spanish Emperor owes payment to His Grace as well."

"You mean that His Grace claims the entire cargo? But that is beyond understanding, the Treaty of Windsor it states..."

"Please, *Senhor* Pessoa, I do understand that in the end, your claim on the treasure may be a good one. His Grace would merely place a lien on it until his own debts are cleared. You will understand that sending this dowry to King João, using the same bank account which was supposed to pay the far larger debt owed to our King Henry, has done nothing to enhance His Grace's faith in the intentions of his debtor."

"So this is why you have delayed our case, while another enquiry is headed by these Cornish *bandidos*? No doubt you appointed members of the Commission who would again acquit their own brothers and cousins, so we must come to His Excellency for justice."

"His Excellency the Cardinal is merely following the new procedures agreed by the King's Council, *Senhor* Pessoa. But as it happens, this delay can only be to your advantage, given the situation with Spain."

"But, Master Secretary, while there is all this delay, these Cornish *bandidos* are sure to be selling the treasure. By the time we win our case, there will be nothing to reclaim."

"I can assure you, *Senhor* Pessoa, that these bandits, as you call them, are in fact men of substance. The estates of Godolphin, Millaton and Seyntaubin must be worth more than five thousand pounds between them. Only a King could dissipate such a sum between now and the hearing."

"But one of them has already mortgaged his estate to the hilt with the Hanse merchants. What is more, it is said he has found the means to start repaying their loan at any moment."

"Your sources in Antwerp keep you well informed, *Senhor* Pessoa, as do mine. But these Hanse merchants, desperate to reopen trade with Antwerp, are unusually compliant of late. Their mortgage on his property will not be released while this case is pending. So you see, all these transfers make no difference, except to give you cast-iron proof of how much he and his partners must owe you."

Not for the first time, a foreign emissary was left admiring the brilliance of the English Cardinal, while wondering just how much it was going to cost him.

"I am immensely grateful for His Excellency's efforts. After all, he must have so many other matters of state to concern him, Master Secretary."

"Your gratitude has been noted, *Senhor* Pessoa, along with the token of appreciation you sent His Excellency this morning. But as I am sure you are aware, a case such as this will not be decided by mere tokens."

Pessoa coloured slightly. The Dürer had been a prized possession; to have it dismissed so lightly felt like an affront. "My dear Master Secretary, *Causa de Estado* is well understood..."

"I am sure it is, *Senhor* Pessoa, but in this case you might succeed better by considering *Causa de* Cardinal..."

Pessoa groaned inwardly. Such an overt hint offended his sensibilities, honed by years of negotiation. He felt taunted into an arched reply. "Of course, Master Secretary, we could always settle out of Court with the other side. Then His Excellency *O Cardeal* would receive nothing for his troubles."

"My dear Pessoa, we have over a hundred of these cases every year. If more of them would settle their disputes between themselves, our new procedures will have succeeded. But in this case, I doubt you will find your Cornish *bandidos* willing to agree terms more amenable than the Cardinal's. Even though we already have enough evidence" – here Cromwell tapped the large folio to his side – "to throw at least one of them in the Tower."

"How can you be so sure, Master Secretary, they will not settle with us?"

"Well, they have appointed John Densell to defend them. Apart from his reputation for winning Star Chamber cases, he's another Cornishman."

They had now returned to the entrance to York Gate and Cromwell left his visitor feeling in two minds. On the one hand, by acceding to Wolsey's rapacity, he could achieve an outcome that punished the defendants. That, for the immensely wealthy King João, might suffice. On the other hand, Cromwell had betrayed no anxiety. His master was evidently unaware of Gattinara's plot. If Lisle had not dared to reveal it, the game was still afoot.

****

Three days after his birth, Honor Basset's new boy had been christened James, in the presence of all the leading women of West Cornwall. As Honour Godolphin tartly mentioned to Ann Seyntaubin, his was neither a Basset nor a Grenville name. But no one else seemed to notice, certainly not the healthy baby wrapped tightly in his swaddling clothes. A few weeks later, the christening robe was returned to the priest at Crowan, where Honor's brief 'churching' ceremony marked her return to normal life and to her home at Tehidy. Mary Seyntaubin and her daughters still visited Honor whenever they could, but Clowance once more resounded to the noise of Ann's brothers and sisters.

The three magistrates were to take it in turns to provide the monthly "cake" for the "French run" from the Mount, but from the outset they had required someone trustworthy and competent to oversee the regular hauling of such a valuable load to the island. John Moyle was the obvious choice and Godolphin and Millaton were quick to agree when Thomas suggested him.

Moyle took care to use a different cart every time and vary the day in the month for each assignation. No one seemed surprised that a food wagon occasionally found itself caught by the evening tide. That the inside of the wagon contained only two armed men and a small chest was another well-kept secret. After dark, it was a simple matter to take the chest to the Breton ship moored along the harbour wall and exchange it for a sackful of gold, the agreed method of payment. Come the dawn, both ship and wagon were already departed.

One man who did notice all these things kept the knowledge to himself, save for a few cryptic messages to his superiors at Syon Abbey. John Arscott had learnt his lesson from his interview with Lisle and had long accepted the loss of his spyglass. But late at night, he would now stroll unseen down to the harbour. He had only needed to spot John Moyle once, to recall his face from that night a year before. Then within two or three months, his sharp brain had worked out exactly what was happening at these exchanges. He started to keep a log, while biding his time for the right opportunity to use it. In fact, given the constraints of the tides, he could even predict the day of Moyle's next shipment.

So the events that July evening took him completely by surprise. Instead of another farm wagon, he saw a procession decked out in the Basset family livery cross the causeway to the Mount. The Basset party, including Mary Seyntaubin and her daughters to help with the baby, swept up to the castle, where Millaton's garrison presented a guard of honour, before they went through to the dining hall.

Several leading members of the King's circle already lived openly with their mistresses. Lisle had persuaded Honor there was no point in denying the happiness of being together, for the sake of discarded convention. Privately, he was deeply worried that

Spanish agents might attempt kidnap or worse against the mother and son, either for blackmail or revenge. So it was that a hundred-ton frigate, flying the King's flag, now entered the bay and headed for the Mount harbour. As it did so, a volley of cannon was fired from the castle battlements. The Vice Admiral of the Fleet's arrival, to collect his lover and child, was being heralded in style.

Thomas waited in the harbour to greet their illustrious guest, while Lisle's frigate moored off shore and the Mount barge was sent to collect him. As the two men made their way up to the castle, the Basset luggage was ferried out to the ship in readiness for departure.

"You have chosen a fine day to round the Lizard Point, my Lord."

"Our passage here has been fair and fast, Thomas, with no Spanish gunships to worry us. As for the Channel pirates, they have far easier pickings than a Navy frigate."

"Are we still at war with the Emperor? I have to confess, it is hard to follow."

"His Grace the King still supports Francis' Italian League, but it suits neither England nor Spain to widen the conflict, however much the Cardinal may want to do so."

"Why should he want that? Wars are expensive, as we all know."

"His Excellency has set his mind on a grand alliance between France and England, to be confirmed by a marriage. My taking the Garter to King Francis was a token of intent. The problem is, the French King has lascivious tastes. His London ambassador doubts King Henry's innocent twelve-year-old daughter would be to his liking."

"If rumours of his divorce are true, could not our King marry a French Princess? I'm told you met several Parisian beauties on your travels."

"Yes indeed, that is the Cardinal's plan. But our King's heart is set on the Boleyn girl. So it is said that the Cardinal is casting around for some means to convince the King to put his country before his concubine. Some say a Spanish Plot is about to be discovered, although where the evidence will come from none is telling."

"These matters of state seem far from our lives, I must confess. The important point, my Lord, is that your frigate can now give Honor and James a safe run along the English coast, free of warships and stormy weather."

"That is for certain, Thomas. I am only too glad to hear that you have volunteered to keep us company on the voyage to Portsmouth."

"Well, I have much business to conclude ahead of our case going to London, for which the promise of a safe passage solves many problems. I am for ever in your debt, my Lord."

"You and Mary have helped to deliver us of the one thing for which I have longed above all others. But it is our affair. To all the world, let James remain a Basset, he could hardly ask for a finer start in life."

They had now reached the courtyard in front of the Mount Church. They observed the tide closing over the causeway below, as Millaton's men were marshalled into line for inspection, before they joined the dinner party in the Hall. Here, Moyle was talking to Ann in the corner. He broke off to have some words in private with Thomas and Millaton, who passed him a key and spoke to some guards. Led by Moyle, they disappeared to the garrison room, where they retrieved a strongbox. This was taken down to the harbour and under Moyle's supervision, loaded out to the frigate and secured on board.

As the sun disappeared below the mainland, rays of light picked out a few remaining fishing boats in the bay, hoping to reap a shoal in the semi-darkness. It was time to leave. A torchlight procession took the party down to the harbour where the barge was waiting. The island villagers had lined the harbour wall to watch them go, a cheer rising when Lisle waved, as they rowed out of the harbour mouth. Soon they were on board and under sail, the gentle breeze promising an easy passage through the night into the steadier waters of the mid-Channel.

****

Lisle's arrival in Portsmouth was greeted with all the pomp and ceremony befitting its Vice Admiral. The frigate moored against the massive harbour wall and soon their train and possessions were loaded, ready for the final stage of the journey. They were now entering the territory where Lisle had grown up and where his Wayte family still held sway. John Wayte had just agreed with Lisle the lease of the medieval Hall at Soberton, set in its own park of more than a hundred acres. This is where he and Honor planned their future. As they rode into the estate, Thomas reflected how far it was removed from Clowance. Quite apart from its closeness to London, a prestigious advantage for a courtier, Thomas had to admire the verdant grasslands and fine young oak trees, sprouting trunks as thick as a man's thigh. He conceded nothing so sturdy could grow on the humid Cornish peninsula.

Thomas' strongbox contained seven hundred and fifty pounds in gold coins. A third each of this immense fortune in ready money belonged to Millaton, Godolphin and himself. He had not yet revealed the facts of its contents to Lisle. To use his Navy frigate to transfer the strongbox had been an inspired idea. But the scheme had been hatched only days before Lisle arrived. Thus far, the cache had travelled in complete safety, greater than imagined. But the last stage of the journey – from Hampshire to London – had been left to Thomas' initiative.

After the rigours of the sea, Lisle had ordered a feast to be prepared to mark their arrival. A quarter of stag to start, a roast pig to follow, sweetmeats and strawberries all formed part of the celebration that evening. Thomas was flattered to be present and to share Lisle and Honor's joy at the happiness stretching before them. Yet he also struggled with the thought of his journey to come.

"My dear Thomas, you wear a vexed and troubled look. Surely you can have no cares this evening, now we are safely ashore?"

"My Lord, there is only happiness to be found here tonight at Soberton. I am just sad that tomorrow I must depart for London, taking my baggage along a road with unknown hazards."

"Then let me reassure you. As a member of the King's Council, there are always piles of papers waiting for me to sign. Master Cromwell, with his usual efficiency, has ordered a pair of royal messengers to collect a portfolio tomorrow morning. Ride with them and I can arrange for you to be escorted right into the heart of the City. Where are you headed?"

"I call at the Inner Temple, my Lord."

"Then it is arranged, for you are only a short distance from their destination. I am sure York House will not begrudge the extra time it takes to see you safely there."

Thomas enjoyed the irony of this proposal. There could be no surer passage than to be escorted by the King's own Guard. If anyone but Lisle had suggested such a solution, his suspicions would have been aroused. Even so, deep into the night, he found rest hard to come by. His head toyed with endless interpretations of this apparent coincidence, before sleep finally conquered suspicion.

The next morning, Thomas rose at six and ate a breakfast of Hampshire sausages, duck eggs and roast chicken, in readiness for a day's travel. He had time to bid Honor a tender farewell and to pay a final visit to James in his nursery, where he seemed blissfully happy with his Cornish wet nurse. Lisle had already departed on estate business. Leaving a note by the Hall entrance, Thomas prepared to ride alongside Cromwell's messengers all the way to London. They appeared quite unmoved by the need to take his strongbox. The pair of seventeen-hand steeds provided for its journey could almost have been sired for the purpose.

By lunchtime, they had reached Guildford. Here it had been arranged to change horses. But first, they stopped for a meal at the new coaching inn in the high street, where to Thomas' relief a locked room was provided for the strongbox. While the King's messengers stood guard, he went through to meet a mix of travellers taking the Portsmouth road.

"So you're a Cornishman, are you?" an old man asked in a thick Surrey burr. "I suppose you'd be goin' to the Mount, then." Thomas looked confused, until he continued, "You know, the Mount above the town here, where you Cornishmen gave the King's father a right thrashing! Of course, there's not many here'd remember a thing that long ago."

"It's still remembered in Cornwall," Thomas responded, failing to hide his pride at the memory of the 'ninety-seven rebellion, when he had been only a boy.

The old man winked. "So where's you be going to next, if I may ask? Because if it's London, mind yourself when you reach Blackheath." He seemed to find this very amusing and soon had his friends laughing at the thought of what was going to befall this Cornishman when he reached Blackheath, until one added "I'm not so sure this time, Jago. Seems this fellow's got the King's cavalry ridin' with 'im, not against him!" The two messengers had entered the bar, their royal insignia causing a ripple of discomfort. Awkwardly, Thomas bought them both a mug of beer, which was downed swiftly. They turned to go, Thomas feeling sorry to have spoilt the mood. But as he left, the old man came up again and shook his hand. "My mother came from Truro. Give the old town my blessing, my son, for I won't be seein' it again."

Their fresh horses were now more eager than Thomas to make their way, as he asked himself whether he was being led into a trap. The two messengers were cold, stiff characters who showed no interest in engaging him in conversation. But they were well-stocked figures and their swords glinted in the sun, as did the handle on the knife each wore in his belt. Thomas consigned his fate to their hands, clinging to the belief that his friendship with Lisle afforded him a protection of sorts.

****

That evening, the normal bustle around the Inner Temple was missing. News had broken of a sudden outbreak of the deadly sweating sickness and some students had already chosen to end their summer term. There was even talk of the sessions at the Royal Courts of Justice being suspended until the autumn. Anthony Wayte reflected that it might do no harm, if more litigants were persuaded to settle, before the delay in their cases dragged them to an early grave. In his experience, the most lucrative work was where his clients had avoided the penurious result of their day in court. Wayte looked again at the letter which Thomas Seyntaubin had sent a week before, giving the rough time of his arrival and explaining the vital need to have access to the Inner Temple vaults. Such requests were not uncommon. Situated on the side of the Thames, between the government at Westminster and the merchants in the City, the Inns were used to providing the middle ground for concluding contracts and settling debts. Thomas' late arrival could easily be accommodated. But when the City bells chimed eight o'clock in the evening, he reluctantly decided that his cousin's friend had been unexpectedly detained.

Wayte had his own concerns about the spread of the sweating sickness and no desire to risk contagion by spending any more time in his cloistered office. He wandered down to the gardens overlooking the Thames, inhaled the rose-scented air and found a bench where he could enjoy the sounds of the river. By the time he returned to the stables at the entrance to the Inn, over an hour later, he discovered that his visitor had already arrived. Thomas Seyntaubin's strongbox had been salted away by the porters, while he had headed straight for his room in a state of exhaustion.

Meanwhile, half a mile upriver, Cardinal Wolsey was also

enjoying the late evening air, in the company of his Secretary, at York House. The Italian campaign was no longer faring so well and he feared that his troubles with The King's Matter could soon be coming back to haunt him. The Cardinal was relieved when conversation turned to the minutiae of the day, as the trees in the gardens at York Place swayed in the twilight and the fountains cooled the night air.

"So tell me, Master Secretary, did our Cornish rebel reach his lair tonight?"

"Yes, Your Excellency. The messengers who escorted him have just handed me Lisle's portfolio, which we had sent them to collect. I believe our plan has gone without a hitch, the fellow not showing a hint of suspicion."

"Very good. At least the gold is now secure – who would have thought he would have been so careless in Guildford! Now we just have to bide our time. This Irish wench, thinking her Captain Millaton has a fortune waiting here, will take the bait and lure him up to London with her. Then she can be taken."

"But do we still need to force a confession out of Millaton? Popular feeling is running high against the French and for their old Queen Katharine. As for His Grace, he seems ever more infatuated with his Boleyn concubine. Let me frame this Cornish crew as the villains of the Spanish Plot, with the evidence I have already. It could prove our best throw of the dice and bring all to heel again."

"Nicely pleaded, Master Secretary. Except there are no dice in the game I play."

Chapter Eighteen

...the premises notwithstanding, the said defendants Godolphin, Seyntaubin and Millaton are instructed to appear before the Court of Star Chamber at the next session.

Sir John Arundell's Commission into Piracy,
Star Chamber Papers

The unexpected return of the sweating sickness cursed London. As people died and the panic spread, legal hearings ground to a halt and courtiers dispersed. Meanwhile, the second Cornish enquiry into the *Santo Antonio* drew to a close and Sir John Arundell submitted his findings to the King. He reminded him that the first Commission had already found for the Cornish defendants. But in deference to the Lord Chancellor, he still instructed them to appear before the Court of Star Chamber in the autumn.

Due to the plague, no amount of artful persuasion could stir Millaton to make the journey to London that summer. But he never tired of playing with the sensuous peaks of his Irish sweetheart and revelled in the new vigour with which she satisfied his lust during the hot August nights that followed. He had no illusions about her motives, as sacks of gold coins piled up in the Castle, awaiting their safe passage to the Capital. But he believed himself to be as capable of satiating her appetites, as she was proving of his. This neediness was not love, but it was addictive.

Correspondence flew between Lincoln's Inn and Cornwall, as John Densell assumed the mantle of their Star Chamber advocate. Throughout the enquiry, the figure of Pessoa had lurked in the shadows, his agents had spied in Helston, and their threats and entreaties had filtered into conversations at the Angel Hotel. Still no evidence had come forth to counter the Cornish defence. Yet John Densell warned against any complacency and urged his clients to seek a settlement. Pessoa, it appeared, was willing to negotiate.

It was now mid-October and still no date for their first London hearing had been set. Thomas proposed a council of war to Godolphin and Middleton, inviting them to Clowance to see what compromise might be agreed, just to bring their case and its worries to a close. It was the first time the three of them had been alone together since that meeting at Godolphin House, when they had devised the scheme to sell the silver. The success of that plan had gone a long way to strengthen the partnership.

Mary arranged a meal of miniature pastries stuffed with pheasant, rare side of roast beef, summer puddings and plenty of claret. As candlelight flickered in the evening dusk, a sense of trust and kinship pervaded the Great Hall. Thomas was loath to test this spirit, but knew he must have instructions for Densell.

"There's only one question for me, Thomas, what have we to fear?"

"According to Sir John Arundel, nothing at all. But as my Lord Lisle said to me a year ago, in this wrestling match there's only one Stickler and his name's Wolsey."

"But have we broken the law?"

"Again, not according to any evidence I've seen. Pessoa was almost careless there, if you ask me, when he didn't even probe what we had recovered exactly. If you like, it's that carelessness which is bothering me."

"You mean, it is as if he had some other means to get the result he wants?"

"The other day, John Densell went to York Place, the Lord Chancellor's London home, on another case. He noticed some etchings by Dürer hanging in the Hall. There was a whole set of them and he was sure they were new from his last visit. So he asked someone how His Excellency came by them and heard they were a gift from a Portuguese friend."

"Pessoa?"

"None other. So John Densell persuaded his client, who he'd taken with him, to ask a few questions of his own and then the two of them swore an affidavit back at Lincoln's Inn."

"So now we have proof positive that Pessoa has bribed the Lord Chancellor. What need have we now of a settlement?"

"All the need in the world, gentlemen. You cannot go into the Star Chamber and accuse the most powerful man in England of corruption – he'll fling you in the Tower for contempt before you've had time to plead for Fleet prison! All the same, if he's accepting bribes, then we can guess which way his judgement will go."

"There are other solutions." Godolphin spoke for the first time. "We could offer Wolsey a bribe of our own."

"Not if you want John Densell as your lawyer, Cousin, nor if you want me as your partner. Apart from the rights and wrongs of the matter, he's warned me how that course simply leads to disaster. Bribery being one of the worst offences, the moment it is attempted you are in the Cardinal's power. Then there is no limit to his demands."

"Does not that apply to Pessoa as well?"

"That's our difficulty. Pessoa, being attached to the Portuguese Court, enjoys some form of immunity. He can be banished, but he cannot be punished."

"These are certainly deep waters, Cousin. Captain, as for our selling more silver and taking the money to London, I've heard enough from Thomas tonight to call a halt to the business. It seems the more we do to reveal our hand, the more one or other of these rascals will demand of us."

"Who knows, gentlemen," Thomas rejoined, "the pot of gold we now have in London may be just the bargaining counter we need to send *Senhor* Pessoa packing." But he spoke more out of hope than conviction, while Godolphin was left silently toying with another solution, one involving Spanish ships, Cornish archers and hidden treasure. But this was not the time to mention the approaches he had received.

****

The Christmas vacation at the Inner Temple lasted three weeks. During term time, the Knights' Hall would assume a strict formality. But this now gave way to the feasting and hospitality proudly described as "the ancient and hereditary virtues" of the Society. In honour of the Templars, members drank from ash or maple cups, some with silver feet, while the Hall was strewn with rushes. Come the evening, candles and torches, helped by a blazing wood fire in the centre, lit up the proceedings.

As the elected Steward this Christmas, Thomas' role was to ensure that the course of these revelries ran smooth, with minstrels in the gallery, singers for the entertainment and students present for their moots. This last was an essential part of their study of the law. With no examinations to sit, as a student Thomas had found that paying the fines for dinners or moots he had missed proved the chief obstacle to being called to the Bar.

In these moots, invented cases were debated by opposing teams of students, before a senior Reader. Tonight, Thomas had invited Lisle and Densell to join one of their Christmas banquets. Anthony Wayte was the Reader for the evening. He framed his moot around a recent case before the Star Chamber. It involved some Devon fishermen, compelled by the Admiralty to surrender half a porpoise caught at sea.

Thomas was sitting next to Densell, with Lisle placed across the table between two former Inner Temple students, Godolphin and Grenville, Honour's nephew. They were finishing their fifth course, fruits and sweetmeats washed down with fortified wine, served on gold plates embellished by the Templar insignia. Then as the minstrels' melody closed, Wayte stood up, silence spreading across the Hall.

"The case tonight is Men of Devonshire versus Admiralty. For the Devon men, we have Masters Wylkowes and Culpepper; for the Admiralty, we have Masters Midylton and Heyworth." Wayte outlined the facts of the case for the benefit of the guests. The question to decide was, who owned the porpoise – the fishermen or the Crown? Wayte called on Wylkowes to present the Complaint of the Devon fishermen.

"The Admiralty claim an ancient right, which gives to the King the value of royal fish, that is to say whales and sturgeons, when they are found ashore. But this is far from being the same as claiming a porpoise found at sea. In the ancient words of Bishop Le Breton, ...*for treasure hid in the earth and found shall belong to us, but if found at sea, it shall belong to the finder...* "

But Master Midylton cited *Prerogativa Regis* and quoted from the *Black Book* of the Admiralty. "The Crown is entitled to half of all that is found, whether in the sea or not..." At this point, Thomas found the fortified wine winning over the line of argument. Even so, he recognised that the principles of the dispute exactly mirrored his own.

He had to chuckle when Midylton raised his voice and said earnestly: "Furthermore, when the fishermen inveigled the porpoise onto their ship, his consent to board was hardly an enforceable contract. The consideration he received was the bait on the fishhook, a consideration so vague as to be illusory."

Culpepper disagreed. "The Rules of Oleron were revived forty years ago," he said. "They state that fish found in the sea are adjudged to the finder. It may be otherwise with *great fish having fat, found dead on the bank of the sea*. But even in such cases, the Rules of Oleron state *regard must be had to the custom of the county...*"

Then Hayworth cited another case, which caught Thomas' attention again. *Salvage in the sea belongs to the King, as a right of the Admiralty. On land, above the high-water mark, it belongs to the Lord of the Manor, but beyond low-water mark, he can have no claim.* Thomas could see Godolphin nodding at him at this point, recalling perhaps his advice in William's garden, on the day their adventure started.

"Between the two water marks, it is *divisium imperium...*" It was hard to follow, but Hayworth now made a vital point: "If the person who seizes the porpoise is in a boat, it's the Crown's. If he has simply waded out to sea, it's the Lord of the Manor's. Finally, when this Right of Wreck attaches to the Crown, it is only until the proper owners of the wreckage appear and can claim it back..."

The last speech impressed Reader Wayte greatly. After complimenting all the students on their wise and witty remarks, he awarded the moot to Masters Midylton and Heyworth, for the Admiralty. There was no need to remind the Hall that their guest Lord Lisle, the Vice Admiral sitting opposite him that evening, might well favour the same outcome.

"It has been a splendid occasion," Lisle said to Thomas as he bade goodbye. "Although I am sure my friend Densell here will be the first to warn against drawing too many conclusions from the fate of a porpoise."

"At least the law seems with us, my Lord. But we two meet shortly, when we hope to settle our purpose." At this, Densell nodded and all bid each other good night.

Thomas returned to the Knights' Hall, where Godolphin and Grenville were still to be found. Like him, they would be staying in chambers at the Inn that evening. "A well-chosen invitation to our two guests, if I may say so, Cousin," Godolphin remarked. "Only I was a little surprised you did not include Captain Millaton in our party. Had you not considered he was in town as well? He's only staying up the road in the Strand."

"I have his address, but I'd imagined he would be otherwise engaged tonight, William."

"Even Jack Millaton enjoys the odd rest from his Irish beauty! But I am sure no harm's done."

"Not at all, William, I realise now how wrong it was of me to leave him out." Just then, the Bell of St Clement sounded ten o'clock. "The night is still young. Let me see if I can find him now." Before Godolphin could speak again, Thomas was on his way, through the stables and walking down Fleet Street, heading

210

towards Millaton's lodgings. He was determined that nothing should put at risk the success of their partnership, for now he considered it, Thomas could easily guess at Millaton's feeling slighted by his omission that evening.

But when he reached the Strand and found the address of Millaton's lodgings, Thomas was in for a surprise. A couple of men had been and settled Millaton's bill on his behalf barely two hours before, informing the inn keeper that "Mr and Mrs Millaton" had decided to make alternative arrangements. It was all most odd and Thomas made his way back to Fleet Street deep in thought. He was not to know that, only half a mile away, Millaton was being held against his will.

****

The young redhead opposite Elizabeth Holland looked at her with a mixture of alarm and curiosity. The elegant room where they were sitting had no windows, only full-length mirrors with gilt frames hung between silk drapes edged with golden lace. The carpet was a vibrant red with an oriental pattern. Each end of a long side table was supported by the subservient carving of a naked man in black ebony. A pair of Venetian glass vases stood on top, while in the centre of the table a scent of jasmine emanated from a light blue urn. Candles burnt in an Italian chandelier and the light from the sconces refracted off the mirrors along the wall.

Elizabeth Holland wore a dress bedecked in tiny diamonds and each of her long cool hands wore a diamond ring on the middle finger. Her low-cut front revealed a firm generous bosom and the emerald pendant between her breasts was complemented by two pretty earrings. Her blonde hair was put back, as if to emphasise her generous red lips and delicate nose. She was tall and slender and about twenty-seven years old. The younger girl felt she had never met anyone so beautiful.

"So tell me, my dear, what is your name?"

211

No one had asked her that question in a long time, not her real name. "I'm not sure what to say, Mistress. Captain Jack, he calls me Pirran, an' it seems to have caught on."

"Pirran, does he? Why is that?"

"Says I'm his Irish miracle worker, Mistress, in the bedchamber, if you know what I mean."

"I know exactly what you mean, Pirran. And does he work any miracles for you?"

"Oh no, Mistress. Boys don't do that sort of thing for me. I know how to make him happy, mind, sounding all excited and so forth. But although he's older, Captain Jack's just another boy in so many ways. A nice one though – and very sweet to me."

At this, Pirran glanced involuntarily at her own finger, where she was wearing the ruby ring Millaton had bought her at Richard Kene's shop that afternoon. "Which reminds me, Mistress, did he say when he was getting here? The message I received wasn't clear about that."

"Men are not to be relied upon, my dear. I shouldn't worry about him. We have all the time in the world."

Pirran was attracted to the musky scent she was wearing, as Elizabeth Holland moved closer and removed her shawl. "It's really very warm in here, don't you think, Pirran? Can I take your cloak for you? I'm sure you will feel more comfortable without it."

Pirran was very happy to remove her cloak and gratefully accepted the offer of a goblet of sweet white wine too. They shared some sugared almonds, as Elizabeth Holland eyed her slim, clean body. Pirran had dressed to please Captain Jack this evening and her thin white blouse allowed her hostess a glimpse of her uncovered breasts. She saw so many girls. Beyond the seductive confines of this inner sanctum, they catered for many tastes in the Old Manor House. But how often had she searched for that one ripe young plum, fresh and unbruised, fit for Elizabeth Holland's own consumption. She smiled at the fortune she had been paid to perform tonight's commission, even as she jettisoned Master

212

Cromwell's crude instructions. As bawd of the most exclusive brothel in Southwark, fortified by its own moat, drawbridge and portcullis, Mistress Holland took instructions from no one.

As for Pirran, there were so many questions she wanted to ask this warm sensuous woman, things about her own body that no one had explained before and feelings she felt awakening for the first time inside her.

****

The next day, Thomas had no time to dwell on Millaton's unexpected departure, between organising the next revels in the King's Hall and preparing for his meeting with Densell. The three magistrates had each taken a purse out of the cache at the Mount, leaving the London strongbox untouched. This was to be used, as Thomas saw fit, to reach a settlement with Pessoa. But John Densell had been a study in discretion the night before, Thomas reflected, as he made the short walk across Fleet Street and up Chancery Lane.

Thomas approached the new Gate House to Lincoln's Inn, passed through its heavy oak doors and made himself known to the porter. The gardens beyond were the most extensive of any of the Inns of Court and he needed careful direction to John Densell's staircase. It was a modest opening to the rooms of one of the greatest legal brains in the country, but once inside his chambers, the rows of leather-bound volumes on the shelves whispered their aura of learning. A coal fire was working hard to exclude the winter cold, as Densell motioned him to sit beside it, easing his enormous frame into his own chair as he did so.

John Densell put his hands together, as if in prayer, and paused for a moment before speaking: "What we have here, Mr Thomas, is an excellent series of what we could call moot points on the one side, set against the power and might of a King and Cardinal on the other. Legally speaking, from all you have told me, what you

213

have done is unshakeable. If you ever chose to return to practice, there are chambers here that specialise in the law of the sea. I have no doubt they would like to meet you. Even so, certainly a year ago, I would not have given your case a chance. The kinship that bound His Grace the King to the thrones of Spain and Portugal would have left you in a hopelessly exposed position."

"So what has changed?"

"Well, first of all, the rift with Spain over The King's Matter. Then there is the weakening position of the Lord Chancellor, who finds his power frustrated by the Lady Anne Boleyn. Lastly, there is the change in your own fortunes and that of your friends. Lord Lisle is now a member of the King's Council. Then last night reminded me that your nephew, Sir Richard Grenville, is to be a member of the new Parliament."

"That's all very well, but my Lord Lisle has made it clear there is little he can do to intervene in a case of law, while Sir Richard is a man to follow his own path."

"You may know that, Mr Thomas, but Cardinal Wolsey does not. It will have stayed his hand the while and may explain why, perhaps, none of you has yet been put in the Tower – or on the rack."

Thomas looked at Densell in astonishment. It had never occurred to him that they could be running such high risks.

"Of course, it probably took them some time to work out who actually had the benefit of your bargain with the Portuguese. They would have suspected Arundell himself behind it all." Here Densell allowed himself a chuckle, a sense of pride in his native county. "It's not many places where the local gentry take on their Lord of the Manor and get away with it!"

"But if, as you say, we have got away with it, why should we settle at all?"

"While King Henry's ties of kinship to Spain and Portugal may be broken, the Cardinal has developed financial ties all of his own making. We now face a blatant case of bribery. In fact, Pessoa has

214

done his best to prove he's bribed Wolsey to my face."

"Why would he do that – and if he has Wolsey in his pocket, what possible settlement could he want from us?"

"Our Portuguese lawyer is desperate for a conclusion to the affair and – as luck would have it – the recent outbreak of plague has delayed every case in the land. Pessoa also hopes to browbeat us into a better deal for himself, than the bribe he has had to promise the Cardinal if it goes to court."

Thomas shook his head in disgust. "It's certainly not the law as I was taught it, Mr Densell. But if you say so, then I have authority from the others to offer up to seven hundred and fifty pounds to settle with Pessoa out of court. We have the money in gold coins, sitting in the Inner Temple."

Densell did not react as Thomas expected to this proposal. He sat looking into the smouldering embers of the fire, as if trying to solve a great riddle. Then he stood up and went over to his desk, to retrieve the letter he had just received from Pessoa. He handed it over silently and watched Thomas' reaction, as his eyes alighted on the critical passage:

> *...Furthermore, provided that the value which my clients recover from the wreckage is more than ten thousand pounds, I am instructed to offer to the said defendants Godolphin, Seyntaubin and Millaton, the sum of seven hundred and fifty pounds in gold coins, in final settlement of the case...*
> *There will be no further offers.*

Thomas understood all too well what these words meant. Pessoa's spies and gossip in the Angel Hotel had breached their defences. How otherwise could Pessoa have known the exact amount of ready money to hand? Yet even as he discussed all this with Densell, Thomas stoutly refused to be intimidated by the offer.

"It would be a humiliation, Mr Densell, to accept such terms.

Besides, the sum proposed may be useful, but it answers none of the problems I need to solve."

"But think of it this way, Mr Thomas. Even on your own evidence, the salvage you collected with the help of Alvares must have already paid for your outgoings. The offer to you of seven hundred and fifty pounds is pure profit, a sum I dare say none of you would have refused for any other wreck."

"There's my point, you see. We will never have another chance like this one, whereas for the King of Portugal, it is a mere pinprick to his pocket. And if this is about his pride, was it not God's doing that wrecked the ship taking his bride's dowry?"

"There's certainly no room for pride in a case before the Star Chamber, Mister Thomas," Densell replied sternly. But try as he might, he could not wring a change of heart from his client. In the end, he was not sure whether he admired or cursed this obstinacy, but he had to admit it came as no surprise.

Chapter Nineteen

Why do you talk of the King of England? If we wished,
we could expel him from his kingdom within three months.
Mercurino Gattinara, Imperial Grand Chancellor,
Letters and Papers of Henry VIII

Thomas had paid a visit to Goldsmith's Row before returning to Cornwall. Mary's delight at her Christmas present put them all in high spirits. Then the news broke in the New Year that Sir John Basset had finally passed away, peacefully and with his family around him. Honor wrote to Mary to describe how Lisle had come down to Devon and how before he died, Sir John had given their union his blessing. "Truly," Mary read from Honor's letter, "he has been my 'most parfait gentle knight'." Thomas made some rueful comment about old Mr Bluett, which brought a light scolding from his wife, before discussion turned to the funeral.

"He was your father's generation, Thomas. All his friends passed on long ago. So the family plan a quiet service, in the chapel at Umberleigh Park, which is where he will lay to rest with his first wife. There's room at the chapel for us, but not for the children. As the new steward at Tehidy, Honor has asked if you would help her to choose five men on the estate to come too. They can lodge with the Umberleigh tenants."

The trip to Devon took some organising and by the time they arrived at Umberleigh, the shock of Sir John's death had already passed. Thoughts were turning to the future for Honor and Lisle.

"We will take all the children to live with us at Soberton," Honor was explaining to Mary, "as soon as rooms can be prepared. But here is the really exciting news, Sister. As Lisle is a Knight of the Garter, His Grace the King has offered Windsor Castle for our wedding, in St George's Chapel! Of course, we want all of you to come, but for your Ann to be a bridesmaid would be my special pleasure."

Mary was thrilled to accept on Ann's behalf, only she could not stop herself asking, "Will His Grace the King attend the service?"

"Not in the main chapel. But he has a discreet balcony, to the side of the altar, where he might appear with his Lady Anne."

Thomas realised that he had one more favour to ask. "Tell me, Honor, would you consider inviting Captain Millaton to the wedding?"

"Really, Thomas," his wife shot back, "you cannot be expecting Honor to drag up all our Cornish neighbours to see your daughter as a bridesmaid."

"Not at all, Sister," Honor replied graciously. "Lisle and I had already resolved to invite the captain. Our visits to the Mount have a special place in our hearts."

"Come to think of it, Thomas, we've not seen the captain since before Christmas. Do we have his news?"

"No, beloved. It's a strange thing, but I missed him in London and he's not returned the note I sent. But I cannot imagine him missing this occasion."

The Christmas and New Year at Clowance, the demands of the estate after his return from the Inner Temple, then the suddenness of Sir John's death had all combined to push Captain Millaton to the back of Thomas' mind. He had written giving the gist of his meeting with Densell to the other two magistrates. Now he was waiting to hear the date for their first hearing in the Star Chamber. Sure enough, when he returned from the Devon funeral, there was a message from Lincoln's Inn. The hearing was fixed for mid March. At least, Thomas reflected, he would have the chance to stage one final Feast Day at Clowance, before their fate was sealed.

But come St Pirran's Day, a gloom hung over the proceedings. In honour of Sir John Basset, Thomas had called for a minute's silence before the wrestling started. But for many of the spectators, it seemed as if he were mourning the passing of something else, his own family inheritance, a line that had stretched back from the Seyntaubins to the Kemyels and so to before the Conquest. There were many who quietly came up to Thomas and Mary that day, to have a word, or to thank them for a kindness from years past, even stretching back to his grandfather's tenure. No one said it but everyone sensed that the ties of time were about to be broken. They had "heard it from a mouth" at the Angel Hotel in Helston.

However, the mood at Clowance lifted when Moyle triumphantly returned with the hurling ball. It was a portent that luck could change and gave renewed energy to the closing celebrations. But the next evening, the Seyntaubins found themselves alone in the library at Clowance and facing the harsh choices that lay before them.

"I dare say Honor would be prepared to rent us the house at Tehidy, if Clowance must go," Mary suggested. "I know she would be loath to lose such a fine steward, now you have started, beloved."

"Then again, my spell at the Inner Temple before Christmas has refreshed my London acquaintance and sharpened my appetite for legal work," Thomas replied, trying not to notice Mary's evident pain at the thought of leaving.

"With so many thoughts and pressures, Thomas, I know it has been hard to face one glaring question, but where was Captain Millaton yesterday? Didn't you make a special point of inviting him?"

"The captain has been avoiding me for two whole months, beloved. I upset him before Christmas by not inviting him to our grand dinner and nothing I have tried since has changed his mind. We've not even sat on the Bench together. To tell the truth, I've grown rather tired of our Captain Millaton and his sensibilities, especially seeing as I am the one doing all the work when it comes to defending our case."

"He may be a rude, awkward fellow for all that I know him, but if digging him out of his lair will save the house we live in, then I cannot think what is to stop you. Was there not something odd about the mood at the Feast? A few months ago, the feeling was we had stood our ground and were set fair."

"That's because people looked at the result of the local enquiry, which vindicated us sure enough. But I agree about yesterday, it was as if everyone knew something except us. Perhaps Millaton has struck his own bargain with the devil, in which case…"

"In which case, Thomas, I want you to go and see him face to face. This is not going to be solved by notes and messages."

Her husband rose from his chair and determined to ride over to Pengersick Castle. The evening light was growing longer and a fresh horse would cover the distance in half an hour. He could ride home by the full moon, perhaps passing by Godolphin House on the way, to offer his commiserations on the hurling match.

By the time he reached the castle, a light in the tower was shining in the dusk. He called out several times before hearing movement, as someone came down the steps to the heavy entrance, now defended by Portuguese guns. It was Millaton, not at all his old confident self.

"Good evening, Captain," Thomas started. "My apologies, for I should have come to see you sooner. It's clear from your look that there has been some great adversity and tribulation, but what it is I forebear to tell."

"Come inside, Mr Thomas, the apology is all on my side, for I have played the unwise man."

He showed his guest to the room looking over the courtyard where they had first sat together two years before. He offered Thomas a glass of wine, then helped himself to one himself, by no means the first of the evening. Thomas sought some words to break the awkward silence.

"How is your wife, Captain Jack?"

"She's dead, Thomas. No, don't look like that. She died some years ago."

"But I thought – we all thought – she lived here, looking after your father."

"No, no, though I admit it was no harm to me that people believed it so. The lady who lives here is my father's housekeeper. My own wife died just before you came back to live down here, as a matter of fact, the same plague that caught your brother. But given my father's needing to stay quiet, as you'd recall, I couldn't risk introducing another woman, even had I wanted to. So I went to London and found our old housekeeper and brought her down. It didn't bother me if people thought we were married or not and it was easier for Honour, too."

"So the housekeeper looked after your father and daughter, while all those women on the Mount…"

"Were just some fun, Thomas. Well, until the last one, that is."

"She's gone too, has she? I hadn't realised she meant anything more…"

"She's gone all right. And I feel like I'm damned in hell about it all." Millaton gave Thomas a grieving look and his guest realised that, stuck in this remote outpost, there had been no one to whom Millaton could turn these past few weeks.

"Let's start with the lodgings in the Strand," Thomas suggested, seeking to thread some sense into Millaton's comments. "What happened that night, when I came looking and was told you had gone?"

"I had left Pirran, as I call her, while I went to check our plans for the evening. When I returned to our lodgings, the porter said a smart-looking gentleman had arrived with a message, offering to escort her to Paris Gardens, where Captain Millaton had arranged a surprise." Millaton paused. "Hearing this, I rush out the door, go down to the river and find a boat to take me across to Southwark. But the boatman won't listen. He only takes me upriver, you see, 'till he reaches the steps of York Place."

"Cardinal Wolsey's house!"

"'Xactly. Only I'm taken in there to see the understudy, that Cromwell bastard."

Millaton spat out the words and Thomas could almost guess the rest of the story as he spoke. Cromwell started by explaining some great matters of state, which made it Captain Millaton's bounden duty to confess to Cromwell's version of events, in return for a free pardon.

"I turn him down of course, even when he offers to bribe me with owning the Mount! Then he raises my father's case, so I talk my way out of that by saying he's dead already. I then offer to resign my commission, rather than take orders from him. So Cromwell comes to the real threat. He's put my Pirran in a whorehouse. If I don't sign the confession he's just placed in front of me, he'll see that she's stewed by every street urchin in Southwark."

Thomas shook his head. It all explained why people had started to believe he had lost. No wonder Millaton had stayed away from the Clowance Feast Day. "I can't say you gave in easily, Jack. Some men would have taken the bribe straight off, to be honest. Godolphin and I won't hold it against you. But what we must know is this. What crimes are alleged against us in the confession that Cromwell made you sign?"

"I haven't a clue."

"What? Do you mean to say you just signed and left, with no memory of it even?"

"I didn't sign."

Thomas was speechless. He slowly absorbed the implications of this. Then he said, with a quiet anger, "They're just cowards, aren't they, Jack? They daren't touch us. So they pick on a poor defenceless girl. Well, at least I'm glad of something, that I spurned Pessoa's paltry offer. But there's no amount of treasure can make up for what they've done to you, let alone what has happened to the girl."

"There's something else, Thomas, for 'tis only fair to warn you. Cromwell had a folio with him, which he kept tapping. Said he had enough evidence to put you in the Tower, whether I signed his piece of paper or no. It could have been just another empty threat, of course..."

"Thank you, Jack. But to make head or tail of it all, we need John Densell."

The advice from Lincoln's Inn forced a change of tactics. Thomas had hoped to confine the Star Chamber hearing to points of law. Legally speaking, as Densell had said, their position was unassailable. But clearly, the Portuguese spies already knew how much had been taken from the wreck and new evidence had been garnered by the other side to sabotage their case.

Densell now proposed a Grand Hearing in the Star Chamber, with full cross-examination of witnesses. This was a gamble. It meant that the offence of perjury would hang like a sword over every inadvertent word Thomas might utter under oath. On the other hand, Densell would be able to probe the Portuguese in person and prove their contract with the Cornish was genuine. Lastly it meant, as always with the law, a further delay. The Grand Hearing would take place in the Summer Term, the date fixed being shortly after that of the Lisle wedding.

****

The wedding day approached. Staging the event at Windsor Castle, so long a distance from Soberton, let alone Cornwall, almost defeated Honor and those around her. The Tehidy estate was to provide venison for the feast, daffodils for the chapel and tenants for the pews. As the new steward, this required Thomas to liaise with the great kitchens in the castle, the Royal Guard on the Windsor Gate and the chaplain's office in St George's. Yet it all came as a welcome relief from his legal worries.

The day of the wedding, sunshine burst through the sixty-six lights in the Great West Window. St George's Chapel was the haunt of knights and the resting place of kings, Garter banners lining the choir stalls and royal tombs either side of the nave. As guests filled their pews, the choir sang over the peal of the organ and seven-year-old Anne Basset started to cry. It had been a long journey from Soberton. Staying the previous night in this huge castle, she would have been too scared to sleep, even if her brothers and sisters had not kept her awake with their excited chatter. Now her sisters and cousins had disappeared, to put on their bridesmaid dresses, leaving her behind with her elder brother, who looked embarrassed.

Just then, through her tears little Anne noticed a kind young woman with dark brown hair and glittering jewels coming towards her, others almost bowing as she made her way. "My name is Anne too," she heard her saying, as she was taken in hand and led up some stairs. "Come with me and we shall sit with your new cousin." Now they were in their own seats, in a balcony looking down at all these people, and this big Anne was making her laugh at all the hats they were wearing. Then there was a noise behind, as a man almost as large as her new father stepped into the balcony and sat alongside her. He smiled through a funny orange beard, which made her laugh again, except he lifted his finger to his lips and Anne knew she must behave. But her eyes kept repeating her innocent flirtation. This left him little time to notice the bridesmaids below, just as Anne Boleyn had planned.

The chaplain was saying some words. After gazing fondly on his own daughter in her silver damask gown, a garland of flowers in her long blonde hair, a bouquet in her hand, Thomas looked up to his niece in the balcony and then around the chapel. He spied the Arundells, down from Court, then Grenville and Waite and a few of his Inner Temple friends. Densell's frame was not to be missed, seated by Sir Thomas More, his friend and colleague at Lincoln's Inn. Godolphin nodded in his direction and there was Millaton too, their betrothed children in tow. Moyle sat in the row behind, his gaze fixed on Ann Seyntaubin.

The chapel choir was singing now, a liturgical arrangement chosen by Honor and Lisle. The tune was the ballad to which they had first danced together at Clowance, "Pastime With Good Companie".

"It must please the King not a little to hear one of his own compositions," Mary whispered in an aside to Thomas.

After the ceremony, the wedding party moved to the cloisters beyond the chapel. The royal couple could not stay and little Anne Basset was released to the care of the bridesmaids, full of her adventure. Finding their way to the reception, Thomas and Mary passed the tomb of Edward IV, Lisle's natural father.

"Here are Lisle and Honor, first bearing a child and now happily married," Mary remarked to Thomas. "But being King actually prevents His Grace, for all his power and glory, from doing likewise."

"How he and his Lady Anne Boleyn must long for children. They certainly liked Honor's pretty little girl," Thomas replied. "Yet they've had all these wasted years, because The King's Matter must first be resolved."

"The Crown comes at a heavy price."

"Which you could say, beloved, makes Lisle the lucky bastard!"

"But only say it to me, Thomas! He's our brother-in-law now, remember."

"Mr Seyntaubin?" An affable, red-faced fellow of stocky build had approached them. He wore a flat bonnet on his head. It displayed a silver badge in the shape of a falcon, perched on a fetterlock. "John Husee is the name, Sir, I'm my Lord Lisle's man at Court."

"Mr Husee, I've heard much of your saying and doing. Mary, beloved, please meet Lord Lisle's Secretary, who undertakes all manner of suit and request on his Lordship's behalf."

Husee was anxious to make his mark with the new steward at Tehidy and to work some pattern into what he hoped would be a long and lasting association. He was a jovial character, who was quick to exchange his knowledge of the courtiers at the wedding for that of the Cornish guests. As they talked, Husee proved compliant in many matters that they discussed, but he had one sticking point.

"When we come to meet in London, Mr Thomas, I am to be found at the Red Lion in Southwark. You will not find me crossing that river, unless it is at the command of the King, for the ferrymen are all thieves. As for walking London Bridge, I wouldn't trust those shopkeepers not to sell the clothes off my back."

At this moment, Millaton appeared and an introduction to Husee was made. Thomas left the captain telling Husee every detail about Lisle's voyage to the Mount in the frigate. He noticed Godolphin joining them. He was not to know that their conversation would soon turn to Southwark and some of its less reputable inhabitants.

Thomas took Mary to find Ann, their beautiful bridesmaid. They found her enjoying the keen attentions of Sir Bryan Tuke, the close confidant of both Lisle and the King. The interest of the older man was not so pleasing to John Moyle, however, standing at her side.

"Thousands have it," Tuke was saying, "from fear, who need not else have it at all, especially if they observed good diet."

"Thousands have what, pray, Sir Bryan?"

"The sweating sickness, Madam, that curse of last summer which took two thousand lives."

"But not your life, Sir Bryan, I am glad to know," Mary replied, "though I heard it from my sister Honor that you and your good wife were both severely afflicted."

"We were indeed, although in my view the sweat was rather provoked by the disposition of the season, and keeping men close, than by any infection. But London has a great deal more to offer than sickness and death, surely. Of this I have sought to persuade your daughter, as I take her to be, this most fair and gentle bridesmaid."

"There's no need to persuade us of that, for all your Courtly arts, Sir Bryan. Although I dare say you may continue with our

226

daughter Ann, who cannot be averse to her admirers on such a day."

Tuke glanced at Moyle as he said, "I can see I am not the first in that queue, Mistress Seyntaubin. But without flattery, may I congratulate your husband on enjoying, in you and your daughter, such great and goodly fortune? As to my friend Lord Lisle, he has found in your sister as fine a jewel as any man may wish or desire."

Thomas decided that Sir Bryan Tuke was one of those men who wished and desired fairly widely, for all his charm and grace. He was surprised when the courtier took him firmly by the arm, leading Thomas to a corner of the courtyard.

"Forgive me, Mr Seyntaubin, for forcing this matter on you, but have you heard of the Spanish Plot?"

"My Lord Lisle made mention at one point, Sir Bryan, of rumours at Court."

"You're quite sure you've heard nothing said in Cornwall?"

Thomas recalled the meeting at Godolphin all those months ago. "You can hear anything you like at the Angel Inn in Helston, Sir Bryan, for all the good it will do you."

"Quite so, Mr Seyntaubin. Well, I thought you ought to know, the Earl of Desmond has just died." Saying these words, Tuke closely watched Thomas' reaction.

"I'm afraid I never met him, Sir Bryan. Forgive me if he was a friend of yours…"

At this, Tuke gave a chuckle, evidently satisfied by this interview. "I see it is you who should be forgiving me, Mr Seyntaubin. We hear more rumours at Court than at your Helston hostelry! But seeing as you are now brother to my good friend Lisle, you should be aware that the Imperialists have been seeking some ploy to put Princess Mary on the throne, before our King produces a male heir."

"And this Desmond had some part to play?"

Tuke lowered his voice and drew closer. "Only six months ago, I came across a man sent out of their native Ireland by this Desmond to secure his pact with the Emperor. Then in April, we hear the deed has been signed. There are to be risings in Scotland and Cornwall, timed to coincide with the Irish invasion, as we gather."

"So what does the King say?"

"He refuses to believe a word of it. His Grace says it is all put up by the Cardinal, to force his hand to Wolsey's way of doing things."

"As for yourself, Sir Bryan, what do you believe?"

"In all honesty, Mr Seyntaubin, this Realm has never been in greater danger. There is a man, Gattinara by name, who would have his Emperor Charles rule all Christendom. He has others to Desmond at his beck and call."

At this point, Densell rolled into view and Thomas quietly took his leave.

"Much as I like my clients to meet such fine members of the King's Council, Mr Thomas, do not forget who they are for a moment. These men have seen life-long friends dispatched to the Tower, yet their first thought as the axe has fallen has been the division of the dead man's spoils."

"I have no doubt you speak wisely, Mr Densell, but surely so grand an event as this, on the eve of our hearing, must give us some shield from the Cardinal's devices?"

"If you are right, then it might explain why I fear we face yet another delay. But the more likely cause is the King's divorce. The Cardinal is so involved in hearings on that matter, day after day, that all other cases are stalled. There is however, one thing I have learnt to our advantage..."

"First disease, then divorce... there seems no end to these causes for delay. But what is this advantage of which you speak?"

"It seems that the Portuguese will send over only one witness, *Senhor* Jeremy de Corfe, saying that as a Gentleman of the King's Chamber, his was the main signature on your contract. But I have argued that Alvares is the man, the one who undertook the negotiation and knew what he was selling. If they cannot produce him in person, we could string this out for a year or more. Only in the end, I fear the Court will accept a written statement on his behalf."

"Can they do that?"

"I am afraid so, Mr Thomas. If the delay really helped you, I would recommend it, but you seem anxious for a result, whether good or no."

"The truth, Mr Densell, is that I have no choice. You see, the Hanse merchants have refused to accept repayments of my loan, out of the proceeds of the wreck, until this case is decided. Without an answer in the Star Chamber, the day will come when their interest charges force me to sell my estate in any case."

"There is one last point, Mr Thomas. Witnesses giving evidence must wait outside the Star Chamber, before the Lord Chancellor proceeds to the start of his session. Look around that hall and see if you recognise any of those who have come to testify against you."

"But I may have no idea what they are about to say."

"But just knowing who they are, may save you from making some fatal error in your answers. Please also remember that you can instruct me to attempt a settlement with Pessoa at any time, but once he sees victory, *the door is closed.*"

****

Jeremy de Corfe probably owed his life to the Grand Hearing demanded by John Densell and certainly his wellbeing. It had taken some time for Pessoa to convince King João, even more his Queen Catherine, that their claim might be tainted by the sight of a witness with his eyes gouged and his limbs broken. The success of such methods in convincing the Portuguese courts could not be guaranteed in England, where people clung to quaint notions of justice which he struggled to explain.

Pessoa skilfully succeeded in claiming the credit from de Corfe for his escape. So what might have proved an awkward journey together, in the carrack from Lisbon to London, instead provided Pessoa with a gratifying display of subservience from the disgraced courtier. If Pessoa ever owned a dog, he decided, he would call it de Corfe.

But weeks of delay in Lambeth, at the residence of the Portuguese ambassador, began to play on their nerves.

"My dear Jeremy," Pessoa remarked one morning with disdainful familiarity, "surely you do not intend to prowl the streets of London again in that ridiculous costume?" Denied the stage they deserved at the Sintra Palace, de Corfe had brought to London all the extravagancies of his Lisbon tailoring.

"*Senhor* Pessoa, I do not mean to offend, but it is not you that I wish to attract today."

"I would have thought, on the contrary, that by now you must have attracted every wench in Southwark by your garb. My concern, de Corfe, is more with their disappointment, when they discover that there is almost nothing inside that absurd contraption on the front of your breeches."

"*Senhor* Pessoa, not all of us have the instincts of a hound. There is a girl, at once so beautiful and so innocent, whom I have been courting for nearly a month."

"I doubt there is a single innocent maid to be found within a mile of London, let alone a mile of Palace Gardens."

"But you are wrong, *Senhor* Pessoa, this girl lives in moated seclusion, guarded by a jealous witch. I am her Prince, come to rescue her for all eternity."

"I see, de Corfe. And after you have tired of eternity, is she to be shared with the crew, on our way back to Lisbon?"

"For once, do not jest with me, my friend. I may have proved luckless in the loss of my place at Court, but you must allow me some way to spend the rents from my estates. No doubt this filly will wear with time, but I shall have a pretty ride all the while, before she is passed onto the stable hands."

"Very well, de Corfe. But without fail return early tonight, for tomorrow our day in this court has finally arrived." With these words, Pessoa reluctantly let his pet off the leash.

A mile away, Elizabeth Holland was admiring the transformation which she had wrought in Pirran in less than a year. The naughty minx had been thoroughly groomed into a lady who could pass for sophistication in any circle in London. It was a task which Elizabeth had undertaken with undiluted pleasure, never ceasing to thrill Pirran with the secrets of her bedchamber. But time waits for no woman and nor did Elizabeth Holland. Now the moment to sell Pirran had arrived, which is where her mistress showed her true genius.

Most bawds cultivated a whore in order to farm her out, collecting rent from the best gentlemen, before trading down. But the chatelaine of the Old Manor House invested for capital gain as well as income. Dealing with the finest customers, whose search for exclusivity was matched by her own discerning standards, Elizabeth Holland was no longer surprised by the absurd prices rich men would pay for her most polished jewels. In a world where a concubine was about to become Queen of England, Elizabeth Holland enjoyed pointing out that her own fees were modesty itself.

"If there is one thing I look for in a man," she explained to Pirran that morning, "it is chivalry. I could not bear to think of my sweetest treasure being mistreated."

"What are you talking of, Bess?" Pirran asked, for between them formality had long disappeared.

"The two of us have dallied long enough, my dearest love. It is a man's world and it is time I found one worthy of you, even though it will break my heart."

"But you promised, Bess," Pirran voiced with rising anxiety, "that you would never turn me into one of your working girls. What do you mean to say?"

"I will keep my promise, Pirran, please believe me. But there are one or two very fine gentlemen who have made a proposal for you."

"A proposal, Bess?"

"Yes, a proposal which in all honesty, Pirran, I cannot refuse in your own best interests, much as it pains us to part..."

It was a well versed performance and soon Elizabeth Holland had Pirran primed for the role she was to play. De Corfe's advantages were easily expounded, until Pirran's fondness for Millaton, already obscured by her infatuation with her mistress, seemed like a faded dream. After all, he had never come. As for Elizabeth Holland, she looked forward to naming her price. A thousand Portuguese ducats would be her record.

Much later, de Corfe could be seen leaving the Old Manor House, a very happy man. For a quarter's rent on his estates he had secured a pleasure which could easily last out a year or more. He had every doubt as to the claims to purity for his new prize, in fact he would be disappointed if she did not prove an artful and inventive lover. But her innocence and reticence were all a part of the game he loved to play. As soon as his day in court was over, he would be back to collect her.

Along the street, his high spirits suddenly turned into a premonition of death. Coming towards him were two of the Cornish magistrates, Millaton and Godolphin, led by a red-faced fellow, who wore a flat bonnet on his head with a silver badge shaped as a falcon on a fetterlock. Fortunately, de Corfe went unnoticed and his shock soon turned to laughter, when he saw the three of them walk up the drawbridge into Elizabeth Holland's den of iniquity. These English and their vices, he thought to himself.

****

The Great Hall at Westminster Palace was alive with the sounds of London. Shop keepers, bargain hunters, dealers, lawyers and bankers each had their stall under the most venerable roof in the capital. In one corner, a court case was in tow, in another two tradesmen disputed the value of a painting. A pickpocket helped himself, as a visitor tucked into lamb chops and ale at one of the tables. A stray dog picked up some scraps, watched with envy by two spaniels on a lead. Smoke wafted up into the giant hammer beams holding the roof together, where shafts of light from the east window picked out the sooted rafters.

Thomas had walked to this emporium. He would not risk the ferrymen, even by the Inner Temple steps, on this most important day of his life. After all, if all went awry, a trip on the river to Traitor's Gate was his to be had for free.

He had come alone. Millaton had already made his sacrifice for the cause. If disaster now befell Thomas at the hands of the Cardinal, he needed Godolphin free of taint, to safeguard his family. This, his cousin William had vowed to do, hand on sword.

Thomas carried no notes. Densell had impressed on him who was now in charge of the case.

"You must unclutter your mind, Mr Thomas, to leave your memory clear to act as a witness."

"But if I tell the truth, I could be walking into their trap even more surely than if I try to outwit them."

"In this Chamber, Mr Thomas, you are paying me to have the wit. You must have the courage. Only cast around that Hall and see whom you can discover there, to sharpen our readiness for their attack."

But if Wolsey had witnesses up his sleeve, then surely they were avoiding Thomas, as he walked through the Great Hall. Soon the throng would be lining the passageway to the Star Chamber, to see the Lord Chancellor make his entrance. So Thomas moved briskly to this side hall, leading up from the river landing into the Star Chamber, to gain an easy vantage point before the crowd filled. He made good time.

Four trumpeters, wearing the Cardinal's livery, came first. They were surrounded by marshals, who divided the crowd and pushed people against the walls. Three barges could be seen arriving at the Star Chamber steps, two either side of the largest, which was slowly pulled up to the centre of the landing stage. As it was secured, the trumpeters let out a volley of sound which filled the hall and commanded silence.

There was a short wait, then four bishops in their robes of office appeared, followed by two lines of priests, heads bowed in silent prayer. Behind them, six pages dressed in the finest gold livery, fanning out into a single line, the rows of onlookers once more pushed back against the wall. Then came the Lord Privy Seal and the Lord Mayor of London, wearing their chains of office. Finally, from the landing post stepped the Lord Chancellor of England, processing slowly into the hall where he paused. A longer trumpet voluntary was now sounded, a musical peroration. This is both God's messenger and the King's, it seemed to say, the man before whom all must tremble.

Thomas' eyes cast about and that is when he saw them. It was Fr Trelobys who caught his eye first, the old priest whom Thomas had crossed as a child. What could he have to do with this? Then he noticed Pengelly, the Helston shipping clerk, a look of shame and dread on his face. Standing two rows away, on the other hand, John Arscott had an air of detached curiosity, as if this scene were some play he was observing. Richard Kene, the London jeweller, was there. Then finally he saw de Corfe, wearing his Court dress and feathered hat. After that, scanning a sea of faces revealed some familiar figures from his service on the Penwith Bench, wreckers no doubt suborned here in lieu of being charged for their most recent crimes.

It was not a pretty list. Thomas wrote out a note to Densell, to pass on as soon as this procession was over. Meanwhile, he could not ignore what his legal training told him. Conspiracy was the least of the accusations which he must now be facing. In skilful hands, it would all be plausible enough, at least for a court whose opinion had already been bought. Thomas cursed his own pride and admitted, finally, that it was time to concede defeat. But at that moment, a note was passed to him. It was from Densell. It read simply:

The door is closed.

Pessoa must know he had won.

Thomas looked back at the procession. It moved again now, more pages and servants coming behind the Lord Chancellor. Solemn music had succeeded the trumpets, a mournful rendition whose funereal tempo matched the pace of this stately train. Thomas steeled himself against remorse. He thought of his pride in his two sons, his love of Mary and his girls. He drew comfort from knowing that they at least would be cared for. He might have lost all, but in this new world what prizes might they regain when he was gone...

Thomas was only partly conscious now of the scene unfolding before him. In his own mind, he had moved on beyond the Star Chamber ordeal still to come. Yet his eyes still registered, as a tall Parliamentary officer in a black tunic broke out from the crowd and marched steadily towards Wolsey. The Cardinal glanced to his side, to spur one of his sidesmen to seize this miscreant before a more heinous offence was committed. But the officer had a scroll in his hand, which he raised.

"In the name of the King!"

Someone motioned to the musicians to cease, only some of them doing so.

"In the name of the King!"

This was heard by all. As the music stopped, they saw the officer march towards the Chancellor and present him with the scroll. He did not bow, an omission which drew a gasp from the crowd. Then as the Chancellor read the scroll, he stumbled and had to be helped back to his feet. He turned round and paced now towards the Star Chamber steps, his train falling back in confusion.

Mayhem erupted in the hall. There was shouting. Thomas came back to his senses, enough to hear it said, "Wolsey is fallen. He's no longer the King's man." Then a great cheer went up, followed by baying and jeering as Wolsey stepped slowly back on his barge to return to York Place. "Wolsey is fallen," echoed through the Palace, into the Great Hall and onto the streets, followed by waves of cheering.

Thomas found the bench along the wall. There he sat down and wept.

Epilogue

But what could he hope for, when such puissant enemies did procure his destruction?
Herbert, *The Life and Reign of King Henry the Eigth*

The porter to the Gate House at Lincoln's Inn led a quiet life, but from time to time some vision would appear at his lodge to brighten his day. This was such a moment, as he opened the door to a lady of such tasteful beauty that he could go a whole month of ageing lawyers before he saw another.

She wore a French bonnet in the new fashion, which hid her hair, as befitted a married woman. There was a gold chain around her neck and her cloak of velvet, laced with satin, had a border of silver thread. He could tell that she was younger and more slender than most and no doubt yet to bear child. But above all, it was the liveliness in her eyes and the assurance in her manner which impressed him most. It was only when he spoke that the porter even noticed her husband.

"Good morning, can you tell us the way to Mr Densell's

chambers? It's Captain and Mrs Millaton to see him."

The porter was only too happy to oblige Millaton and his wife. There was a string of people ahead of them, he said, pointing the way across the gardens on this cloudless autumn day. Soon, theMillatons had found the Densell staircase and joined the Godolphins and the Seyntaubins standing by the coal fire. Densell motioned all of them to take a seat.

"I know there were many times when we thought this moment would never come," Densell began. "But this morning I have received, from the new Lord Chancellor, the official discharge of the case against you. Sir Thomas More is not only my great friend, he is also a great lawyer. The evidence of the bribery between Pessoa and Wolsey was sufficient on its own to secure our victory, in his eyes. But I am pleased to say, Sir Thomas found for us on the sanctity of the contract as well. The actual amount you recovered from the wreck, he said, was almost immaterial. What counted was that you undertook to pay tangible consideration. Indeed, fifty pounds is by common consent a generous payment for any salvage."

"So can we now pay our mortgage, Mr Densell?" Mary asked.

"Certainly, Mrs Seyntaubin, the Hanse lenders can raise no objection after this. All you need to do is raise the balance required."

Godolphin coughed. "Captain Millaton and I were wondering, Mr Densell, if we could come to some arrangement here. After all, neither of us needs our share of the strongbox sitting in the Inner Temple vault, not in London in any case. Would it not make more sense if the Seyntaubins took the strongbox and we'll take the balance of their silver hoard from Clowance? Then we will be all square."

Thomas and Mary immediately thanked them both and Densell's clerk was put to work to draw up a simple contract between the three magistrates. Meanwhile, wine was produced to celebrate their success.

After this contract had been signed, Godolphin looked at Thomas and asked coolly, "By the way, Thomas, I suppose you're sure the strongbox still contains all those gold coins, aren't you?"

"It never left my sight, William, all the way from the Castle on the Mount to the Inner Temple vaults. Except, that is, for half an hour in Guildford, when it was under lock and key with Cromwell's messengers..." Thomas' voice trailed off, as he said these words.

"Well, I'm not worried, Thomas," Millaton said, as he blew the ink on their contract dry. "According to this agreement, we are to take your silver and you are to take the strongbox. Now tell me, William, who was it who told us – was it a year or so back? that provided you deal *contents unknown*, 'tis the other fellow's lookout if you enter a bargain which he later regrets."

"No doubt about it, Jack, I remember it well," Godolphin rejoined. "Besides which, I think the Lord Chancellor has just confirmed that what counts in these cases is – what's his term? 'tangible consideration'." With this, he winked at Millaton.

Thomas looked between Millaton and Godolphin and realised in a moment that all this had been planned. He had sold them the silver in his cellar in return for a strongbox which, as like as not, was now empty. Not saying another word, he rushed out of the door, down the stairs and ran all the way from Chancery Lane to the entrance to the Inner Temple.

"Mr Seyntaubin?" The porter at the Inner Temple was puzzled to see Thomas in such a state, as he leant against the desk to recover his breath. "There are some gentlemen inside who want to see you, Sir. They have gone up to Mr Wayte's chambers."

Even more alarmed, Thomas drew himself up and found his way to Anthony Wayte's rooms. He cautiously opened the door.

"Ah, Mr Thomas, these men have come from the Hanse merchants in the City. Now, if you don't mind, would you just sign these documents here? Then the mortgage on the Clowance estate is discharged in full."

"But what about the strongbox?" Thomas could not help himself from asking. "Surely they want to check it first?"

Anthony Wayte looked surprised. "But I thought you knew, Mr Thomas. Mr William Godolphin came in here three days ago. He's made all the arrangements on your behalf."

Thomas looked at Anthony Wayte, then at the Hanse merchants and sat down. Then he burst out laughing.

Author's Note

"What if the past – defined as our knowledge of it – does not exist until the historian writes it? ...Our knowledge and understanding of the past (as *found* in the evidence) is in substantial part the product of our own minds" *Alan Munslow, 'Editorial', Rethinking History (1997)*

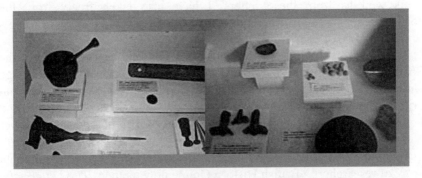

*Artefacts from the **Santo Antonio** discovered by local diver A.C. Randal and preserved by the Pengersick Trust*

The missing treasure from the *Santo Antonio* has remained a puzzle for nearly five hundred years. *Custom of the County* portrays the most convincing explanation of this mystery, consistent with all the facts it has now been possible to establish.

John Chynoweth's research,[1] more than forty years ago, was a key starting point. The more recent scholarship of Dr John Guy and Sir John Baker QC, into the workings of the Star Chamber[2] under Wolsey and the early records of the Inner Temple[3] provided vital clues. I am indebted to Sir John Baker and to the Inner Temple Library for their assistance. Mary Robertson, the Chief Curator of Manuscripts at the Huntington Library in California,[4] also gave me her valuable time and insight.

An important background source was the Lisle Letters.[5] The Bassets, the Seyntaubins and all Lisle's friends and family sparkle in its pages.

Through their intimate letters, one comes to know their personalities as well as any circle in the Tudor period. The 1981 edition by Muriel St. Clare Byrne, a fifty year labour of love, was described as "one of the most extraordinary historical works to be published in the century".[6] Her analysis of the circle's style of speech is superb. Yet St Clare Byrne can also commit omissions and skirt conclusions, in her prim aversion to the hint of scandal. In our more open age, I have taken the robust approach.

As well as from these letters, I have also taken freely from the contemporary writings of Leland, Vergil, Cavendish and Carew, to bring a sense and style of the period closer.

The Royal Institution of Cornwall was a mine of information. For the Spanish and Portuguese, the British Library (and the Cambridge University Library) provided rich pickings, both of scholarship and original material, concerning João III and his Court, his agents Pessoa and Fernandes, the use of torture and lastly, the bribes he spent to recover booty lost at sea.[7]

Without the internet search engines, this project might have required an army of researchers.[8] British History Online now includes *The Letters and Papers of Henry VIII* and *The Calendar of Spanish Papers*. Both proved vast treasure troves in their own right, from Henry's anger over the Spanish debts to the extent of foreign plots against him. The *Letters and Papers* also provided an ironic clue as to how the treasure was finally sold.[9]

Malcolm Smitheram at Godolphin Hall and Guy Evans at Pengersick Castle, both friends of old, revealed the historical secrets of these two extraordinary places. My son Henry, while on guard at Windsor Castle, arranged a personal tour of St George's Chapel. My daughter Kitty, a law student, introduced me to a moot after a grand dinner in Hall at Middle Temple. My brother James St Aubyn let me loose with the family records at St Michael's Mount, where the guides were ever helpful, as they were at Hampton Court.

The Star Chamber at the Palace of Westminster was destroyed by fire in 1834. The site has since been named Star Chamber Court, where I was once confronted by a solitary figure emerging from the evening shadows. It was Peter Mandelson, surely the Cardinal Wolsey *de nos jours*.

244

These are among the many diverse experiences that convinced me to write an historical novel, rather than a narrative of events. In so many ways, this is real history – disciplined evidence-based deduction imbued with personal insight, but with no claim to absolute certainty – history at simply a different point along the spectrum, one which has the academic scholars at one end and the dedicated romancers at the other.

These characters, who deserve their liberation from the archives, face new twists of fate in the next ten years. They are drawn into the orbit of Henry VIII at the very time when, unleashed from Wolsey, he is at his most dangerous. In fact, one of this Cornish circle is sent to the Tower on charges of treason, even as his daughter becomes the object of the King's desire.

It all really happened and it all continues in the second novel in this trilogy. So my last and greatest thanks go to my wife Jane, without whose unstinting support this venture would never have started. Also to my late father, who passed on his abiding love of Cornwall, along with his rare collection of Cornish books, papers and manuscripts, which have played their part.

March 2010

Footnotes

1 James Chynoweth, *The Wreck of the St Antony*, Journal Royal Institute of Cornwall, n.s., v(iv) (1968), 385-406. See also by the same author *Tudor Cornwall* (2002). See also *Court and County* (1987) and *Tudor Cornwall* (new edition, 1969), both by A.L.Rowse.

2 Dr. John Guy, *The Cardinal's Court* (1977). See also, I.S. Leadam, *Select Cases Before the King's Council in the Star Chamber* (1903).

3 Sir John Baker, QC FBA FRHistS FBS, *Prospography of the Inns of Court* and *Dictionary of National Biography re: John Densell, et al.* See also *A Calendar of the Inner Temple Records, Vol. I (1896),* ed. F.A. Indlewick.

4 The Huntington Library, 1151 Oxford Road, San Marino, California 91108. The image on p. 75 is taken from *The register of the most noble order of the Garter*, 1724, RB125774.

5 Muriel St. Clare Byrne, *The Lisle Letters*, 6 volumes, (1981).

6 *New York Times*, review by J.H. Plumb, June 14, 1981.

7 For example, J.A. Goris, *Etudes sur les colonies marchandes à Anvers* (1925).

8 See British History Online (*http://www.british-history.ac.uk/*). But how else to find, for example, J.A. Browner's *Wrong Side of the River* in *Essays in History*, vol. 36, 1994, University of Virginia, or to witness a Cornish wrestling match on UTube?

9 *Letters and Papers, 37 Henry VIII,* No. 828, p. 408. One St Clere complains to the Privy Council that "in Devon and Cornwall certain gold is ignorantly molten with the tin, and so unawares conveyed abroad to the profit of strangers". He is granted letters, "to permit him 'to put his cunning in ure' for one month and to certify the result". But he is to work through "Mr St. Aubyne and John Militon in Cornwall", with results we can deduce.

Custom of the County

The Manifest of the Santo Antonio

(transcribed from the Star Chamber Papers)

All in Tudor money, when farmland fetched £1 an acre (£5,000 today) and a labourer earned less than 2p a day.

8,000 cakes of copper	£3,234
18 cakes of silver bullion	£2,250
3 garnishes of silver vessels, basins, ewers, pots, bowls and other plate, and a chest with ready money	£3,576
Precious stones, pearls, chains, brooches	£2,664
Rich cloth of Arras tapestry and other jewels of gold	£766
Holland cloth and other linen	£610
Satins, velvets and other silks	£400
Camlets, says and Satin of Bruges	£250
friezes and flemish cloth	£520
fine English cloth in many colours	£916
English cottons and linens	£255
2,100 barbers' basins	£164
3,200 latten candlesticks	£418
6 barrels of stopper nails	£40
A pipe of padlocks and weights	£20
2 pipes with packthread, needles and compasses	£50
A great chest with swarms and other musical instruments	£30
4 sered pipes with armour for the King of Portugal and his horses	£210
Pitch, tar, tallow and wainscot	£37
Brass guns, iron pieces and other artillery	£2,470
Sum total	£18,880

redandblackpress.co.uk

Red&BlackPress™ is a new publishing house dedicated to promoting historical writing which combines quality and accuracy. We are especially interested in works with a connection to the West Country.

Custom of the County is our first publication.

The book is available in a hardback edition, a softback edition, as an e-book or as an audiobook. Visit our website for more details, *www.redandblackpress.com,* where you can also buy on-line. Read comments by other readers, discuss the history behind *Custom of the County*, check our diary of events and receive information on forthcoming publications, including the sequel to this novel.

The Royal National Lifeboat Institution *has launched an appeal to raise £1.8M towards the cost of a new Tamar class lifeboat for The Lizard lifeboat station crew. Proceeds from the sale of* Custom of the County *through the Red&BlackPress website and participating booksellers will be donated to this appeal. More details may be found by visiting www.redandblackpress.com.*